The Rogue's Last Letter

DARIA VERNON

BOOK TWO of *THE REWARDS OF RUIN*

The Rogue's Last Letter: Book Two of The Rewards of Ruin
Copyright © 2021 by Daria Vernon

Cover Design by www.daybedbooks.com

Print ISBN: 978-1-7359814-8-2
Digital ISBN: 978-1-7359814-4-4

www.dariavernon.com

Without my mom this book would not have come together.

Thank you for the many hours of plot brainstorming.
I will forever treasure the fact that "Secret twin!" is your default
epiphany whenever we're stuck.

1

London, England
April 1787

> *. . . If anticipation were food, I would not be a starving man. Your promise of a kiss tumbles around my head every minute of the day. Whatever alley we need slip into, whatever carriage we need duck behind, I am ready for that kiss. Were I a king, I'd have you fetched to London sooner. Were I a bird, I'd fly to you myself. That it is yet three months till our paths will cross—I cannot bear. Time seeks to destroy me, but I will be patient, Primrose, because the rewards are so great . . .*

Lady Allison Weldon refolded the letter and dragged her pinched fingers along its well-worn crease. The parchment crinkled as she set it aside.

Oh, Harry. So young, so raw, so earnest. She could pass judgment on not one of those traits because she shared them all. How was it then, that such a seemingly honest man had broken her heart?

. . . three months till our paths will cross . . .

. . . three months . . .

It was three months *now*. It was London *now*. And still not a word from her distant lover. She had responded to his last letter. Had shared her dreams of where and how they might conceal their kisses. Had told him of the notches she'd daily carved into her window casement at Tallyside—one to mark each of the eighty-six days before she would arrive in London for the peak of the social season. Now, eighty-seven days later, she blushed at such girlish folly, because no response had ever come back from the Bow Street Runner at Eight Dryden Street, London.

Perhaps some trouble with the post, she thought. *Perhaps—*

She'd sent another letter. *But nothing. Nothing after nine months of correspondence.*

To think on it overlong was to evoke an irritating queasiness. She pressed a palm to her stomacher, finding strange comfort in the sharpness of the silver spangles that adorned it. She'd done the piece herself. Had decorated it with evening primroses, the flowers that Harry had likened to her by way of their being *"oh so golden and bright."*

"Allison, darling!" shrieked a voice from downstairs.

Allison winced. Her mother's voice always cracked when she shouted. She didn't bother answering but merely heeded the call, descending to the entry of their London townhouse.

Lucinda, Countess Weldon, was already a tall woman, yet could not resist the towering modes of hairstyle that made her taller yet. Tonight, her graying blonde locks were covered accordingly by a creamy abomination whose topmost curls might be clipped by any doorway. Allison's nose itched as she reached the foot of the stairs. *Had Mother doused herself with every perfume on the dressing table?* The overpowering miasma struck Allison like a whiff of hartshorn salts and did nothing for her anxious nausea.

The countess stood in the marble-floored entry with their first footman, Hayden, who patiently held open the door. Allison was reluctant to draw any nearer than the staircase's lowest step, so repelled she was by her mother's scent.

"My Allison, but aren't you ready early? I worry your hair will wilt before you reach the doors of the assembly room. It is our first night back in the city and I wish for you to shine, my dear."

"I promise to leave here looking as fresh as you see me now."

Lady Weldon's powdered brow arched upward in that skeptical way her daughter knew too well.

Outside, a pair of men were lowering a sedan to the street and opening its top and front. The grand woman turned to Hayden who was pushed somewhat aside by the breadth of her burgundy skirts. "It is time for me to go and make my social calls before our appearance tonight. Your father will be leaving shortly to make his own rounds and—" she swiveled on her heel, "Hayden, you will call a sedan chair for Lady Allison at eight sharp."

"Yes, Your Ladyship."

A moment later, the door clunked shut behind Lady Weldon's little train of taffeta.

Hayden was quick to avoid Allison's gaze, but she swooped down the final step and blocked his egress. "Hayden."

"Lady Allison?"

She was already palming a fat handful of shillings in the pocket that hung beneath her petticoats. She withdrew them and pressed them into Hayden's waiting hand.

"You will call a sedan chair for me not at eight but at seven."

His fingers curled around the fistful as his dark brown eyes lowered to meet hers.

Hayden had been born with a split in his lip and it had been repaired in a crooked, but serviceable manner when he was still an adolescent, working as a groom under his father. Allison was a very young child when she'd heard him crying out under the knife of the family surgeon. It had given her nightmares. Yet, once he'd healed up, she decided he had the most lovely smile, even as no one else seemed to agree. It was the smile he wore now as he acquiesced to another of her habitual bribes.

He sighed. "I will call a sedan chair for you at seven."

He delivered an exaggerated bow fit for the court, and Allison met it with a strained and teetering curtsy.

"Do not twist your ankle, my lady. Your mother will have my head."

"Where do you suppose she keeps the other heads she has collected?" Allison tried not to laugh or break their stare. She knew this game and hated to lose it.

Hayden thought on it. "One of the wine casks has taken on a strange odor of late."

Allison snorted but inched herself lower. She *would* make him laugh first.

"Mr. Hayden! Do come!"

Both of them were drawn sharply upright by the earl's voice from the rear of the house.

"He needs for you to reach something up high, I wager," murmured Allison.

Hayden nodded his agreement and heeded the call, shillings jangling in his livery pocket.

Allison returned upstairs. What a blessing that their dreary butler had been left at Tallyside to look after it while they were away. With Hayden helming the townhouse, she had access to freedoms she might not otherwise enjoy.

She had an adopted elder brother, Stefano, but he'd worked in shipping on the Mediterranean for so much of her life that she hardly saw him. So it fell to Hayden to be the target of gentle sisterly harassment, and he was quick to tease her in kind. Their conspiratorial exchange had briefly diverted her from the stirring in her stomach. Now, as she resettled on the edge of her bed, that stirring was back—a potent reminder of a plan too bold for her. A plan that would be enacted at seven.

The extra hour would grant her time to visit Dryden Street. Time enough to find Harry's apartment—to gaze upon him and discover what emotion he might elicit now that her passion had been tainted by confusion and ire.

Of course, she hoped it might all be some misunderstanding. Hoped that one letter, then another, had been lost in the post. Perhaps Harry shared her confusion about a lack of correspondence. Perhaps they would share laughter over it. Perhaps his eyes would light up as they fell upon her, and hers would brighten too, as she heard his lips move around the word *Primrose* for the very first time . . .

Orrr he might be a rogue and she a fool.

She sighed. They had not met in the conventional way. After all, how conventional could it be for one of her set to cross paths with a Bow Street fellow?

She'd first laid eyes on him a year ago in Bartswell, when he was not yet a proper Runner. It had been a night of mayhem, a night where she and her cousin, Beth Clarke, had narrowly avoided grave disaster at the hands of disgruntled scoundrels. Then suddenly, there had been this young man, Harry, slicing through all of the chaos with the crack of a whip and rescuing Beth's love, Rhys, from an unjust arrest.

He had been marvelous—a sudden star in a dark night. Inexperienced, yet brave. Young, yet wise. Surely his heroics had lent something to her attraction, but she also knew him through Beth's stories. Of how he was the gentlest member of Rhys' highway band of thieves. Of a distant, ill-fated mutiny . . .

Allison had approached him that night to flirt, to bat her lashes and soothe away terrible new memories with light conversation and compliments. But they exchanged no compliments. And they spoke not of favorite refreshments nor games, but of the loneliness of long journeys and the faintness of childhood memories. And all with a wistful good humor that felt like a natural state.

They spoke a mere couple of hours, yet Allison had walked away feeling known and had whispered to the young hero where he might post a letter.

He had posted nearly four score letters since.

Then nothing.

Allison took a deep breath, quelling the burn of rising tears. If only she could have her cousin's advice.

It was because of that night in Bartswell—because of its scandal—that the name *Beth Clarke* was banned in the presence of Lady Weldon. Since then, Tallyside's butler had ensured not a single note bearing the ruined name ever reached Allison's letter tray.

Now Allison could finally write, but no counsel would be reaching her in time. No, tonight she would be crossing uncharted waters alone, seeking answers from their source.

She looked across her room to the dressing table's mirror. Her mother was right, her hair would wilt. She replaced a sunny tendril into the strand of pearls strung through her coiffure and confronted the girl in the mirror.

Here she was, taking the matter into her own inexperienced hands. It was precisely what Beth would have encouraged.

The thin cushioning of the sedan chair's box did little to prevent bruises as another rough jostle saw Allison's head banging into the side.

"Have a care!"

The men carrying the box either didn't hear or ignored her. What had gotten into her? She sounded like her mother.

They were almost to Bow Street and Dryden was not far. Her stomach tightened. The inside of the little box was suffocating, yet she found herself equally disturbed by the prospect of being free of it—of being alone at sunset in Covent Garden.

The fear was confronted sooner than expected as the floor of the box, rather unceremoniously, met with the pavement. The front opened up and one of the carriers offered a hand to help her from her seat. No sooner was she standing than the men hurried off to find their next fare.

Allison stared up the brick facade of Eight Dryden Street. She could feel how her golden gown drew the gazes of the passersby. She stuck out like a gilt flower, so decorated she was for the ball. Conscious of her visibility, she lowered her head and knocked on the tall green door.

A full minute seemed to pass before it cracked.

"Who want?" The words uttered by the meek feminine voice made no sense at first and Allison stammered.

"I—I am here to see—I wonder where Mr. Plymouth might reside, if you please?"

Tired eyes examined her from the shadows inside. Flicking up and down, they approved enough of what they saw that the door was flung open. A thin, neatly dressed woman with gray curls jutting from beneath her mob cap pointed at the staircase.

"U'stairs," she said, "but I don't want trouble." The woman slammed the front door behind Allison and ducked into the nearest room, slamming that door too.

The building appeared quiet and well-kept. Allison stepped onto the staircase and looked up past its many turns and landings. She forced a swallow of courage past her dry throat. Harry had once written about the view from his dormer windows. *'U'stairs' must mean the garret.*

Each upward step increased the tremors in Allison's hands. Never in her life had she fainted yet felt suddenly bared to the possibility. Her thoughts grew layered and chaotic. *What if—? What if—?*

She found only one door at the top.

She raised a fist to knock, and her eye caught the glimmer of the garnets on her bracelet. This was absurd. She was dressed to draw the eyes of the ton's finest bachelors. Yet here she was in a tidy lodging house, seeking a Bow Street Runner who might have deliberately discarded her.

A memory of his smile flitted through her thoughts. His smiles started in his lips but ended in his deep blue eyes, which became so lit by his spirit that they dazzled like fireworks. She could not fathom such eyes being insincere.

With that one fleeting image of a smile, the garden of her hopes was watered. Her nerves settled and her bile retreated. If she were to be a victim to her own naiveté, so be it.

She knocked.

A little gasp puffed from her throat—the door had moved away from her knuckles at the first gentle rap. It opened with a well-oiled whisper and stopped when it was but a few finger-widths ajar.

Allison glanced over her shoulder, toward the staircase, as though someone might be there to offer reassurance.

She rapped again, this time against the doorjamb.

No sound came from within.

"Mr. Plymouth?" she called. She lowered her voice to try again. "Harry?"

No answer.

She flattened a palm against the door and eased it open, only for it to be stopped by something on the other side. She jumped back. Something was not right.

Somewhere downstairs, a door opened and closed loudly, startling her again. She wished to be anywhere else but in the stairwell where she felt so exposed and out of place.

She pushed the door slowly until, again, she met with resistance. There was almost enough space to push her head through the crack and have a peek, but the idea of putting any part of herself through the portal before she knew what lay on the other side was wholly unsettling. She shut her eyes and reopened them with a surge of courage. Then she put a shoulder to the door and shoved.

The resistance began to give, but there was a cascade of disturbance on the other side: the *tinks* of broken glass, the shuffling of papers, the groaning of heavy things against the plank floor . . .

Her progress struck another more solid blockage. The door would give no more. *No matter.* There was room enough to slip through.

Her next cautious greeting was swallowed up by the sight that confronted her.

It was difficult to absorb it all at once. The carnage.

Golden twilight cut through the two dormer windows to Allison's left, flattening each layer of the room's destruction into its own shadowy, twisted shape.

It was a toppled bookcase that had blocked her entry, its documents and tomes scattered far into the room's center. Pages, ruthlessly torn out, were thick on the ground. They were disturbed by her skirts as she entered.

A rug was scrunched against one wall. Chairs, splintered to bits, were haphazardly strewn before the little fireplace. A flipped table. The bed's mattress was decimated—fiber and down erupting from its insides in a gory manner.

She wandered far enough into the room to find one of the strips of waning sunlight and stand in it as though it might comfort her.

The words the landlady downstairs had uttered clanged like an alarm bell in Allison's skull: *"I don't want trouble."*

What trouble happened here? Was Harry safe? Was *she*?

She drifted to the next window, to where the glitter of something caught her eye. There, a little clerk's desk lay on its broken face with a dagger standing upright from its wooden back. Allison crouched down to study its gleaming brass pommel and a grip inlaid with a checkered pattern of nacre and lapis . . .

Her hand went to touch it, but something stopped her. A dark awareness was coalescing; if she let it take hold, she would not retain her senses.

Her knee gently bumped the desk's side drawer, which was thrust out like a little tongue, spilling stationery all around her where she knelt. She swept a hand through the papers, finding them mostly blank, but for one—she unburied it. It was a letter, or the start of one, with *Dear Primrose*, sitting lonely at the top. She brushed the words with her thumb only to see the word *"Dear"* disappear beneath a jet smudge.

On examination of her fingertips, she found several of them stained with ink. Daubing them on the paper did little to clean them. She dropped the letter and stood, snatching up her gold skirts in a sudden panic for her hem. A toppled ink pot rolled around near her toe.

So absorbed was she in the little mess, that she almost did not catch the *click* of the pistol behind her.

"Don't move." The male voice was gentle but authoritative. "I don't know who you are, but you are going to tell me everything, including who sent you."

Allison heard the door close. Footsteps.

Her heart clenched as she awaited further instruction, as she hoped she might be asked to turn around before this stranger was upon her.

"I only came for Harry," she said.

The footsteps halted on a crunch of broken glass. They didn't move again and the absence of sound was hard to bear.

"Why?" asked the voice.

"Because he—he promised me something."

Harry Plymouth's mind was addled from many nights without good sleep. Reality was hard to separate from the nightmares of mutinies and murders. It was enough to worry a man that any moment might be a dream. Was this?

One golden curl tumbled down the woman's neck from where her coiffure had lost hold of it. That seemed right. As did the rich and sunny concoction that enveloped her. Her petite stature—that too. Her voice—he did not quite remember her voice from a year ago, but he remembered he liked it. He thought he might like this voice too. Though he hated now to hear how it trembled.

Yes, from the back, she was every bit his Lady Allison—his distant Primrose. Yet he expected at any moment that she might turn and reveal some villain's face instead. Such were his nightmares. Such was his life now.

"What did he promise you?" he asked, lowering his pistol.

She turned then.

And it wasn't some wicked face that greeted him. It was *hers*. It was *her* green eyes, bright and gentle, shimmering in the sun's waning rays. They danced as she assessed him. Then they flared, widening at the very moment recognition struck.

He flinched as she moved toward him. *No. She can't be here. It isn't safe.*

But his arms betrayed his judgment, folding around her as she collapsed against him. For a moment, he was lost—blessedly, lost. Then his senses awoke to the crispness of the taffeta beneath his fingers. He gently extracted her.

"Allison. You should not be here."

"Is that all you have to say?"

Not remotely. But now was not the time.

The urgency of the situation wrapped around his neck like a tightening noose, and now here was his lovely Allison standing dangerously close to the same gallows.

Her fingers threaded through his, bringing with them a veil of peace, rescuing him from hell, for just another moment.

"Harry. What is all of this? What has happened?"

Her face was the shape of a heart and her lip trembled over a small and pointed chin.

"You look very lovely," he said, as though all sense had fled him. There was an echoing emptiness to his thoughts—a mind full of cobwebs.

For one second, her eyes lit up in the way he hoped they might, but then her expression collapsed into one of pity as though he were a senile man who needed to be led to his dinner plate.

Another thought—useless in the moment—escaped the cobwebs. "I'm very sorry."

He wandered away from her and picked up a book of no consequence. He placed it in a deliberate position on the mantel, as though the one gesture might render his whole room back in order.

"Harry, you are frightening me."

He turned on her.

"Am I?" His thoughts, his actions—they all felt so nebulous amid the deprivation of sleep. "It's no wonder. I'm rather frightened too."

Allison approached, the need for answers swimming in her eyes. She opened her mouth to speak—

A sound from downstairs, though—

Harry cut off her words with a finger to her lips, finding them warm and tremulous. He turned an ear toward the door. Someone was downstairs. A man. Arguing with another in the stairwell.

Allison's lips flinched beneath his finger and he responded with a whole hand across her mouth. He hoped the desperation in his eyes conveyed his regrets before he whispered his instruction.

"Someone's coming. It is very dangerous. Do you trust me?"

The sight of her wide and glassy eyes above his firm grip would haunt his nightmares for the rest of his days. If anything should happen to her, fear would be the last expression he would ever know to grace her face.

He could not let that be.

She nodded beneath his hand and he removed it, taking her wrist instead. He raised his pistol and led her silently to the far dormer where his desk was toppled. He slid the sash upward and helped Allison to it, using the desk as a step. For a moment he panicked that she might not fit with her enormous skirts crowding the way. But her frock collapsed miraculously, the way a cat seemingly loses its bones whilst creeping beneath a gate.

He joined her on the roof outside and closed the window until only a small gap at the bottom was left.

Allison had already flattened her body to the roof's slope, bracing her heels against the short parapet that made any falls unlikely.

Harry stretched an arm around her.

"We must move away from the window," he whispered.

She nodded and crept away with him close at her heel—too close, apparently, because he stepped on her dress, disturbing her footing. Before her chirp of surprise could become a scream, his hand was across her mouth again. There was no time to linger on the anguish it caused him to handle her in such a way, but rather than having to force away the thought himself, it was eased when she settled her body against him.

There was a *bang* as someone inside flung the door open, only to be met with the immovable toppled bookcase.

Harry raised his half-cocked pistol and waited for the sound of a footstep to conceal the click as he pulled back the flintlock's hammer. He slid his hand from Allison's mouth and stroked her cheek instead, all while keeping an ear to what was unfolding inside.

He expected to feel her shake apart in his arms like a clockwork toy rattled by an over-tight spring. But, no. She was utterly still, as though she dared not even breathe.

Two pairs of steps entered the room. One, heavier, like boots.

The other, detectable by their carelessness as they shuffled through broken ceramic on the floor.

"I don't think he's been back," said a man.

"No, I don't suppose he has." This voice was more refined than the other and nearer the window. It was the voice with the boots. "But he left your blade out for you, how kind."

Harry heard the groan of the desk against the floor as the dagger was plucked forcibly from it.

"Anything else you'll want me to be looking for?"

"No. The letter you found is enough. It is a mere souvenir, besides. We knew he was our man."

Harry's flesh went cold. *The letter.* He had pushed away the fear for days, but now the final thread of denial was cut. This hell. This nightmare. It was about the mutiny of years ago.

How he wished he were free to curse, to shout, to rush the men with his pistol and strike them down—it would have been the perfect chance but for Allison. Instead, all he could do was listen when the men neared the window again:

"Shall we leave a note?"

"A note?" The question was laced with casual disdain.

"You know, a threat?"

"Yes, Giddy, we will leave a threat but not on paper."

The clumsier steps crossed to the back of the room, near Harry's destroyed mattress, then crossed the length of the room again, toward the mantel.

They continued their conversation, but Harry could not hear clearly until the clumsier man passed by the window.

"Almost done. We'll get you to your Willis' soon enough."

There came the sound of wood knocking against wood. For a moment, it was just another innocuous detail, then Harry realized what sort of threat was intended. His heart twisted in his chest. There were more *snaps* and *knocks* as the legs of Harry's broken reading chairs were committed to a pile of firewood. He wondered whether Allison could hear it, if she understood the outcome as he did.

The men inside worked quickly and exchanged no further pleasantries. Minutes passed. The sounds of footsteps either disappeared or were deadened by new sounds. A whiff of smoke reached the window. It was too dangerous to wait any longer, even if the men were still about.

Harry rolled away from Allison's side and threw up the sash, leading through the window with his pistol hand.

Dropping into the room, his eyes softened with relief even as they burned against the smoke. The men were gone. They'd not waited for their fire to take hold.

Harry scooped up his ruined counterpane and dashed to where the pile of burning rubbish trailed from the hearth. He beat at the encroaching flames until they retreated. He smothered the rest of the pile with a rug.

Coughing, he braced his hands on his knees, exhausted over the remains of the crisis. He turned to retrieve Allison and was stopped short by what he saw.

A leg.

Just a leg. Bare to the thigh. A pointed, slippered toe searching for the desk they'd used as a step. Her frothy dress had been caught up in the window frame, even as she used one hand to try and force her pocket hoop through the opening.

One leg. One strong leg, with treble-clef curves. One ribboned garter below the knee, coming undone.

"Harry?"

His thoughts snapped back from paradise as he rushed to assist her.

He extracted her in as chaste a manner as possible, which was not saying much. When she finally had both heels on the floor and faced him, it was to display the sort of blush that put roses to shame.

The embarrassment was his fault—*Dash embarrassment!*—the threat to her very *life* was his fault.

She smoothed her skirts distractedly. The silk now had a great many snags in it. Without thinking, Harry reached out to brush the dust of dried bird excrement from her hip. She paused her own ministrations to observe his.

Her sides expanded as she took a deep breath. Then she lifted her chin to reveal an unexpected and unnerving smile.

"Well. This *has* been interesting. I do not suppose my courage has earned me any actual answers?"

He didn't know what to say. He didn't want her any more involved than she now was. So he stood there. Stricken.

"No?" she asked. "I supposed not."

She smoothed her skirt once more and moved past him, but he cut off her path at the door.

"Where are you headed?" he asked.

"To a very large party, where I hope to make guano and ruined silk the latest fashion."

Harry didn't mean to, but he laughed.

The smallest thread of a smile came to her lips too.

"Let me see you there," he begged.

"For my safety?" she asked.

He stretched a hand between them to cup her cheek.

"For my sanity."

2

Allison's fingers searched for any loose strands of hair that might be nervously tucked back into place, but preening was futile. With each bump of the carriage, another tress seemed to escape. She pushed another aberrant lock behind her shoulder in surrender. There, it might at least mingle with the few curls that had been artfully arranged to trail down her neck.

Throughout the useless exercise, she'd kept one eye on the man across from her. The meager light of London's oil lamps lit his profile as his shoulders rocked back and forth against the squabs.

This was not how she remembered the Harry of a year ago—this downtrodden man wearing naught but his rumpled shirtsleeves and open waistcoat. No, what she remembered were bright, closed-lipped smiles cutting through his otherwise bashful expressions. Blue eyes that hooked into her gaze like a well-fitted latch. A young man confident in the moment of action and sweetly uncertain in the moment following. This man, sagging beneath the weight of burdens unknown, wasn't him.

Some things were the same, surely. His hair was still a mess of shades, if a bit longer now, a bit more disheveled. Some of the strands were as bright and flaxen as hers. Sun-kissed. But there was a sandier color beneath and a darker shade yet at the root. It was this much darker shade that matched his brow—a brow presently resting in dark contemplation.

His face had changed little, yet he seemed tragically matured, as if his youth at four-and-twenty had resided entirely in his eyes, which were now as flat and unreflective as stone.

No, this was not the lovesick poet who had written her for many months.

A theft of Harry's spirit was evident, and Allison wished to know the thief—wished to see them brought to terrible justice. Her hand flexed into a fist as though she might seek out and strike the offender herself. A little voice in her head—her mother's voice— chided her for such a thought. Allison's hand relaxed and she cast her gaze outside.

Harry had instructed the driver to circle the park so that they might have time to talk. Instead, they continued to share nothing but tense silence.

Allison drew her lips between her teeth, as though that might quell the imprinted sensation of Harry's hand clamped against her face. The feeling persisted. She sifted through her emotions, curious which one was appropriate to feel at present. None seemed to fit.

In the midst of their peril on the rooftop, a sickening toxin had risen within her. For all the ways it had left her ill at ease, it had somehow left her more clear-headed too. Nearly an hour on, she still struggled to bend toward the whimsies and impulses that typically commanded her. She possessed an uncommon sense of control. Patience, even.

Without this sudden change, she might now be questioning Harry until his ears bled. But some steadier voice told her: *patience.*

It was eight o'clock. Her parents would be expecting her at Willis' soon, but her usual anxieties over tardiness were buried deep beneath other concerns.

Allison reached for her hair once more. Vanity, even the futile pursuit of it, was easier to sit with than uncertainty. She twisted a fallen tress around one finger, silently begging it to take a pretty shape. It did not comply.

Abandoning that, she tugged upward on her voluminous skirts, fishing for her loosened garter beneath a sea of taffeta. At her fussing, the whites of Harry's eyes flashed in the dark.

Ah, so that caught your attention.

Allison tightened her fingers on the gathers of silk and allowed a breath or two to pass before she resumed. She then proceeded slowly, drawing her skirts up with sensual purpose. She could feel Harry's gaze on her, following the hem upward.

Her stays were no impediment to reaching her garter, yet she paused before her fingertips brushed the ribbon that had slid down her calf.

She performed a soft sound of displeasure. *"Mmph."*

"Are you all right?"

She looked up at Harry, pleased to see that his features had opened up into a warm expression of concern. Something lighter. Something more *Harry*. But she stifled her pleasure.

"I cannot quite reach my ribbon."

Harry stretched an open hand low across the space between them.

"Give it here."

Allison leaned back, lifted her foot, and allowed the heel of it to drop into his hand—rather inelegantly, she feared.

Any embarrassments were whisked away, however, as Harry wrapped a hand firmly around her ankle. *Here* was a new sensation.

His warm grasp rotated around her ankle, then her calf—his arm twining like a serpent around her leg until his palm cupped the back of her knee. It was a sensitive place, she decided, yet she'd never noticed before.

She watched, transfixed, as he repeated the motion—his hand, opening and closing as he followed the curve of her calf. He was completely absorbed in the task.

For the better part of a year, she had imagined the abandon with which she would fling herself into her lover's arms. She had stirred her courage into a froth, confident she would not just flirt like the devil and retreat—as had been a habit of years past—but would give herself over to him . . .

Completely.

But now, at the touch of the man she'd dreamt about, her desires were not so lucid. *The newness of it. The intimacy of it.*

Her skin tingled as his fingers brushed past the boundary of her stocking, touching the flesh above her knee as he worked to smooth down the knit silk. It was . . . daunting.

A long drag of air escaped her. She'd not even been breathing.

Harry's pinched fingers lifted the embroidered ribbon from where he'd set it on his knee.

"A bow?" he asked.

"Sorry?" As Allison replied, she realized she'd leaned rather far forward, as had he.

"I've never tied a lady's garter. How do you wear it?"

"Oh. Yes. A bow. The flowers go in front. I wear it below the knee."

Harry cupped her heel more firmly and pulled her foot into his lap. The gesture nearly tugged her from the seat's edge. There was a staggering lack of grace in her new position and she strained to keep her neck looking long.

She observed his work and cocked her head. It wasn't going to stay up unless—

"Tighter," she whispered.

At her direction, the ribbon squeezed her leg. Harry's knuckles brushed against her kneecap as everything was cinched into a tidy bow. The task was complete, but he did not give up her leg. Instead, he smoothed a hand over the now taut stocking.

"Forgive me, Allison. For everything."

She nearly didn't hear him, lost as she was in the novelty of being touched.

She shifted her attention from his hands to his face. "Forgiveness might be much easier if—"

"Yes. If I explain."

She stole her foot back from his lap before another brush of his hand could rob her of all senses. With one swift motion, she hoisted herself back into a fashionable posture. She was not blessed with her mother's stature and as a girl had suffered many hair-rufflings by Hayden and her brother, Stefano. Therefore, the maintenance of an erect posture felt critically tied to the sense that she was ever at all taken seriously.

Harry continued. "I know it is not the reunion we had in mind. I know my letters stopped and I'm very sorry for it."

Allison folded her hands in her lap and waited as he took a shuddering breath. His head slumped forward, showing her the top of his disheveled mop of hair. She wanted to rest a hand on his knee, wanted to comfort him, yet fear was contagious and she could hardly comfort herself.

"I don't want to invite you into my purgatory, Allison."

"But what *is* your purgatory?"

"I wanted to keep it from you entirely." He raised his voice to compete with the clamor of the hack. "Three months back, when the letters stopped—it was the first time I caught an intruder in my room. It was late at night and I woke to a figure over my bed."

Allison's thumbnail dug into the palm of her opposite hand.

Harry continued.

"We fought in the dark. I could not see him, but he had a good deal of size on me. We grappled upright until he caught a heel and fell. Before I could seize on his disadvantage, he gathered his feet and fled."

Harry raised his head and his eyes—his brilliant young eyes!— looked hollow as a ghost's.

"Who was it?"

"Before tonight, I'd no answer to that. I brought it to the attention of Bow Street, but the chief magistrate, Sir Wright, dismissed my intruder as a thief."

"But you disagreed, even then."

"I did not realize my intruder had a dagger until I rolled away and heard it tear into my mattress. Once he was gone, my eyes adjusted to the moonlight and I saw the blade stabbed into my bed. Yet I could not convince the magistrate, even when I brought him the weapon . . ."

Harry shook his head and stared down at his fist, as though he still held something there.

"The dagger in your room? In the desk?"

"Yes. Though they took it with them when they left tonight."

Allison's mind lingered on the vision of a dagger hovering over the heart of the man she loved. Long needles of guilt worked their way between her ribs. For months, she had been nursing her snubbed affections, all while he had nearly been murdered.

Gratitude followed. Everything might have been so much worse.

"After that . . ." Harry wiped his brow as though exhausted by the very idea of recounting. "Some days passed uneventfully. Then I was investigating a murder in the rookery. I was making inquiries at a tavern when a brawl started, seemingly without cause. When I stood to help restrain a man, I felt something sink into my back."

Allison's hands did not fly to her lips, nor did she gasp. Her thumbnail merely dug into her palm a little harder. How could she feel as though she were still two hundred miles away from this suffering man when he was right here?

"It was a piece of glass and did not go deep, but whoever did it was quickly lost in the crowd."

"And the magistrate still did not—?"

"'It is the rookery,' he told me." Harry went quiet and his gaze flicked toward the window, searching for something reassuring out there in the night. Allison refused to let him slide back into tortured silence, not when he was finally speaking.

"And then what?"

"I tried to believe in coincidence against my better judgment. For weeks. Tried to tell myself the incidents didn't mean anything. I saw shadows over my shoulder everywhere I went and didn't know if they were real. I continued working. Then I came home one day and found my inkpot on the other side of the desk—a small thing, but . . ."

"Not where you would leave it?"

He didn't reply.

"And when was the sacking of your apartment?"

Harry shook his head as though to shake off a spider. Then he sighed and met her eyes. "I'm sorry I did not write."

Allison shifted in her seat and straightened her skirt down with her palms. "That is not what I asked."

"But it's what you most want to know, is it not?" he snapped, eyes suddenly wild.

Allison flinched and heard her reply come out under her breath. "Not anymore."

Harry was acting a cad, biting at her like that. He knew it. He could see it as though he were outside of the whole scene looking in. But it all felt so dreamlike. He was too tired to be himself. He relinquished his forehead to the comfort of his palm and shut his eyes hard, trying to remember what he wished to say. "Please allow me to apologize for that much."

She answered with her stillness. Her silence.

He summoned the energy to fill the pause. "I was too unsettled to write you, even after that first intrusion. Some instinct warned against it. Things were taken, Allison." *He winced as he said it, as he contemplated just how much of the truth he could bear to tell.* "I did not wish my stalker to find anything with your name on it. I fear I am now a dangerous man to be tied to."

A lock escaped Allison's hairstyle as she cocked her head. "Harry, you are not an aristocrat, therefore, you are *already* a dangerous man for me to be tied to. I've not shied away from it."

His chest expanded weakly, with something that might have escaped as a laugh in better days. No. She'd not shied from it. And that's precisely what he feared—her appetite for reckless proximity.

"Dangerous, in a way, but it's not the same," he said. "I do not believe your mother would outright murder you for a dalliance with a Bow Street Runner."

"Perhaps you do not know her as I do." There was the hint of a smile before her face moved into the shadows. Then it was as though she'd disappeared, as though she'd never been there at all and he were talking to himself.

At last, came her voice from the dark. "Nothing with my name on it? Harry, what of my letters to you? Where are they?"

Any notion that he was hallucinating dissolved. Much as his imagination tortured him of late, he knew his mind incapable of inventing such a pained quiver in his Primrose's voice.

It made the answer impossible to utter aloud. *Burned.* Her letters were burned.

He had knelt at the hearth as it glowed, sated by the meal of her words. Regret had fallen over him like a velvet drape. And just as the last scrap of vellum was curling at its edges, his hand had darted into the flames to retrieve it. It acted independently of him, knowing his wishes better than he.

Harry rubbed the tip of his middle finger with his thumb, absently soothing the spot where the blistering was its worst.

The scrap he'd retrieved was now his dearest thing, reading—

> *hands*
>
> *wishes redeemed*
>
> *no poet, but*
>
> *days in the sun*

It was, that very moment, in his boot.

"They are gone, Allison."

Her face emerged from the shadows as they passed into a better-lit plaza. Her expression was unmoved. Had she already known before she'd asked?

But no, her eyes were changing now, glittering, catching more light in their—in their tears.

Harry's instincts again found his body moving without the consent of his logic. He dropped heavily onto the bench beside her, crushing her gown. He pulled her against him.

"Lady Allison, please. It does not mean they meant nothing to me."

"When have I ever been *Lady* Allison to you?"

Harry didn't want to say it, didn't want to keep her near to him with that word. But as she shook in his arms, he knew he was too weak not to give her what she needed.

"*Primrose*," he whispered.

Allison softened into his shoulder. "Tell me the rest of it, Harry."

The scent of her hair was unbearable against his face—like a bed of lemon verbena crushed against him. It was the first time he had ever had her in his arms and he had never imagined it being so anguished as this.

"I began to sleep with my pistol, half-cocked, in hand," he began. "One night, I woke to hear the door's lock being fussed with. I crept over and waited for the intruder to succeed at picking it. I held the knob, but it never twisted in my palm. I tore open the door and met only darkness at the threshold. Some days, I fear I've gone mad. That none of this is real."

"Yet there is a wound in your back from a piece of glass that says otherwise. Your pursuers are men, flesh and blood."

"Yes. My pursuers. My *hunters*, more like."

Harry felt her flinch at the word *hunters*.

She pushed away from his embrace, giving them space on the seat. "And then what?" she asked.

"I slept in alehouses for three nights after. When I returned ten days ago, I found my home in ruin."

The memory was not easy to revisit. As soon as he'd lain eyes on his apartment—on that blanket of torn papers and ledgers on the floor—he knew what had been taken. Even through a fog of denial, even through afternoons spent desperately sifting and searching, he knew.

Allison rested a hand on his. "I cannot fathom all you've been through. But it is as I said—these pursuers, hunters, whatever have you—they are *men*, mortal as the rest of us. A specter may not be caught and arrested, but a man may, and that is a fact on our side."

Our? wondered Harry, but her mind worked too quickly for him to interject. "Did you catch much of the men's conversation tonight? From your nearness to the window?"

Harry nodded, marveling at the ease with which she led him to engage. "I believe one was in the employ of another. And I heard a name. That's something."

"Which was?"

"Giddy."

Allison snorted. "Giddy?"

Harry didn't satisfy her need for confirmation. Her insistence on being a help to him was fast shaping into his own regret.

"As the employer or the employed?"

"The latter."

"And the name means nothing to you?"

Harry shook his head.

"But *why* you?"

Harry could not look at her as he responded—as he *lied* to her.

"My best estimation is that I arrested someone who saw the noose and someone connected to them isn't happy about it." Such was the delusion he once clung to as he sifted through his papers—a delusion pierced through by certainty the moment the evening's would-be arsonists mentioned *"the letter."* Allison was aware that Harry had mutinied years ago with Rhys on the *Diligence*, but she did not know fully his part in it. Nor did Rhys.

Allison looked around herself in quandary, perhaps mulling over his thin, dissatisfying answer. "The person after you must have a great deal of resources and possibly influence," she suggested.

Harry suspected as much himself. "A finely crafted dagger speaks to that."

She straightened. "So, where do we start looking? You *do* know that everyone who is anyone is in London for the peak of the Season?"

Harry's cheeks warmed as his eyes skimmed the luxurious fabric that took up more space in the carriage than they did. *Yes, he was aware who the Season had brought.*

"*We* do not start looking anywhere," he said.

"But if this is a person of influence, you *must* have my help."

"I disagree. I cannot put you in harm's way."

Allison cocked her head and adopted a skeptical expression that was far below her breeding. "You did not disagree with my argument just then at all. You simply made up a new one!"

She was right on that and likely right about his need of her help, too. All this truth did little to quell his building irritation. "This is my *profession*, Allison."

"A profession you have professed to not doing much of these past months."

"Had you not been in my rooms tonight when those men arrived, I'd have finished it. It would be *done*!"

Allison crowded into the bench's tiny corner, eyes wide, with nowhere to escape from his sudden wrath.

Harry retreated in shame, giving her space on the bench. It was another unfair response. He'd been within a hair's breadth of his hunter before and had naught to show for it. He could not know how it might have played out tonight.

He put a helpless hand in her lap and wished she were still in his arms. She did not meet his hand with hers—did not accept his pathetic olive branch.

"Where will you sleep tonight, Harry?"

"My room, of course."

Allison swatted his hand from her lap.

"On Dryden? With your place looking like that and dangerous men visiting it with the frequency of a brothel?"

"I still pay to let," he said.

Her delicate jaw dropped. "You are mad."

"Yes, Allison. *This.* All of this—" He gestured as though the toppled bookcase were still at their feet. "It drives a man mad. So please explain how you think it daft of me to spare you from it? You would have me watch these shadows follow you? You would have me know they might creep into *your* chamber at night and hover over *you* with a dagger? Rend your life apart? In what world would I allow you to be cut down like that?"

The words came fast and forceful, and tremors shuddered down his arms. He closed his eyes and took a steadying breath. Bringing himself down from the cliffs of anguish, he tried to focus on the way Allison's shoulder felt against his arm. As his own trembling calmed, he noticed hers. He took her hand in his.

"Allison, Primrose, what we knew through our letters was *perfection*, but my side of perfection is broken and thus so is the purity of that bond. All that was good about it is carried only by you now. Preserve yourself. In doing so, you might salvage the last crumbs of sanity I have left."

Allison shook her head gently at him and stroked her thumb against his hand.

"You can *solve* this. It's what you do."

It certainly should have been that way, but months had passed, each day only driving him deeper into darkness.

"I'm not like Rhys. I'm not as good at it. I do not see the details as he does." Whether as a seaman, a highwayman, or a Runner, Harry had never felt worthy of his friend's mentorship.

"You were named a Runner for a reason, Harry. Your position was not merely handed to you by way of being Rhys' shadow." He let her words settle over him, hoped they would rouse some untapped energy within him. They did not.

Allison's shoulders sagged as she faced him. "Harry, one day this will be over. Do not push me away before that day."

Rejecting her was the last thing he wanted to do, but whenever he caught the flash of her green eyes in the dark, he saw nothing but terrible outcomes.

"That day in the future . . ." he mused. "Until that day, I am poison."

Allison tore her hand from his and rapped on the wall of the compartment. The coachman stopped, and before Harry could voice his protest, she was hopping out into the busy promenade at the edge of St. James' square.

"Allison, please get back in the carriage. You'll be seen."

"I was already *quite* seen on Dryden. I felt like a harlot going up the stairs to your door, and I am certain I was assumed one by any who saw." Allison straightened her skirt with a frustrated tug and frowned down at it. "Or perhaps I shall amend *harlot* to *courtesan*, because, well—just look at this frock."

Harry almost smiled at how the sudden prod of vanity had quite wrecked her line of argument. Or perhaps the welcome tug at his lips was more about the frock itself. He *had* looked at it. How could he *not* notice this lemon tartlet of a gown that framed her bosom like the finest piece on view at the Royal Gallery. The sight of her traveled through his sleep-deprived body like a jolt of lightning, raising him up for one sweet second before he was plunged back to the London streets.

"The people on Dryden do not have a rat's chance of knowing your name or reputation, but we are in your territory now. These are *your* people, Allison."

She finally paused to examine her surroundings: an elegant pair strolling from the left, a bubbling group of dandies throwing their laughter from the right. She straightened self-consciously, perfectly framed by the window of the hack, standing a few yards off.

Harry tapped his knee impatiently and leaned out from the paneless window. "What will it take to get you back inside?"

The amber light of a street lamp highlighted one side of her expression—a half-moon of indignation. She strode to the window, chin lifted.

"I would *prefer* to ride with the man I met in the stables at Bartswell last summer. The man who rescued my cousin's husband from arrest. A young hero. Confident and kind. I would *prefer* to ride with the man who wrote me since, talking of love and elopement." Allison stood on her tiptoes, making a dramatically mock inspection of the hack's interior. "But I do not see him here. I see only a defeated soul who will not fight and will not ask for help."

Her sarcasm stirred nothing in him. All he felt was his own

lifelessness, a testament to the very truth of her speech. He stretched an arm down from the window to caress her cheek.

Members of the fashionable set crisscrossed on the path behind her, but she seemed again to take no notice. Her focus had him feeling like the only man in London. He waited, wondering whether some flitting hope might arise from basking in her gaze. It did, and he snatched at its promise as though it were a firefly.

"Help me, Allison Weldon."

Allison took his hand and used it to leverage herself onto the carriage's step. It forced him to look slightly up at her rather than down.

"Kiss me first."

It was a command. A dangerous bridge to cross, yet there he was, pressing up through the window to find her lips.

They were feather-light against his, but even at that whispering touch, some understanding was exchanged.

He saw her side of it now. Memories of his own hopes and dreams crashed into him like white water. Nights spent awake, thinking what he'd say in his next letter. Sharing his joy with her when he was formally appointed to Bow Street. Waiting anxiously for her every note. Sometimes the letters were as mundane as a description of her room at Tallyside, but he devoured them all.

Allison pulled away and examined him—*what sort of impact had the all-too-swift kiss had?*

He'd only ever been kissed by the occasional flirtatious barmaid. And at Allison's own admission, she had never been kissed at all. Their kiss should have been more than it was. It should have been all they had imagined on their nights awake, but it was not.

The temptation to lower his lips and try again was a powerful one, but there remained all he'd told her. All he'd warned about.

She was right. Without inoculation against his despair, his nightmares would be made irreparably real. Her words slid over his restless body like warm sanity. Or was it more like cold water to the face?

Of course he could root out those responsible. *Of course* there would come an end to it. To encourage her involvement, however—

"Where next?" The coachman's voice was curt. Impatient.

Allison lowered herself from the step momentarily to be let back inside. "Still Willis', thank you." She'd hardly shut the door behind her when the hack jolted back into motion, spilling her into Harry's lap.

Harry caught her by the waist to steady her, but his thoughts this time were far away from the feel of her. "Allison, who is Willis?"

Her eyes glittered with wry curiosity. "Willis is not a person, so you needn't be jealous. Rather, Willis' Rooms is a popular assembly hall, the most elegant in London. It will be a name on everyone's lips this time of year."

Harry's hands tightened on her waist.

"Harry?" The glittering curiosity in her eyes went dark.

"The men in my room. They mentioned Willis'. They spoke of going there *tonight*."

Allison stared into his eyes, unreadably stone-faced until her whole body jolted with a *"Ha!"* She shoved him so hard that she'd have slid to the floor if not for his grip on her. "I *knew* you needed me."

Harry's mind immediately sought for the ways he did *not* need her. He could go to Willis' Rooms himself. He could get Mr. Crofty to accompany him, to legitimize it. He could—

He peered down at his rumpled shirtsleeves. A headache was forming and he pinched his brow in the hope to ease it. He could find no argument to best her, so he indulged in sarcasm. "Pray, when you converse with dukes and such tonight, will you put in a word and ask if any are trying to murder a Runner?"

"I shall."

Her easy response to the jest unnerved him. She pulled away to throw herself clumsily onto the opposite bench.

"In all seriousness, I cannot in good conscience drop you there knowing those men are about."

Allison shrugged. "And why not? No one saw me at your rooms. They were confident you were not home, therefore, no one—well, no one *of consequence*—saw me. I shall be safe." She caught on to his unchangeable dissatisfaction and shifted her voice to a soothing pitch. "There will be other balls, other fêtes, many opportunities to go and ask your questions. These things all draw the same people."

"Much as I wish to, I have not the resources to go as I am. I would be a distraction. I would need a way to notice them before they notice me."

Allison smiled prettily. "Why, Harry Plymouth, are you saying you need an invitation?"

Clever Primrose, striking upon the very thing that he could not deny needing. The satisfaction across her lips told him she knew it too.

3

It was but two seasons ago that Allison had nearly trembled out of her shoes on the steps of Willis' Rooms. To enter the hallowed assembly hall without confidence in one's perfection was to induce the sorts of anxieties that might see one slip straight from the heights of society into Bedlam.

Tonight, however, she was confident—confident she was *not* the vision of perfection. Somehow being so far from the glossy standard left her feeling shockingly invulnerable to it.

Funny that, how being nearer to perfection is the very thing that might make one strain harder to reach it.

Half of her hair had tumbled from the strings of pearls woven through it, and the sheen of her gown was now dulled by snags. Yet as she gazed up at the brightly lit facade of the assembly hall, her body was steady. It didn't matter. None of it mattered.

"There you are!"

Allison turned to her father's voice. Lord Weldon.

Something unusual, though—

"Father, you are without your wig."

His frown developed before she'd even finished speaking—he was *aware.*

"Apparently, the trunk containing my wigs was never loaded up with our things at Tallyside."

Allison placed a reassuring hand through his arm. His graying curls were not unlike the color of his wigs, but it was a spot at the back—now more scalp than curls—that pained him. He wasn't as tall as his wife and was no doubt mindful that most of society would have a good view of his dome tonight. Men, even earls, were not immune to sensing their lack of perfection at Willis'.

Allison tugged gently on his arm. "Wigs are losing their place in fashion. You will be ahead of the mode tonight." Her words, only half true, brought a weak smile to his face. "Please forgive my tardiness, Father."

"My darling, do you think I stepped outside for air? No. I am tardy too. I do not particularly fancy going in there, but here we must." He patted her hand. "Because you need a husband and I need a drink. Let us go find your mother, shall we?"

Yes, she *did* need a husband. Were one to ask her mother, a husband for Allison was the whole point of the family's time in London. That Allison's father needed to return to London to sit Parliament—well, never mind that.

Allison's mother was nowhere to be seen as they were announced. Lady Weldon had no doubt already planted herself like a nettle somewhere deep in the wool of the aristocracy.

The countess was a woman rigidly driven by reputation and decorum. For her efforts, society had crowned her with a wreath of universal approval. By the time they reached London each year, the countess was parched for the company of her admirers.

Allison and her father glided into the assembly room. Chandeliers floated overhead like gaudy coronets, painting the high, rosy walls with their ever-shifting light. Latticed balconies overhead splashed over with the abundant fabric of ladies' dresses squashed against them. Another such balcony contained the musicians, who worked their strings with enthusiasm. A cotillion was in progress in the grand room's center, and the excited crowd barely afforded the dancers enough space to execute their figures. Willis' would surely never lose its luster.

The hack had dropped Allison at Willis' with a heart limp and sore from all she'd learned, yet she remained weak in the face of spectacle. Looking from one vibrant silk to the next, from one handsome, smiling face to the next, inhaling the perfumes—it all united to caress her wounded heart. She had anticipated the need to conjure a facade for the evening—to invent a smile—but the comforts of the Season were working their magic on her, in as genuine a way as they might.

She had departed from the carriage on a triumphant note—extracting a promise from Harry to meet on the morrow. Allison would send a hack to Dryden with instructions to bring Harry to her.

He had not acquiesced to her offer of assistance in any formal capacity but was in dire need of access to the ton—something he could not achieve without her. She tilted up her chin, basking in the feeling of usefulness. Things had seemed rather grim there for a moment, but they were going to solve Harry's problem together and clear the way to the union they had dreamt of.

Allison's eyes skimmed the teeming hundreds. *Now, if only one of them would wave a rare dagger in the air, calling, "Over here!"—that would be divine.*

Her father excused himself from her side and started on a trajectory toward the refreshments. With her chin still uptilted, she caught sight of her mother's sanguine gown among those pressed to the rail overhead. It would have been a passing observation if not for her mother catching her eye and beckoning her up with a wave.

Few people loitered in such transitory spaces as the grand staircase. They were all too desperate to be in the thick of the excitement, be it upstairs or down. Allison acted under this same impatience as she hurried to the balcony. The hum of voices and laughter swelled as she ascended.

She rounded the corner into the upstairs hall with such enthusiasm that she made full, staggering contact with a man rounding it the other way. As she ricocheted from his shoulder, he struck out a hand to steady her, catching her by the elbow.

Her pulse leapt in mortification as she looked up and met the man's eyes. The stony quality of his expression was a fitting match for his statuesque features and silver gaze.

"Forgive me," she breathed.

Her balance returned as she settled into his grip. He did not speak, only nodded curtly and released her, continuing his route toward the stairs.

Mystifying. He was surely the least blithe character in the whole establishment.

She shook off the encounter and steeled herself to enter the throng of people packed onto the balcony. Thankfully, her mother's high tresses were visible above all and Allison knew where to aim herself.

"My dear Lady Allison, here at last." Lady Weldon's elegant hand slipped between the bodies of others to find Allison's wrist and draw her upstream.

Allison immediately took note of a very fine lady at her mother's side. The woman was tall like her mother, but perhaps a little younger. It was hard to say with the powder and stained lips. Her features were soft and youthful in spite of thin lines that cut across them. And her smile? Angelic.

"Lady Allison, may I introduce the Marchioness of Merton." Allison quickly dipped her head, taken aback by the title. The woman's reputation preceded her. Her fame—and rumored infamy—was unparalleled.

"Lady Merton, it is a pleasure to—"

"No, no, Lady Allison." The woman waved a palm through the space between them, letting a few drops fly from the sherry glass in her other hand. "The pleasure is mine. Your mother has been impressing me with tales of what a fine young lady she has raised. I have been eager to make your acquaintance."

The words were lapped up by Allison's ears like a pretty song, but a cloud fell—was it sarcasm? Allison suddenly felt what she had expected to feel on the steps outside: paralyzing inadequacy.

She hoped that her skirts, crushed up as they were against others, might escape any close scrutiny. Her hair, however, was a loss, lacking the volume that was practically a test of admittance to these circles.

Allison's nerves led her to speak quickly. "Your gown is very fetching, Lady Merton." The minty concoction trimmed with a blush pink was in fact something Allison might seek for herself on a day when a dressmaker could convince her out of her penchant for yellow and gold.

"My favorite colors," said the marchioness, gazing down at her dress as though noticing it for the first time herself. She rolled her stained lips together in a smirk that struggled to conceal how foxed she might be. "And might I add how dazzling your stomacher is. Embroider it yourself did you?"

Allison nodded and hoped she did not appear over-eager. Her stomacher was the only thing left pristine after the night's misadventures.

So much had happened since sunset. Glancing at her mother, the weight of it hit Allison all at once. Lady Weldon had no idea at all. No idea that her only daughter had been pressed between a man's body and the shingles of a Covent Garden rooftop not but two hours ago. *In danger.* The awareness of it went off like a firework inside of her—a secret.

And the marchioness had no idea either.

This notion appealed to Allison. So often she felt like she walked through a world where everyone knew something she did not. Suddenly, she possessed intrigue. It felt like an initiation.

"Lady Allison, I believe you need some wine." The marchioness snapped her fingers over the crowd at someone Allison could not see from her height. Moments later, a glass was delivered by a train of hands over the group. The marchioness made a mock frown as the small glass was passed into her hand overhead.

"Champagne instead. Do you like champagne?"

"I like everything," said Allison.

Lady Weldon was quick to make a correction on her behalf. "Nonsense, I assure you my daughter is very discerning."

Allison truly wasn't though. Perhaps in dress but little else. She loved most things. She was aware of this trait and equally aware of how her mother found it to be a flaw.

"It is much more pleasant to go through life liking things than not liking them," said Lady Merton. "Tell me, Allison—"

Allison's lips parted in astonishment at the marchioness' rapid familiarity.

"—do you like minuets?"

"Yes."

"Tea houses?"

"Yes."

"Fanny Burney?"

"Oh, yes."

"Wars?"

"Ye—No! Of course not!"

The marchioness was laughing, but Allison sensed no derision and laughed with her, nervously taking half of her champagne in one dram.

"Fine," conceded Allison. "I love *most* things."

"And what about handsome men?"

Allison cocked her head at that, playing too coy to respond. *Oh yes.* And she had one in mind. But the Harry she envisioned was not the one she'd just shared a carriage with. It was the Harry of a year ago. Harry the poet. Harry the idealist. A Harry she suddenly worried no longer existed.

The marchioness stared at her, her eyebrows doing a little dance of anticipation. Apparently the question about handsome men was not rhetorical.

"Of course," said Allison, demurely as could be managed, "handsome men, too."

The marchioness gestured down to the dancers in the hall below. Allison squeezed past her mother to get to the rail. It was the sight she dreamt of every year—this omniscient view of the dancing, the drinking, the murmurs, the music. And yes, *many* handsome men.

The marchioness put her palms on the rail beside Allison's and leaned down to her ear conspiratorially.

"Which do you like best?"

Allison sensed a trick. "Is one of them your marquess?"

She looked to the marchioness' face just in time to see what she'd swear was a roll of the eyes. Lady Merton quickly recovered a look of sly glee.

Allison tried again. "Your son, then?"

The marchioness' expression flattened like a desert. "I have no sons." She followed the proclamation with an emptying draw from her wine glass.

Allison's heart fluttered at her misstep, but again the marchioness returned to her glittering smile. "I do, my dear girl, have a *godson*, however." She winked.

Allison tried not to let dread reach her eyes. The marchioness' original line of inquiry had been pleasurable, but to pick out someone of importance to her was most unnerving.

Lady Merton leaned in again. "I shall give you a hint. He is among the group dancing now."

Well, that narrowed things significantly, yet how could she ever . . .?

She leaned over the rail for a better look. Only three men struck her as being young enough and only two of those wore the sort of finery that put them at the top of the nobility. But one of those men was—

No. It was the same man Allison had crashed into in the hallway. He was the most graceful dancer on the floor, yet, even at a distance, his joyless expression was evident.

"I believe you have picked him out," said the marchioness, close to Allison's ear.

"In the blue frock coat?"

The marchioness nodded.

"And who is his family?" asked Allison, straining to summon politeness when the topic of conversation was such a dry man.

Lady Merton raised her glass to her lips once more, only to find it empty. "He is the son of the Duke of Montagu, Viscount Faulkner."

"He is very handsome."

"And an exquisite dancer." The marchioness settled her back to the rail. "We must see to it that you get a turn on the floor with him, Lady Allison. You will find him very light of foot."

And very heavy of soul, I'd wager.

Lady Merton reached out a hand to brush Allison's cheek, catching her quite off guard. Allison waited for her mother's indiscrete whisper at her ear—the encouragement to seize upon a duke's son being offered up on a silver tray—but it didn't come.

Lady Weldon had been swallowed up by some other circle and ferried off to another part of the balcony.

The marchioness pushed back from Allison, assessing her. "If you do not mind . . . how many years have you?"

Allison's cheeks heated. She despised the question. At three-and-twenty, the ton found her to be wearing her unwedded status thin, yet Allison's friends—Beth, Rhys, Hayden—they all had a decade on her. It left her feeling young and unwise.

She braced herself to answer, but the marchioness was already waving it away. "How vulgar of me. Allow me to rephrase, dear— would you find a man of six-and-thirty unsuited to your tastes?" She punctuated the question with a sip from her glass.

Allison enjoyed the marchioness' attention, yet found herself wishing the woman were not quite so foxed. She knew precisely who

Lady Merton spoke of, for her eyes still lingered wistfully on her elegant godson below.

"Age differences are not unusual." Allison did not know what else to say. What was a thirteen-year difference in the aristocracy? It was *nothing*—provided one is speaking of the man's being older. God forbid it be the woman. But Allison was well aware of how she withered beneath the gaze of those older than her, of how she fretted under some perceived authority they carried. No, she did not want someone older. She longed to have a person she could stumble alongside. One with whom to learn and grow.

"You *must* meet my godson."

Allison quashed a reflexive sigh and fabricated a smile. "I would be delighted for the introduction."

The marchioness beamed at her words. There was something curious about how often the woman's features shifted. From this lady of a higher station, Allison was receiving mostly warmth, yet there were troughs detectable between the woman's waves of elation.

As to what a dance with the dour Lord Faulkner might look like, Allison was not kept in suspense overlong. In the absence of Lady Weldon, Lady Merton took up the responsibilities of social guardianship with a drunken vigor. Yet, however much they smiled at the various gentleman who greeted them as they traversed the hall, Lady Merton's single-mindedness about her godson was apparent.

"Lord Faulkner," sang Lady Merton. "I have found for you the most lovely sunflower in attendance."

Not my flower of preference, thought Allison, *but no mind.*

Her hand was placed into that of Lord Faulkner by the marchioness.

"May I introduce Lady Allison, daughter of the Earl Weldon."

It came as no shock when the introduction did not elicit more than a polite nod in her direction. "Delighted," he said, "but we have already met."

The marchioness opened her arms in a melodramatic gesture and Allison was quick to speak. "Not properly, he means."

Lord Faulkner finished the thought. "Yes. It was anything but proper."

Allison was about to smooth over his words with an explanation but was cut off by a violinist testing his strings in the musician's balcony above. Lord Faulkner lifted her hand, apparently deigning to entertain her with a dance.

The dance floor became a garden of vivid petticoats as partners took their places for a minuet. Lord Faulkner's back was straight as a birch as he lifted her hand high and placed his other behind his back. The first note sang across the echoing space, and all the dancers regarded one another with bows and bobs.

A smile, gentle and fleeting, stole across Lord Faulkner's lips. Not a genuine thing, but a polite thing—a contribution to the dance. His well-bred presence matched the refinement of the hall. It would be no tragedy to look at him for the ensuing minutes, and it would perhaps spare Allison from actually talking to him.

His frock coat was a sapphire blue with gold and green embroidery. One of the finest garments in the whole of the assembly room. His chin was cut as though by a sculptor's chisel and his nose was just as sharp. Everything was made of perfect angles. His face. His posture. The cut of his collar. Some part of her wanted to reach out and muss something—make him disheveled like the rogue she'd left in a hack. She did not want someone of marble, but of clay. Someone with the marks of life on them. A freckle. A sunburn. Anything.

The marchioness was not wrong about Lord Faulkner's dancing skills. It was enough to make Allison overly conscious of her steps.

Yet, she sensed her own skills were improved merely by his lead.

The rest of the minuet proceeded so elegantly that it passed in a blink. Allison curtsied. Lord Faulkner bowed. Their transaction, complete.

"Thank you for the dance, Lord Faulkner. Lady Merton was not in error regarding your steps."

"A pleasure, Lady Allison."

She had hoped he might walk away. Instead, he stood courteously by. Escape was up to her. She looked around. "I believe I see my father." She punctuated the fib with a bungled repetition of her curtsy and whirled away.

Perhaps she'd not have been so discomfited by the man if not for Lady Merton's foisting him upon her. After all, she danced with dozens of men each season, and at least half were as dull as Lord Faulkner. Instead, the danger lay in what her own mother might have to say about it. Allison could imagine her mother's gray eyes sparkling—*A future duke?* On her mother's terms, it was every ambition become real.

Harry would be a different story. Suppose Allison should express a wish to wed a baronet? That would be enough to make Lady Weldon shatter a saucer or two and isolate herself for days, unspeaking. A commoner though? Unthinkable. And her mother would never even know what Harry had been in his past life. A well-justified mutineer, consigned to the gallows and spared at the last. Member to a crew of highwaymen. Lady Weldon could not fathom such things. *"Bow Street Runner"* would be plenty enough to strike fear into her stiff, aristocratic heart.

Lady Weldon had met Harry the same night as Allison in the stables of Bartswell, one year ago. Yet the likelihood she had any recollection at all of him was slim. Her mother could recall the face of a fellow countess in perfect detail after a decade apart, but any person without rank was committed so frailly to memory, she might not even get their hair color correct after one day.

Allison took a seat on a bench along the wall. A sweet-looking chap in a rust coat flung a smile in her direction, but she averted her eyes. The spectacle of Willis' had a hold of her, but the gentlemen, for once, did not.

She wished for it to be tomorrow, when she would again see Harry. She imagined him with restful eyes and a hopeful heart. The chance of either was slim, but she would find a way to help him to that sense of peace. Whether in the lifting of his spirits or for an invitation to her circles, Harry needed her. It was a truth, inescapable.

4

The luster of a ball at Willis', which had initially seemed so intact, faded quickly for Allison. By night's end, she had been through the motions of a great many dances, and just as many hopeful suitors had raised her hand to their lips. For each and every one who did, she could only imagine Harry in their place. It was a wonder his name had not popped from her lips.

Now, an empty crystal glass listed in her fingers as she smiled and mused about the less complicated diversion of the evening—Lady Merton. Allison had somehow caught the notice of the marchioness, a woman whose reputation was so perfectly amalgamated—educated and elegant, yet woven through with small threads of vague scandal that no one dared to pull lest the whole illusion come undone.

Allison's eyes wandered up to where the clock was hung at the ballroom's end, but festoons of flowers obscured the view. Likely for the better. The hour was sure to be a painful bit of knowledge.

Besides, a little party was now approaching: her parents, the Lady Merton, and a robust man of about sixty, the Duke of Montagu, she suspected, for he had Lord Faulkner in tow. *Oh, jolly.*

Allison abandoned her glass and rose to meet them. Her mother swooped forward to take her arm, as though she thought Allison unable to balance herself.

"The first of many magical evenings this summer, do you not think, Lady Allison?" Lady Weldon turned to the group before receiving her daughter's nod. "Magical company does tend to make for magical evenings."

Lit by the eagerness to introduce her daughter to a duke, Lady Weldon locked eyes with him, but Lord Faulkner beat her to it.

"Lady Allison, my father, the Duke of Montagu."

"A pleasure, Your Grace." Allison curtsied, feeling her mother squeeze her arm until she had dipped sufficiently low.

The duke reminded Lady Allison of her sporting promise made to Harry. *I do not suppose you wish a Bow Street Runner dead, Your Grace?* The thought made her stifle a laugh as she rose back to her full, if diminutive, height. Harry had not been amused by her jest about interviewing dukes tonight, but at least *she* could be entertained.

"A magical evening indeed," Lady Merton agreed, "and tomorrow we will all meet again." She turned her eyes to the duke. "I look forward to your cook's ratafia cakes, Your Grace. They are always a favorite."

Montagu raised his jowls in smug acknowledgment but seemed reluctant to meet her gaze.

The duke did not strike Allison as the ratafia cake type. It was true a little paunch above his belt betrayed his partaking in them, but his demeanor was mismatched to anything so frivolous. He was of medium height but built like a siege engine. It was difficult to imagine a dainty ratafia cake pinched between his strong, calloused fingers. His features were equally indelicate, yet, beneath the gruff expression and sagging jaw, one could recognize the traces of where Lord Faulkner got his angles from.

Allison's thoughts caught up to the conversation. "Oh? Are we all to meet again tomorrow? How lovely!"

Lady Merton surged forth, rather giddily. "Yes! We have decided to commune in Hyde Park, because this evening has not sated my exploration of these new friendships." Lady Merton looked to Allison's parents.

"That is wonderful," said Allison.

Not just wonderful but perfect. What better way to convene with Harry than to have him fetched to a place so open and public as the park? The news shook the boredom from Allison's bones as her mother led her toward the entry with the rest of their party.

"It has been a long night, though, and we are all prepared to depart," said Lady Weldon.

Allison caught a glimpse of the previously obscured clock. An hour past midnight and many still danced, but the stamina of the nobility did not shock her. Previously, she would have counted herself among those who could dance until daylight.

Soon their little group was on the steps outside, watching the line of private carriages crawl their way forward, one at a time, to carry the well-heeled masses away. Allison's mother was at her side but swept suddenly away to discuss the aforementioned ratafias with Lady Merton. Her absence left Allison alone at Lord Faulkner's shoulder, surely by design.

The minutes between the two of them stretched mostly silent, but from the corner of her eye, she would swear she was being examined. If ever there were a way to make her more uncomfortable, this was it. At last, he said his piece:

"Pardon, Lady Allison, but there is something messing the side of your dress. Might you permit me to remove it for you?"

Well, *that* was unexpected.

Allison nodded mutely, then watched as he dusted something from her hip. Doubtless, it was the remnants of dry bird excrement from her little rooftop excitement. Lord Faulkner scrunched his face in an unpleasant way as he worked. Task completed, he withdrew a kerchief from his pocket and fastidiously cleaned his fingertips.

"Was that all of it, Lord Faulkner?"

"Yes, Lady Allison. I believe that was the most of it." He rocked awkwardly on his heels, returning his eyes to the street. "Lady Allison?"

"Yes?"

"You may call me just Faulkner if you wish."

They exchanged wan smiles, but she neither accepted his offer nor made a familiar one in return.

A moment later, Lady Merton came to them, and—thank the gods for it—not a moment too soon. Faulkner excused himself to join his father. The evening was humid and the marchioness fanned herself so vigorously that Allison shared the relief of its breeze.

"How did you enjoy your evening, Lady Allison?"

"It is always a splendid time at Willis'."

"I have a prediction," whispered Lady Merton.

"Dear Oracle, do share it."

"I expect the Season will make great friends of us."

The marchioness gave Allison's arm a convivial squeeze. Whether it was the wine or the late hour, something had taken the edge from the anxiety Allison felt in Lady Merton's presence.

"I would like that," said Allison.

A dark-haired woman in green-striped taffeta came prancing down the steps, arm-in-arm with her drunken husband. She turned before reaching the street to address Lady Merton.

"Please, do let me know as soon as possible, Beatrice, whether or not you have a man to fill the gap. I am desperate." The woman pouted for effect.

"You will be the first to know when I strike upon a recommendation, Olivia."

The woman's look of concern shifted to fawning gratitude as she lugged her teetering spouse toward their carriage.

Allison examined the fine lady at her side. *So, Beatrice is it?*

"May I inquire, Lady Merton, as to what your friend asks of you?"

"That is Lady Gossington. She needs an extra footman for an evening soirée in her vast gardens—a night which will put all before it to shame." Lady Merton swung her head excitedly toward Allison. "It is in two nights' time—a celebration you must unquestionably attend. I will see to your family's invitation."

"I would enjoy that immensely." But Allison was stuck on the other bit of information that had been flung her way. "In regards to a footman . . . I may be able to secure such a one."

Enthusiasm clouded Lady Merton's gaze and Allison spoke up quickly to temper the great lady's expectations.

"It is not a certainty, but I shall look into it at once."

Lady Merton took a step back to regard her. "My, my. Amiable. Fashionable. Resourceful. What elegant trait do you not possess, Lady Allison?"

A fondness for your godson, thought Allison. She stifled a secretive grin. "You are too kind, Lady Merton."

"If only Lord Faulkner had his eyes on one such as you."

Not for lack of everyone's trying. But Allison put a hand to her breast and feigned interest. "How do you mean?"

"He thinks himself engaged, but Caesar does not approve of the match."

"Caesar?"

Lady Merton shook her head vigorously, as though rattling something back into place. "Apologies. If you did not notice with Olivia, I tend to be over-familiar in close company. By Caesar, I mean the Duke of Montagu."

"Ah. So his father does not approve of Lord Faulkner's choice, and I take it you do not either."

Lady Merton smiled down at her. "How keen you are. I do not, but what say does a godmother possess, really? As a mere friend of the family, I have little part in it."

Beyond Lady Merton, the man in question's carriage had pulled up to the steps. Lord Faulkner strode down to it without sparing a goodbye for anyone in their party.

His footman had difficulty in shutting the compartment door and was snapped at by the coachman. "Ay! What's keeping us?"

"Patience, Giddy."

Allison had just looked away from the little scene when that name—*Giddy*—slapped against her ear.

When she looked back, the carriage door had finally cooperated and the footman was hastily hopping on as the horses pulled it into motion. All she had view of was the back of the coachman's shoulders in a pale shade of livery. Gray, perhaps?

Had she heard correctly? Had she heard *Giddy?*

"Hrmm."

The polite clearing of Lady Merton's throat drew Allison's attention. She flipped through her memory of the last several seconds, trying to remember where their conversation had left off. *Ah, yes. Faulkner's betrothed.* "May I ask what is so disliked about Lord Faulkner's choice?"

"Her rank."

Ask a silly question. Get a silly answer.

The marchioness went on. "A baron's daughter does not suit for a future duke. There is also the matter of fortune—a dreadful imbalance between the families. It is difficult to believe her feelings are true with so much wealth at stake."

"Is she fetching?"

Lady Merton tightened her lips and nodded. "She possesses that much." Then a look of cheer returned to her face, once again marking the swift turns of expression the marchioness was so fond of. "But I fear I am a dreadful gossip and our carriage has arrived."

A man approached from behind her, offering an arm, which she readily took.

"There you are!" exclaimed Lady Merton, playfully whacking the gentleman's arm with her fan. "Lady Allison, may I present the Most Honorable Marquess of Merton, my husband."

"Pleased." Allison dipped in acknowledgment and the marquess acknowledged her in return with a dip of his head and a placid smile.

He was tall and possessed a decent kit of features that were framed by dark auburn hair pulled into a queue. But his eyes did not glow the same way his wife's did, and his dullness was as readable as a ledger's page.

"Lady Allison is the daughter of the Earl Weldon." Lady Merton gestured toward Allison's parents with her fan. "We will be joining them in Hyde Park tomorrow with the duke."

"Will we? Sounds pleasant." They were the only words Lord Merton spoke before fixing his eyes on the line of carriages.

Lady Merton forged ahead without him. "I look forward to tomorrow, Lady Allison. I have a strong feeling the weather will be perfect for us."

"What you say is how it must be, Oracle," said Allison.

Lady Merton's laughter rang out like a chorus of glass bells. "*Oracle.* You said that before, and I love it. Until tomorrow, Allison." The lady winked before being led down the steps by her husband. The marchioness had again called Allison by her Christian name after merely one genial evening. Even her own mother hardly uttered her name in public without its honorific. A frisson of warm pleasure eased across Allison's cheeks.

There were many reasons to ache for the morrow.

Harry flopped his upright mattress to the floor. The hard landing forced a plume of its downy innards into the air. There was hardly enough filling left in it to keep his back from the planks. He sighed at the sight of it.

There had been a luxurious sense of escape in seeing his Primrose earlier that night. In her presence, everything had felt different—had felt . . . put together. Now he was back to where everything had been rent apart. He'd barricaded his door with the remnants of his broken furniture, all while traipsing through the ashes of attempted arson.

In Allison's absence, he was returned to a state of unrelenting vigilance—a state which wore his sanity threadbare. Would he sleep at all? Not likely.

She was right. He could not go on like this. If he allowed this to be his daily existence, then whoever was after him would be granted their desires: *his torture and his death.*

It was time for him to gather his bones and arrange them back into the semblance of a fighting man. If he could not protect himself, then he could not protect her either.

He wished he could ferry her safely to the other end of the earth, but the reality was that she had walked into his world just as his hunters returned. Her life was now at stake and it was his fault. He should have warned her by letter, should have trusted her. Instead he'd vanished, lighting her well-known curiosity like a fuse.

The sheen of a dried puddle of ink caught his eye near the toppled desk. It might just as easily have been blood that was spilt. His. Hers . . .

She did not know the worst of it. She didn't know what had gone missing from his room—a letter to Rhys, written but never sent. It had, almost a year ago, been slipped between the pages of Rousseau's *Confessions* to be safekept—a wry attempt to not misplace it, for it too was a confession. But the courage to send that letter never came and it languished on the shelf, fading from thought until the destruction of his room. Harry knew not how his tormentors had found him, nor who they were, but he knew that they wanted revenge.

Harry crouched down to light the stub of a broken candle next to his flimsy pallet. He removed his boot and watched the burnt little scrap of Allison's letter flit to the ground.

He'd never intended to leave her adrift. For days after the first intrusion, he'd poured his thoughts to paper, struggling to find a way to tell her he must put their courtship on hold, for her safety. Then came another incident, and another . . .

He hid her letters in a hole behind the baseboard, but after the destruction of his room, it did not seem precaution enough. Whoever wished him dead might make dangerous use of the name of one so precious to him. So he'd burned them, and the memories were gone, but her name was safe.

Harry dropped the scrap back into a boot and put them to the side. He lay down.

A young hero. Confident and kind. That was what Allison had thought of him. What she'd *expected* of him.

He stared into the fragile flame that flickered on the stubby candlestick, wishing it possessed enough fire to lend some to his empty heart.

Unlike him, Allison had not lost one mote of her enthusiasm. How had her eagerness to render aid ever caught him by surprise?

Recognizing this optimism in her, he had, early in their correspondence, devised a game called *Buoyant Belle*. He would name to her some rejected thing like a broken pair of spectacles and she would craft an earnest compliment, describing its merits.

She could find the beauty in anything. He once challenged her with "dung heap" and she replied with: *Dung heap, the height of your peak is matched only by your skill at making the garden grow. Your warm heart keeps many worms alive and many hearths lit.*

Harry laughed aloud, recognizing the hoarse sound almost too late to realize it was his own. His heart beat faster. There was hope for him yet.

What sort of fool was he to think he could catch his hunters from such a state of mind? Somehow, he had to summon the spirit to thrive even in the shadow of his enemies.

Allison lent him that spirit. Just in being herself. His eyes slammed shut against a selfish thought—he needed her to continue loving him even as he held her away. He *wanted* nothing but *needed* everything. Including, perhaps, her help.

And she had slyly struck upon how to do so—an invitation to her circle. Undoubtedly, her busy mind was already working out where to have him dressed in the finest silks.

In the morning she would send for him. The very thought tipped the scales against his fears, if ever so slightly.

The candle's tiny flame flickered and smoked. The stub of wax, a flattened puddle.

In another second, it was out.

5

Sunshine poured down from the sky like lemonade, spilling over Allison's cheeks in a way that would surely cue her mother's fussing about the unsightliness of freckles. She blinked against the light. The distant murmur of strollers along the Serpentine mingled with the *whoosh* of a humid breeze. New blades of grass tickled the back of her neck. Young birds squeaked their calls from the nests above. Everything was beginning, rather than ending. So how did so much melancholy cling to such a fine day?

Optimism was as natural to Allison as the azure sky she stared up at, yet her insides were atwist with achy confusion. The gravity of her strange night had not fully struck her before dawn. She had, many times in her life, woken from a dream to think it real until, gradually, some distant, nebulous sense of truth would fall over her. Such it was that morning as the dawn pried her eyes open. For the span of one breath, all had been glorious. She was in London. She had a stack of love letters attesting to the most marvelous affection she'd ever known. A whole summer with her lover lay ahead.

But then memory's claw scratched out the dream, reminding her of Harry's unfamiliar state. A man possessed. A man made more of fear than flesh and bone.

Fear ruined everything. It was precisely why Allison had hardly subscribed to the emotion before. But last night? Last night she had been afraid. She'd not understood it in the moment, but her nightmares were revealing. Even now, her heart ticked up in tempo at any recollection of the rooftop.

Her nails curled against the cover of the book laying open on her chest. Harry might have warned her. If he did not realize she would seek him out, then had he ever truly known her? It should not have been this way, all dashed expectations and wilted hopes.

At present, he would be in his miserable conveyance, headed toward her corner of the park. Would he be disappointed to find her frustrated with him? Should she care?

A shadow disrupted the spill of sunshine overhead. Her mother's perfect predictability.

"Allison, basking supine in the grass does not show you off to the best advantage." Her mother's eyes did not meet hers but skimmed her up and down. "You will develop more freckles, besides." *Ah, there it was.*

"I'm sorry, Mother, but the others have not even arrived yet. I vow to be more social when they do." Allison lifted *Les Liaisons Dangereuses* from her chest, weakly displaying it for her mother.

"Oh please, you've not read a word. It is upside-down."

Allison lifted the book higher to confirm—it was indeed upside-down. She frowned. Amid the bustle of a soirée, Allison's whole existence might go unnoticed, but one-on-one, her mother was a monster for the details.

Lady Weldon's lips softened. "You are taking care not to get grass stains on your *chemise à la reine?*"

"Yes, Mother."

Her mother was loath to see her in such an unstructured garment at all, but had conceded to the choice as a matter of the mode.

"The weather is lovely." Lady Weldon smiled genuinely at the branches overhead. "Very like our time in Florence, do you not think?"

The tension in Allison's fingers softened as she gazed up at her mother. "Some of the very best days of my life," she said.

Lady Weldon nodded. "Mine too." The fly fringe on her dress flicked in the breeze as she turned away, removing herself to a spot she had chosen for their party some distance off and nearer the water.

Allison had convinced her parents they should arrive before the others and enjoy some time alone. It would make it easy to steal a moment with Harry. Regrettably, it had also left Allison too much time alone with her thoughts.

She sighed to the sky and lifted her novel, right way up. She opened it just in time to deflect a flying chestnut from its cover. Her head snapped up, looking keenly for the squirrel at fault. Instead, she spotted a mischievous blue eye peeking around the nearest trunk.

A quick look over her shoulder confirmed her mother's distance. When she turned back, Harry had stepped out from his spot behind the tree.

"Your projectile might have struck me had I not opened my book just then."

"That *was* the idea."

"And what did I do to deserve it?"

"You had me fetched in a tiny sedan chair rather than a hack."

Allison grinned and shrugged. "I thought it prudent to keep a low profile. No one tries to see into those things and they can travel off the park paths."

"So they can."

His smile was subtle, but his eyes sparkled with a playfulness that Allison could have leapt at the sight of. He wore a proper coat now, in a gray the color of a glowing storm cloud. It made the deep blue of his eyes spring forth. Perhaps it was the benefit of daylight, but he did not seem so withered. His gentle brightness was fast eroding her resolve to be upset.

"You seem rather more alive this morning. Sleep better, did you?"

"Alas, not at all." The smile didn't fade from his eyes despite his words. "I slept perhaps worse than ever before, but there were—how shall I put it . . ."

Allison waited patiently to hear how he shall put it, and as she did, he swept down to join her on the grass.

". . . better dreams to be had, even in the waking hours." A meaningful gaze ensured that his sentiment landed.

Allison imagined such a compliment being paired with a caress of her cheek, or some other tenderness, but it never came. There was still a trench between them.

She shifted to sit up and drew her knees under her. "Have you thought on what I've said? Will you let me help you?" She knew that her eagerness was showing in a way many found to be taxing and a widening of Harry's eyes revealed that her urgency was noted.

Suddenly fearing his retreat, she reached for a distraction.

"I'd feel better," she said, "if we move back against the bushes here. To be better concealed."

He shut his mouth, which had been ready with protests, and

moved toward the bushes with her.

"Allison . . ." It was an apologetic tone. Not what she had hoped for at all. "You *have* helped. You slapped me across my face with sanity last night and made me realize I must acknowledge some brightness in my life in order to take out my demons."

"There are no demons, Harry. It is men who chase you, that is all, and—" She stopped herself. His playful eyes had dulled to something more tragic, something gloomy like the misty color of his coat. How could it be so easy to sense a man's angst, even when his words were so sweet? No one had ever warned her of this horrible pit in the stomach that accompanied love.

She waited for him to speak on the feelings that swam in his eyes, but he gave up nothing.

She was happy to end the silence. "I know you do not wish for my help, Harry, but you need it. You admitted last night that you must infiltrate society. You cannot do this as yourself. You must be someone else, the way you once were as a highwayman . . . and I have discovered just the invitation, which I shall share momentarily." He opened his mouth again, but she was quicker. "I also insist that you must not stay in that terrifying place on Dryden. A change of scenery would not only be less depressing but would keep you *safer*, more hidden."

She took a deep gulp of breath before pouncing on her next point, and Harry quite nearly took advantage of the pause, but her words dashed out faster than fillies at Newmarket. "Lastly, I have struck upon something else important. You told me last night to ask the 'dukes and such' whether any are after your skin—"

"Oh God, Allison, tell me you did not."

His look of horror left her grinning violently.

"I did not. Because I did not have to. I overheard something that might be nothing, but . . ." Her voice went up an octave, toward twinkling tones meant to dangle her words like a carrot before him. She shrugged, innocent and smug.

He relaxed back on his palms and sighed. "I concede, Allison. You have my interest. What did you overhear?"

She curled her fingertips into the grass at either side of where she knelt. "*Giddy.*"

"Giddy?"

"Yes, do you not remember? The men in your room?"

For a moment, Allison worried he did not; his face was contorted into an almost pained expression of concentration. But then, his jaw went slack and his hand went raking through his hair. Wild eyes met hers.

"Yes. I remember. The accomplice."

She nodded, trying to hold smugness back from her lips. "It was the name you heard, was it not?"

"It was. You heard it at the ball?"

"Yes. *Giddy.* Can you imagine? How easy was that?! And here I had never even heard the name before."

Harry grabbed her shoulders, focusing her. "Who was he? A nob?"

"No. A coachman. I could not say whether I recognized the voice. You were nearer the window last night and heard much more."

Harry's body slumped. She did not know how she could lose him with such a revelation, yet, somehow, he was slipping away. He gave her a withered look. "Perhaps Giddy is short for Gideon. There might be a great many Gideons in London."

Allison frowned. "Please, do not dismiss this. You overheard 'Giddy' and you overheard 'Willis'.' Coincidence seems unlikely. We know the men after you are resourceful and last night, the room overflowed with men of means."

Harry rallied a weak smile. "Who did the coachman work for?"

The answer to that question had kept her thoughts racing all morning. "That is the thing," said Allison. She lifted her watch from where it dangled on a gold chatelaine. "He will be here in ten."

Harry's face went limestone pale. "Allison. *Who?*" His tone was sharp enough to scare a bird from the branch above.

Allison threw a quick look over her shoulder, ensuring his voice had not drawn attention.

"The son of the Duke of Montagu. An icy acquaintance foisted upon me by other parties with some zeal."

"His *name*, Allison."

"Viscount Faulkner."

Harry shook his head. "I wish I could say it is familiar but alas. Regardless, keep away from him. He could be dangerous."

Allison wrapped a hand around his. "Only a moment ago you were in doubt that my evidence had any bearing at all."

Harry stared at his boots. "Every coincidence turns to terror as soon as I know you're involved. I know not how to stop it." He returned his eyes to hers. "It's why I do not want you to help me in any way besides your being there when all of this is over. Staying safe and existing."

His words had started like a caress, but that last word—

"*Existing?* Harry, when first we met, I had been kidnapped by some brutish acquaintance of yours and thrown from a cart. Merely existing does not quite align with my habits. If *existing* is all you wish of me, then we have much less in common than ever I thought." She snatched her hand away from his.

Harry buried his face in a palm and shook his head. Abruptly he became the man he was the night before, as hollow as a wraith wandering the banks of the Styx. For the first time, Allison wondered whether she could truly lift his burden. She could hide herself away and wait and hope—just as he asked of her—but what good was that for her own burdens? No, she desired to see him just as safe as he desired to see her. She could let go of it no more easily than he.

She squeezed his hand. "We care for one another the same. You're in anguish at the thought of harm coming to me, but my fears for you are no less valid than yours for me. It is why we both must be active in seeing that all turns out well in the end."

Harry churned his lips between his teeth and nodded. "You know, I never should have named you Primrose. You're deserving of a flower more fiery than that."

"I like Primrose just fine." Allison settled down from her kneeling position and scooted herself to Harry's side. The nap of his coat was pleasantly slubby as she rested a cheek against his sleeve. For a moment, his scent overtook the essence of the summer air. It seemed to suit a different season—cinnamon, perhaps, mixed with something she could not pin down.

Harry idly plucked a handful of grass and sighed. "Best tell me the rest."

"You cannot stay in that terrible place."

"Where would you have me go?"

"The mews house."

"What mews house?"

"Why, mine of course." That morning she had cornered Hayden in her habitual way and asked if extra space might be available in the servant's quarters.

Getting no response, she lifted her head to look at him. Harry's mouth had fallen so wide open that she posited she might fit her whole fist into it—just the sort of thought she might have blurted at a younger age.

Harry shook his head strongly enough to cause hair to fall before his eyes. "No. Absolutely not. I would be bringing danger right to your door."

"Well, not *my* door exactly."

"A garden's distance is not—"

"We will be very careful."

"You say that, but there's a chance that one of the men after me is about to meet with you? You said as much."

Allison folded her hands and flicked her thumbnails against one another, concentrating on the nervous exercise. He had a point. She was not prepared for him to be *right* about something.

"I am not meeting *alone* with him. Our parties merely took to one another last night at Willis' and are soon to be gathering near the Serpentine. Think of it as opportune! Besides, Lord Faulkner ever coming to our townhouse is a ridiculous notion." Or so she hoped. Yet the aggressive matchmaking of hovering socialites was not to be underestimated. "How may I convince you?"

Harry twisted to face her and a terrible series of cracks clicked up his spine. He rubbed his neck in response to the adjustment. "How good is the bed?"

Allison smiled. "Better than what I saw in your room." She placed a hand on his thigh. It was firm and the dark fabric of his breeches was hot under the sun. She lingered on both qualities before remembering her question. "Are you worried someone will follow you?"

"I've not had a great deal of faith in myself of late, Allison, but I would be a poor Bow Street Runner if I could not lose a man for one afternoon." His eyes flared—another worry, rising. "What of your mother? Will she not recognize me as the deputy present a year ago?"

"*Aha,* now you've struck upon the *real* danger. At least she does not know your previous life as a highwayman."

"Or a mutineer," Harry added. The tone matched her lightness, yet there was a sardonic cloud in his eyes.

She patted his thigh. "Truth be told, my mother is terrible with faces. Or at least, terrible with *untitled* faces." She gave his thigh a squeeze. "And you are somewhat more muscled than when last she saw you."

Harry's lip ticked up at that.

"Besides, she does not make a habit of frequenting the mews."

Allison was conscious of making an expression that typically brought gentlemen to their knees before her, but Harry averted his eyes and placed a hand on hers. "I will consider the lodging, but only if you promise you will not be scaling any trellises to sneak into my room at night."

Perhaps he did know her after all. "That is ridiculous. Our mews house does not even *have* a trellis."

He laughed, then studied her. Each time he did, she wondered whether she was about to lose the battle for his trust. He sighed.

"Well, may as well get on with it. What of this invitation you mentioned and how does one dress for one of these things?"

Even as Allison celebrated the small victory, she braced herself to disappoint him. She hoped the glint in her eyes would work its magic. "Your attire will be seen to by the hostess."

Harry pinched the bridge of his nose. "Tell me you did not bring someone else in on this ruse?"

"Oh goodness no. I only mean, well, that you will be in livery."

"Pardon?"

"The hostess needed a spare footman and you seemed a robust candidate . . ." Allison squeezed his thigh again, hoping that between that and her dazzling expression, he might be less thrown off. He was not.

"You got me invited . . . as a servant?" His hiss was sharp enough to sting her ear. He stood up, growing more animated by the moment. "First you have me brought here in a sweaty box, and now it is your desire to see me as a servant?"

A guilty smile peeled across her face as she looked up at him. She summoned the last of her charms and rapped one of his boots with her knuckle. "I think you will look fetching in stockings."

Harry breathed out a fierce puff of air, like a bull about to gore a matador. There was something about his hard, building furor that was infectious to her. Something thrilling. Something . . . *arousing*.

"What is it?" he grunted. "Why do you just sit there staring at me like that?"

Her lip went between her teeth and she shrugged. "'Tis a good view."

The corner of his mouth quirked up, caught at last by the hook of her charm. Placing his hands on his knees, he bent over to be level with her eyes. "There shall be recourse for all of this."

Her heart kicked. "Is that a promise?"

He reached out for her cheek and she closed her eyes, antici-pating. Hoping.

Then a voice came rolling over the knoll and through the hedge. "Allison?"

Allison shoved so hard at Harry's knees that he staggered. Her frantic motions were enough to signal he must get out of sight and soon he was.

Lady Weldon reached the crest of the knoll and waved down at Allison. "Darling, everyone is arriving." Her mother hefted her skirts to make an approach, but Allison put up a hand.

"I shall be right there. Do not trouble yourself. I must finish my page." Allison lifted her book.

Her mother's shoulders sagged. "I beg you to be social." She carried her disappointment back over the knoll, disappearing.

A nut struck Allison in the arm. "Ow!"

"That one is for having me set up as a servant." Harry leaned against the tree trunk he'd again emerged from behind.

"The intention is to be discreet, is it not? Does being a footman not make sense? Why does the idea chafe so much?"

He did not answer, but checked over his shoulder as though looking for his hunter. "You'd best get back to your family. But first, tell me . . ."

Allison held her breath, wondering if her efforts would be in vain.

"How is it I get to my new lodgings? A manure cart this time?"

Allison grinned. She had him. He was coming. He trusted her.

"I shall send my man Hayden for you. Be at the same corner at six tonight." Harry stepped forward, extending a hand to help her up. She dusted her white skirts. "Now, excuse me while I go tolerate the company of a dreary man who may or may not have anything to do with your nightmares. I presume we will be watched?"

Harry raised his palms innocently. "Who can say?"

His twinkling gaze made the little hairs on her arm shift. Didn't he know she could always feel his eyes?

Cresting the little knoll, she saw her party spread out on blankets beyond. Her mother and the marchioness wore faded mossy hues, nearly matching. Their skirts puffed and pooled around them in a way that made them seem as one. Each was flanked by a dutiful husband. Lord Weldon, gazed up at the sun, the way his daughter was wont to do, while Lord Merton helped himself to a basket of strawberries. The merry dukedom of Montagu sat apart from the rest—Montagu on a small stool, and Lord Faulkner leaning politely against a tree. They wore matching owls' expressions.

"Apologies for my tardiness. I was enjoying some reading."

"What are you reading?" Lord Faulkner drew himself away from the tree and straightened.

His interest was, at minimum, unexpected, and she flipped the book around in her hands to remind herself which she had brought. "*Les Liaisons Dangereuses.*"

"*Est-ce-que tu aimes ça?*"

"I do, so far. Yes."

She expected more from him then, but that was it. That was all the man had to offer.

"Allison, you must sit and enjoy a cake." The marchioness was somehow even more radiant by day. Her hair was in a more natural state, silver and black, yet it did not make her look old or severe. Rather, it made the bee-stung pink of her lips glow against her pale skin. A light dusting of rouge matched the pink and white stripes of a pierrot jacket that she'd paired with her mossy petticoat.

Allison made her way daintily to the other side of the blanket, to sit where the marchioness had patted at a spot for her. Lord Merton shifted to make room.

"What an absolute blessing to see you again so soon." Lady Merton stretched out a graceful hand and brushed Allison's cheek with the backside of her knuckles. "You look so awake and glowing considering the late night we had."

"As though *you* carry any blemish of the late-night hour."

"If only you knew how my ankles pain me after all that dancing. I was hoping to walk to the lending library after our time here, but I fear Lord Merton would have to carry me."

Lord Merton put a tender palm to his wife's shoulder. "Do not think I would not do it."

The Duke of Montagu made snuffling noise, as though a sneeze were en route, but it never came.

"If you have something specific in mind, I would be happy to do the errand for you before we depart."

The marchioness put a hand to her heart. "That is the friendliest idea. Thank you, Lady Allison."

Allison was, as always, delighted to be useful, but when Lady Merton's gaze shifted to Lord Faulkner, there was a stab of regret.

"Lord Faulkner, you should accompany her."

"Delighted to." His flat tone did not complement the statement.

"*My*, such compelling enthusiasm." Allison only noticed she'd said it out loud when her mother gasped. Faulkner himself seemed unaffected.

Lady Merton laughed. "Oh dear, Faulkner, I do believe you've been exposed."

Faulkner set his eyes on Allison. "I may not make much of a display with my words, but I assure you they are always genuine."

Allison flushed under his earnest gaze and cursed herself for the slip of sarcasm. Suddenly, she was very conscious of being watched—Faulkner's eyes in front of her, and Harry's eyes, somewhere unknown.

6

Harry shifted on the low stone wall where he sat, but the re-adjustments brought no relief to his haunches. It was over an hour since he'd selected the spot as the place from which to keep eyes on Allison and her dandy party. He'd carried on him a copy of *The Daily Register* and now held it open, peering out over top of it.

The group was seated on a blanket just beyond the Serpentine's promenade. At such a distance, Allison's gauzy chemise gown pooled indistinctly around her. But up close, the secrets of its frothy white layers had not been lost on him. The sun at her back was like the key to a cipher—revealing all the tempting shadows of where her curves were drawn. Including those same strong legs that had dangled through his dormer window. His heart beat faster at the memory.

Perhaps he'd been under some enchantment by that dress when he'd capitulated to her plans.

Fears still reared up at the thought of her involvement in the matter, but he forced them down. He could see to them later.

True to herself, the sash at her waist was a wheat yellow, and her curls were piled high with a scarf of gold and aubergine wound through. He liked her penchant for yellows and golds, not least because it suited her. There was something else to it, though—a sureness of self that he admired.

Initially, it had been difficult to tear his eyes from her. The way her chin tipped back with laughter. The way she smoothed her skirts upon sitting . . .

But as time drew on and the sun beat down harder, his eyes and mind wandered. He found his focus pulled toward their blanket on the grass. He was so far away, yet could see how its texture shimmered in the sun, how its vivid dyes rivaled nearby flowers in brightness. If this is what people like them lay on the grass, what sorts of textiles must they sleep in? Harry remembered the feel of embracing Allison in her frippery the night before. The silk had been cool to the touch. Had a distinctive rustle when she moved—

Harry scoffed. *As though I've never touched silk before.* But he could not immediately summon a time he *had* touched silk before. He returned his focus to Allison.

There was a certain unease in watching her from such a distance—in spying on her even when she knew. Yet even as Harry tried to force the dark sensation away, he unwittingly opened himself to all the ways in which he liked it.

She was popping strawberries into her mouth and he imagined himself near enough to see her lips go more crimson with each succulent bite. He imagined his tongue stroking between her lips with that sweet taste still coating her mouth.

Between bites of berries, her white sleeves flitted about like doves' wings—the animated gestures of a story she must be telling.

Everyone laughed. Everyone loved her. Everyone except perhaps a fellow that remained standing for much of the afternoon. Something in his hawkish features and general separateness warned Harry this must be who Allison spoke of: Lord Faulkner.

The duke's son wore a frock coat even more gleaming than the textile the others were sat upon. Green as the elm leaves overhead and cheerful with its border of embroidered flowers, it was a cheer that did not reach the man's eyes. The scowl did little to harm his features though, even Harry could see that. The viscount's straight nose resembled that on every finely sculptured bust on every mantel in Mayfair. Harry's own nose skewed slightly left of center. A trait courtesy of a licking he'd received in his days as a swabbie boy.

Lord Faulkner was taller than Harry and, like a man sitting for a portrait, his posture did not once waver. Indeed a duke's son must have sat for many a portrait, immortalized in oils while the rest of the world aged and disappeared around him.

Harry supposed it was the duke who sat beside Lord Faulkner on a stool. A formidable man, with a face more sun-bitten than most noblemen. Perhaps he had spent a youth on the sea as Harry had but, unlike Harry, had been handed esteemed ranks by the Crown.

The man's face fell into a scowl between bouts of laughter, but at least he *did* laugh, unlike his son.

Allison rose up from the ground in a clumsy way that brought a smile to Harry's face . . . until Lord Faulkner stepped forward to help her. The viscount then unburdened her of her novel and offered his arm. She took it.

The journal in Harry's hands dropped to his lap.

Lady Merton passed another small book up to the viscount. And then every member of the little gathering waved the pair off. Allison and Lord Faulkner were going somewhere. *Together.*

Harry folded the paper as calmly as he could manage and replaced it in his waistcoat. Then he hurried across to the gravel footpath to fall into a distant and careful pursuit.

This was all precisely what he didn't want. Allison was embedding herself in his awful situation and it was changing everything.

She was right about many things, including the need to lay to rest the man Harry had been for months—sleepless, useless, defeated. But was it any better to feel what he felt now? This throbbing need to sink his teeth into anyone that dare be a threat to her?

He'd spent years as an apprentice to his friend, Rhys Bowen. First, in carpentry on their merchant vessel. Next, as an accomplice to mutiny and highway robbery. And finally, as a deputy to Rhys when he became a Runner. But it was less than a year that Harry had been on Bow Street himself and the mundanity of the profession had caught him off guard. He'd been so ready to be challenged, yet the murderers of London were, it turned out, mostly not the cleverest bunch.

He was a bastard son, having passed his earliest years in the garret of his father's London residence. The mistress of the house never deigned to look him in the eye but threw him one blessing in the form of allowing him to be tutored alongside her son for four years.

The other, older lad paid his lessons no heed. He had the security of a future that would be handed to him on no conditions. He was free to spend his youth spouting bad poetry in coffeehouses by morning and in alehouses by night. His lyrics pained the ear but got the attention of the girls he flattered, which was all he'd ever sought.

For Harry, it was different. The words in his lesson books were engrossing. They came to life on the page, sculpting themselves into beautiful places and people and ideas. Knowledge was the food he'd never known he was starved of. Those four years of education had been a precious window to another world; he would hold on to them for all his life and study where he might.

The dream ended when his father left and the mistress sold him into impressment at thirteen years old. It was a long time before he'd see a book again.

When Rhys first brought him to the Magistrate's Court, Harry's mind had come alive with the anticipation of a new challenge. He would be an investigator. He would carve away the artifice of London, and its underbelly would reveal itself like a hidden vein of ore. The puzzle excited him. But upon bringing his dozenth pickpocket into the jail, he realized not all was as he'd hoped.

Now there was a ghost in the streets—the very sort of target he'd been waiting for. But it didn't feel like an exciting puzzle when he was the sufferer. Rather, it was haunting and confusing. It left him feeling like a pawn rolling, aimless, on the chessboard. For weeks, he'd been plagued by the notion he was not up to the task. Investigation was Rhys' milieu, not his, and perhaps he'd best stick to the puzzles in a book, to mathematics, to ciphers . . .

But seeing Allison's hem swish as she strode across the street with this man—this potentially dangerous man—awakened something fierce inside him. It was as though God himself had reached down and stuck a key into his chest, winding his clockwork tight. He was ready to work. He was ready to fight. He was ready to make sure Allison was all right in the end. All other hopes, including that of sharing a life with her, were utterly secondary.

He reached the edge of the park, where it met the road, and watched between crossing carriages as Faulkner held open the lending library's door for Allison.

* * *

The scents of leather and glue were an overwhelming pleasure to Allison as she and Lord Faulkner stepped inside the library. She opened her eyes after a long and lingering inhale. "Do you not love the way they smell?" she asked.

"The way what smells? The books? I am not certain I have ever noticed." He looked to the desk. "The clerk is busy."

"Perhaps I shall—" Allison paused and restarted, remembering to force politeness. "Perhaps *we* might have a look around then?"

He nodded. He loved to nod. It must spare him from those exhaustingly pesky things known as words. His tongue was surely well-rested. As was the total of him. He'd not a single blemish. If he possessed any wrinkles then he did not express himself often enough for them to be revealed.

She studied him as he turned his attention to the nearest shelves. He stood erect as a lamppost, with her copy of *Les Liaisons Dangereuses* and Lady Merton's exchanges clamped efficiently beneath one arm. Never before had she met someone so stony in both appearance and character. He would suit well to being a monument, and she imagined that once a duke, there might be many lining up to sculpt him. Yet he did not leave her nervous—not the way so many others of some seniority did. He was greater than her in age, rank, height . . . yet the strongest emotions she felt around him were exasperation and . . . pity? It was all very odd when she suspected him a murderer.

He did not strike her as dangerous *per se*, but he was the least mirthful member of the nobility she had ever met. Her eyes wandered to the grim line he made with his mouth. What could he have to scowl about with so much wealth and public affection at his fingertips? He led a charmed life but was altogether un-charmed.

Was he indeed a vengeful man? A man bent on killing someone?

Allison's heart kicked. She was playing a silly game, convincing herself of this man's villainy. Was there really so much evidence as she thought? Or did suspicion spring from the desire to prove herself cunning and useful?

"What is it?" he suddenly asked.

Allison froze, wondering whether she had uttered one of her thoughts aloud. "What is what?"

"I could not help but notice you staring."

"No, I—of course . . ." The stammer would only intensify if she went on.

Thankfully Lord Faulkner had already relaxed his gaze to a book in his hand. He snapped it open with a flick of the wrist, and his eyebrow quirked up as the pages settled. "Hmm, I see what you're saying now, Allison. The smell is very nice. Evocative of many pleasant memories."

So, the man had feelings after all. Allison, ever aware of her habit to make an agog face, consciously shut her mouth.

He looked at her. "They certainly hope for us to take to one another, do they not?"

Allison knew just what he spoke of. She smiled in agreement. "I am relieved it has been said out loud. It was rather stressful not to have that in the open, did you not think, Lord Faulkner?" She replaced a book on the shelf, without having so much as glanced at it. At its loss, she missed having something to do with her hands.

"That is precisely why I bring it up. And I would like to reiterate that you may call me Faulkner when we are in private."

"Whilst we are putting things in the open, does your request mean that you *wish* for us to take to one another?"

"I ask it because it is my preferred term of address among my friends, Lady Allison." A smile peeled across his face as he reached for a book on a high shelf. She might never have known his teeth to be so straight, he'd been hiding them so fervently. He passed the book to her: *The Female Quixote.*

"Have you read it?"

Allison's hand sank with the weight of the tome. "I've not."

"If novels are what you prefer, I think it a very fine story."

"I shall take it home today, then. Thank you, L—" She sighed. "Thank you, Faulkner."

He nodded and she nodded back, meeting him on his terms, speaking his terse language.

"The clerk is free now. Shall we make Lady Merton's exchanges?"

Allison put the book under her arm and let Faulkner follow her. "Lady Merton must be a dear family friend. It is plain she cares for you very much."

"She is. It has been a blessing to know the Mertons all my life. My mother died too young for me to know her, passed away on the Continent, so the extra connections were a boon in my childhood."

A *boon* seemed an odd way to put it, but she understood and tried to see, in those stiff terms, what his version of affection looked like.

Her shoulders softened. Perhaps this was not the man who sought her lover's torment? The coachman, Giddy, suddenly popped to mind. A thought spilled out:

"Will you be taking your carriage home today?"

He nodded, but alarm crossed his face. "The landau, yes. Do you need a ride? Did your family walk to the park? It is at your disposal."

The rush of concern caught Allison off guard. She suddenly

realized her question was not the sort one asked when "just curious"—a thing she might have noted before blurting it out. And now he thought her in need of his landau. She was unprepared for this opportunity, dangerous and tempting.

No truth could get her where she wished to go, not to meet her ends. Her cousin Beth had oft made a point of what a pathetic liar Allison could be, but here she thought to try.

"You know, Lady Merton mentioned her ankles being sore from last night, and I fear now that mine are the same. I shall take you on your offer. Thank you."

"'Tis no bother. My footman will take Lady Merton's exchanges back to her and will share the message that I am seeing you home."

"My ankles will be singing your praises."

Faulkner bent to sign the book register. He did so in haste, with unwarranted urgency to see Allison home. Her lie had worked, though perhaps the viscount was an easy mark. Did such a man even take enough notice of human behavior to catch falsehoods?

As he returned the quill to the desk, an irritated sigh puffed out of him. He withdrew his kerchief to wipe ink from the side of his left palm. Likely a common habit for one left-handed as he.

A moment later, they stood beside his landau in the alleyway. Faulkner loaded his footman's arms with Lady Merton's books and carefully explained the message that must be passed on: *Lady Allison was delivered home due to sore ankles.*

Another man, also in livery, watered the horses.

Allison cocked her head at the men, unable to comprehend whether their lavender livery was near enough to what had looked like gray on Giddy. Neither man struck her as familiar.

The coachman from Willis', had been less delicately built than most men in service: tall, with a short neck and large, rounded shoulders that threatened the seams of his coat.

Allison's heart thrummed. She had to get a look at the coachman but could not actually let Faulkner take her home. Not if Harry was to stay there. "Where is your coachman?" she asked.

Faulkner raised a pitying brow—was she daft?—then gestured with his eyes to the man watering the horses. "He is just there, of course. We will be getting along shortly."

Allison's little plan now looked rather more like folly. What had she missed? Was she helping Harry or merely distracting him with nonsense while a real fiend encroached from the shadows?

She churned over these thoughts as she was handed up into the carriage. Faulkner passed her books up to her, then alit on the opposite seat. The landau lurched into motion.

When the unknown coachman asked, "Where to?"

"Savile Row," slipped from her lips, an automatic thought.

Damn. She should have lied her way out of the carriage before she was ever even in it. Too late now.

She sensed a familiar warmth at her back and wondered where Harry was. Guilt caught hold of her. His heart would be in fits upon seeing her get into the viscount's carriage. She looked over her shoulder, down the alley, and saw no one.

"Will you be attending the Gossingtons' garden fête tomorrow evening?"

She snapped her head back to face Faulkner. "Yes. My whole family will be there, thanks to your godmother's invitation. I look forward to it."

"Me too."

A *"Ha!"* escaped Allison without her control.

Faulkner's dark eyebrows knit in confusion.

"Forgive me," she said. "If I am honest, I did not believe you looked forward to anything social. I've not been under the impression that you gain happiness from the presence of other people."

Nodding, he looked around him. "That is a fair assessment from your perspective."

Allison folded her hands neatly in her lap, waiting for what came next, but there was nothing. "What, then, *is your* perspective? What do you enjoy in this life?"

He leaned forward, showing her the iciness of his silvery-blue eyes.

"I enjoy my privacy, Lady Allison. I would go so far as to say my secrecy, even."

Allison could not tell whether it was threat that laced his voice, because his tone was always so much the same—cold and flat no matter his words. She recoiled against her seat. Nowhere to go. Her heart skipped as the last glimpse of Hyde Park disappeared around a corner.

"I apologize. Such personal questions are impertinent," she breathed.

He settled back in his seat, but the tension in Allison's chest remained.

"I took no offense, but I answer truthfully. I do not dislike the company of others, I just do not often get to select it."

"And I am an example of that very thing. I have been twice foisted upon you and should not have taken advantage of your offer for a ride. We will be seen together and it is precisely what our families want."

"Lady Merton is not my family."

"But you know what I mean."

He did not answer.

Allison looked around her. Well-heeled groups were strolling, taking advantage of the spring air. Several looked up at them and nodded cordially. She wondered whether any actually knew Faulkner or only *wished* to know him. He paid them no mind, but Allison's head bobbed at every nod that came their way.

They were fast approaching the townhouse.

"Which way from here, my lord?"

Lord Faulkner referred the driver's question to her with a look.

Her eyes darted around at the local shops and she hurried to speak. "Here will be fine!" She shouted it loud enough for the coachman and he drew up the pair of horses. Before Lord Faulkner had the chance to put words to his confusion, Allison sputtered her next lie.

"I noticed the dressmaker's shop and was reminded I must retrieve something there. My residence is very close now—" *It wasn't.* "—and I am certain my ankles can last the remainder."

"But you are alone."

Ah, so she was. Didn't everyone just *love* to point that out to a young woman? As though they were incapable of noticing their own aloneness, particularly in moments of sweet silence.

"I will be straight to the dressmaker's door under your watchful eye. I heed your concern. Either way, I assure you, I will keep my reputation sparkling."

"Sarcasm is unwarranted, Lady Allison."

Sarcasm? Just what had he heard of her reputation? His dark tone kept her in her seat.

"I do not ask for the sake of your reputation. A good name is overrated. I ask for your safety and because you are in pain."

Allison's lips tightened. She detected just the slightest knit in his brow—was it emotion? Was it *care?* His good intentions stabbed her irritation into submission. "I realize that now. Thank you, Faulkner."

As she managed her petticoats with one hand, Lord Faulkner

hopped down to help her out. His landau did not disappear until after she crossed the threshold to the dressmaker's shop—a modiste she had utterly no business with.

7

Allison kept one eye looking past the display in the shop's bay window and idly fingered a piece of fabric until she felt it safe to step back outside. Regrettably, an eager assistant found her first, clasping his hands in delight.

"How may I best serve you, my lady?" His eyes darted to the cloth in her hand. "Ah, that is a fine one. Real silver in the threads, you know? And recently used in a court dress." The man toyed with a measuring ribbon around his neck, prepared to wield it at any moment.

Allison smiled. "It is my first time here. I will only be browsing, I think."

"Let me give you a tour! There are many luxurious textiles to see, and we are some of the fastest in London at finishing gowns. You could have a whole new wardrobe before the Season is up."

Allison brightened her smile against her irritation and prepared her next polite decline—

"The lady said she will just be looking around."

The man in front of Allison shrank, disappearing into his over-embroidered coat like a turtle into its shell. He looked past her shoulder to where the command had come from and she turned to follow his gaze.

Harry leaned against the sliver of wall between the doorway and the shop's magnificent bay window. The sun outside lit the edges of his hair in halo, highlighting the most golden strands.

Allison smiled a particular smile, the one she employed to delay admonishments.

"Riding in his landau? I thought you wished to spare me from the grave of my own dread, not help me to it?"

She shrugged. "I will admit, perhaps I was a bit too intrepid just then." An understatement. Her heart still rushed from recklessness. The rush was pleasant now only because it was past.

"I do not need you to spy for me, Allison."

"Only the latter part was spying. Accompanying him to the lending library was regrettably beyond my control. And were you not spying on me also?"

He could not hide it—that brief smile behind his eyes. He hastened to move his gaze to the book in the crook of her arm. "May I?"

She passed it his way and his face lit when he saw it was *The Female Quixote.*

"Something you've read?" she asked.

"Yes. Rather enjoyed it. You will love it."

"That's good news. I took it on Lord Faulkner's recommendation."

Harry's lips tightened and he returned it to her with a little toss, like rubbish into a bucket.

"What did you learn from your excursion?"

"Well . . ." Allison let her skirts twirl flirtatiously as she pretended to examine another pretty textile. "You do not *need* my help, so perhaps I should not say."

"You didn't learn anything of use, did you?" He leaned down behind her ear. "You are dreadful at pretense."

Her skirts brushed his legs as she twirled back to him. "I will have you know I just lied very successfully to Lord Faulkner. More than once." Her voice withered as she encountered Harry's face so near to hers. Stray locks of hair, molded roguishly by a gloss of sweat, fell into his eyes. They were nearly in her eyes too. He smelled like the sun.

"And what did you learn?"

She sighed, conceding. "His coachman today was not the one called Giddy."

"So . . . nothing?"

"If I tell you he was left-handed, are you one of those superstitious ninnies who would think him a murderer based solely on that?"

Harry's face went pale, his eyes, distant, even though her sarcasm had been too thick to miss. She could not believe her words gave him pause. He was far too self-educated to make dubious assumptions based on one's handedness.

"Harry, you cannot seriously hold that against him."

But he was shaking his head. "No, Allison, I do not think handedness makes anyone the devil's offspring. I do, however, recall where the inkpot was moved to on my secretary that first time. It would have made much more sense for one who wrote with the left."

Allison remembered his mentioning it, but hadn't given it another thought. This was precisely why *he* was the investigator. A spark of pride went off in her chest. If only he could see his own talents as she did.

"Oh," was all she could say.

Harry took her hands in his. More customers had entered and she coyly turned her face away from them.

"He may be a dangerous man, Allison. Please do not be so *intrepid* again."

She nodded, but . . . "Harry?" She stroked her thumb across his hand. "I wonder whether I may be wrong."

"Wrong how?"

Her chest tightened. It was not an easy thing to admit after her runaway certainty at the park.

"Wrong about Lord Faulkner," she said.

Harry's hands went slack in hers and she tightened her grip to keep him with her. "Not just wrong because of the coachman, but because . . . because his character, it does not quite—I'm sorry. I don't know what I am trying to say."

"And what *is* his character, as you have found it, Allison?" There was a desperation in his words that told her he did not merely ask due to the mystery at hand.

She tried to put Faulkner's nature into words and the best she could conjure was, *serviceably amiable.* Hardly a resounding endorsement. But another word continued to arise, unbidden, whenever she tried to ponder the man: *Lonely.*

Such a compassionate judgment was of no help to Harry. Or to her. She shook it off.

"Never mind it. It is probably just my usual doubts."

"Do not doubt your instincts, Allison. Perhaps you didn't see this Giddy today, but—well, I have had time to sit with it, and my own confidence is growing. My confidence that you have struck on something."

Allison, still terribly confused, braved a smile and tipped up her chin to better show it to him. Did he truly think so? Or was he trying to cheer her?

"Still," she said. "I shall not take such risks again." She pulled her hands from his to place one on his arm. "I only did so today because I was certain the best Bow Street Runner in London watched over me."

His hand slid up to her face. It was too much. Too public.

"Not here," she whispered. She straightened, retreating from his intimacy with a prudent backward step. "Would you walk me the rest of the way home? Then I will not have to send Hayden for you later."

Harry stepped away too, clasping his hands behind his back as if to make them obey.

"Lead the way, Primrose."

Harry stared out the doorway of the mews house, across a small, darkening garden. His eyes scanned up the imposing white cliff that was the back of Allison's home . . . Allison's *second* home.

The groan of wood against wood brought his attention back inside, where the Weldons' footman, Mr. Hayden, pushed a heavy chest across the floor toward the stable. The rust silk of his livery was dark as soil wherever he perspired. "Apologies," he said. "We've had naught but storage in this room for years."

"Can I be of any help, mate?"

The footman straightened and stretched his neck to one side, generating a crack that, judging by the softening of his brow, seemed to bring with it some relief. "I would not object to help, no."

Harry grabbed the chest's other end and tugged—an attempt that resulted in little else but the overworking of one tight muscle in his forearm. "Good hell, is it full of horseshoes?" Tensing his thighs, he gave it another go and the thing, at last, began to move.

"Here will do," said Hayden, and the chest clunked into place against a carriage horse's stall. The animal within startled and shortly after came the sound of shit hitting the straw.

"Terribly sorry about your housemates, Mr. Plymouth."

Harry dusted off his hands and rolled his shoulders back. "I'm not offended by a bit of dung. I've slept with the horses before."

Hayden quirked his head, waiting for elaboration. Harry obliged, not to be taken for a dandy:

"I'm a bastard, Mr. Hayden. I've slept in prisons. I've slept on ships through storms. I've slept in crumbling places. Cold places. Crowded places. Desolate places. I grew up in a garret, where the mistress would not throw me one candle for the night. And I live in a garret still." Harry gestured to the small but tidy servant's room he'd be occupying. "This, I believe, will suit me fine."

A lighter voice broke into the conversation. "Yet you could not sleep in that garret with a murderous stranger tormenting you? Odd."

Harry dropped the bushel he'd just lifted and raised his eyes to the silhouette in the door. *Allison.*

He'd not expected her to revisit the rear house since showing him to it that afternoon. How long had she stood there? She'd overheard him speak of the garret—had she heard more? Heard him call himself a bastard?

She knew the rest of it. The mutiny. The highway robbery. But his bastardhood, his *real* name? Not ever. Not yet.

He stepped toward her, drawn forward by batting lashes. He tipped her chin up to him and she loosed a sharp breath that struck him warmly in the neck.

"Yes, Primrose, I am fitful with a vengeful stranger about. I suppose we all have our limits."

The conspicuous rattle of a clearing throat brought Harry back to the reality that they were not alone. He stepped back. He didn't understand all the rules of Allison's class and cared not to discover them through a footman's censure.

"We needn't be anything but ourselves here, Harry. I trust Hayden very much." She winked at the footman. "He gives me much more reason to trust him than I have ever given him to trust me."

"Pleasure to be of service, Lady Allison." Hayden clicked his heels together in a mockery of decorum and turned his eyes on Harry. "It is absolutely the truth. She's a menace."

"What can I give you for enabling our little endeavor, Mr. Hayden?"

"I am already the most suspiciously wealthy footman in London."

"Then why sleep in our servant's quarters?"

He shrugged. "I am saving up. As an ambitious man, I wish to improve my prospects for retirement from a small castle to a big one."

The curative elixir of Allison's laughter settled into Harry's veins. A night of peaceful sleep felt suddenly within reach.

"I would nudge you toward that retirement if my own freedoms did not so hinge upon our little alliance."

Any sign of jest dissolved. "Please. Allow me this one as a favor."

She dipped her head. "Thank you, Mr. Hayden."

He turned his attention to Harry. "After my rounds inside, I will bring a light repast. Will there be anything else?"

"Yes—I mean, no. I have plenty, thank you," said Harry, unused to any form of deference.

The footman's departure was apparently all the permission

Allison needed to glide boldly into Harry's new bedchamber. By the time he stepped to the door, she'd already alit on the edge of his humble bed.

He planted a shoulder against the doorjamb. If he took so much as a step into the small space with her sitting there, he wouldn't know how to keep himself away. Perhaps she knew that. Perhaps she wanted it as badly as he.

"I was not expecting you back again tonight," he said. "Please say your family is not home."

She shrugged, avoiding his eyes and any guilt that came with meeting them. "As it happens, they did not return after the park. They must have continued on to the Mertons', or elsewhere."

"I will have to go back to Dryden tomorrow to fetch some things."

Allison took a deep gulp of air and smiled, but it was evident the sort of fears that she harbored behind her mossy eyes.

"I will be cautious," he swore.

She nodded.

"It's strange to be alone with you, in such a safe and—" Harry cast a glance through the window at the little garden. "—well-appointed place."

"Is it a bad sort of strange?"

"Not at all. Only it feels like I mustn't touch you."

He turned just as she lowered her cheek thoughtfully to one shoulder.

"I understand." She sighed and flung her own gaze toward the window. "I understand that you worry about me, Harry, but there will be a solution. The things against us are outside of us, are they not?"

He *did* worry about her. But the problem on his mind was another entirely. It was the problem of the towering townhouse across the yard. It was the problem of the honorific uttered before her name by all else but him.

The night he'd first met her, she'd been wearing as fine a frock as ever, yet she'd also just been tumbled through the mud by an accident. She'd looked like a spaniel only half dried after a swim. Ratty and rebellious.

But they were no longer flirting in that village stable—no longer in *his* world. He was now in hers. In Mayfair. And she radiated the opulence of her lifestyle. From the crispness of her golden sash to the snowy white of her chemise gown, it was always perfection that leapt out at him.

And what of him leapt out at her? Was it the stains of sweat yellowing the edge of his collar? The darning of the wool at his elbows?

She was right. A servant's position would grant him useful discretion at the garden affair. It would let him mingle with the gossip-knowers belowstairs—those who knew all their masters' goings-about. Yet, the idea left a discomfort in him—a roiling in his center that he could not correct by will alone.

As though hearing the buzzing of his thoughts, Allison stood and went to him.

He was not taller than many men, but Allison's small stature made him feel built like a tower. She got on her toes and pressed her lips to his cheek. It soothed him straight to his boot-soles.

"Tomorrow, Hayden will bring you the livery for the Gossington fête. And *I* shall endeavor to keep myself from the mews." She ducked her head and brushed past him through the door. Away.

In his imagination, he had stopped her. He had wrapped one arm around her waist and lifted her firmly against him. He'd kissed her passionately, lost his balance, heard her laugh. He'd staggered with her to the hard little bed and fallen to his back with her atop him, netting him in her gossamer layers—

But in reality? He'd not even reached out. Had he, would he have found her white dress sullied by some grime of his? He looked down at his hands, rough yet clean.

Outside the window, she trotted across the pavers, before disappearing into the maw of a portico with Doric columns for teeth.

There was that unease again.

Why was it so difficult now? When he had known her to be an earl's daughter from the start?

He'd seen different lives align in love before. Allison's cousin, Beth, had come to love his friend Rhys, the leader of his thieving crew, in a dilapidated hunting château. But Beth had more freedoms as a woman aging out of the possibility of wedlock and was a rare, independently wealthy woman. Her father held no title and a lax attitude toward her upbringing.

Lady Weldon was anything but lax. She'd been there the night he'd met Allison, and he'd witnessed, first hand, how the countess worshipped at the altar of reputation. Scandal was not something she would trifle with.

Harry had risen up from his bastard childhood, from his past of deck swabbing and thieving. He'd made a name for himself as a Runner and his humble living was one beyond his wildest dreams. Was it not selfish to aspire to a union with one such as Allison?

She'd not understood what the destruction of his rented room had meant to him. She'd never seen it with the hearth glowing nor sat in one of his upholstered chairs, specially made. She'd have loved his collection of books. But how could she know what any of it had meant to him?

She was cultivated and scrutinized in a way Beth never had

been. She was groomed for dances and dukes. The courtyard beyond Harry's window was a chasm between their worlds. He was an interloper—an impediment to some destiny that seemed so obvious whenever he looked at her: greatness, and an overflowing cup for the rest of her days.

His eyes stung. If not careful, he would choke on his own self-pity. It was, as Allison had so astutely pointed out, the very thing that could determine his success or failure. Perhaps not only with the search for his hunter, but with her as well.

8

Assenting to tea with her mother was, without question, Allison's most desperate act of the week. A few moments spent with Harry the day prior was apparently all it took to drain every other activity of enjoyment. A new anxiety took hold, leaving her nauseous all day. The only cure for it would be to steal to the mews and see Harry in his livery before he left for the Gossingtons' that evening. What would he look like in robin's egg blue? With silk puckering 'round his hard thighs? With silver braid setting off his stormy blue eyes?

Waiting was always a hell for Allison, whose mind would berate her with daydreams until everything came to pass. Still, she summoned patience. She'd fashioned herself the accomplice in a rather serious investigation, and what did that call for? *Discretion.* She could not fawn over Harry all day in the mews while unknown eyes lurked in the shadows and a vigilant countess flitted about.

Certainly it made Allison a wreck, adhering to virtues so uncommon of her, but her most natural virtue of all was that she *could* commit to the important things, regardless of personal distress.

Five o'clock. I will allow myself to go to him at five o'clock.

But the seconds ticked by like hours.

Her dresses bored her. Her books bored her. She even bored herself. So at three, when she told her mother *yes* to tea, she committed herself to no greater boredom than that from which she already suffered.

Or so she'd thought. It was half past four.

A teacup gently vibrated on its saucer in her lap as she looked sidelong through the drawing-room window.

Harry's legs. Harry's shoulders. His smile, crooked and bashful. Robin's egg blue. A detectable bulge behind his fall. It is pressed against her hip as she slips a hand past the edge of his—

"Allison, I wish you would not rest the tea so carelessly in your lap. Thank goodness it is not a public habit."

Allison tilted her head at her mother, who straightened indignantly at the glare.

Allison raised her cup for a sip. "Tell me more of last night."

Lady Weldon was keen to do so. "Oh yes, the parlor games! Did I already tell you of the blackberries? If I did not—"

"No, you did," offered Allison brightly, knowing there was a half chance her mother would recount it anyway. After Allison—and apparently Faulkner—did not return to Hyde Park, the remainder of their party had proceeded to the Mertons' residence on Charles Street for wine, parlor games, and light wagers on who could do the most interesting things with blackberries.

Lady Weldon launched into a repeat of the story and Allison took a long sip of tea, nearly spitting it out when she caught sight of a very specific landau drawing up out front. *No.*

She set aside the tea and stretched a hand to rest on the lap of her mother's dark green round gown.

"It pains me to stop you, but—"

"So many disruptions today, Allison! I was in the midst of a story."

"And a riveting story it was, but there is someone—"

"Well, there, I have lost it." Allison's mother threw up her hands. She was still searching her thoughts for the missing blackberry anecdote when the expected knock came at the door. Allison excused herself and for the first time since morning, her mind was not in the mews.

She joined Hayden's side, delivering him a look as he went to open the door. She was all of ten-seconds prepared when it opened on Faulkner's refined features.

"*Ohhh*, 'tis you," she cooed, before realizing her tone might be a tad much. "What brings you?"

"I hope my errand is not over-forward, but you left your book behind in the landau yesterday."

"Odd. I would swear I read the first pages of *The Female Quixote* last night."

"Not that one," he said and Allison noticed the book under his arm—the gold-leafed spine of *Les Liaisons Dangereuses'* second volume. She could have kicked herself for the mistake.

He thrust it forward.

She took it, regretful of the dismissal she was about to make. It *was* kind of Faulkner to bring it, but she could not have him feeling welcomed at the townhouse. Not yet. Somehow her certainties and Harry's doubts had flopped round, and now Allison did not know what to believe about the viscount.

"How kind that you brought it." She carefully avoided his name, lest she rouse her mother, the matchmaking dragon, from her blackberry stupor by the window. Allison stole the door's handle from Hayden, who stepped aside. She closed the door partway as she lowered her voice. "And what generous soul has lent you our address?"

"Lady Merton received it from your mother yesterday. Again, I pray it is not too forward of me."

Allison studied him. His stony gaze was so mismatched to the begging of any forgiveness.

"Thank you for taking the time from your doubtless busy day to come here. Perhaps we can discuss literature this evening at the Gossingtons'?"

Faulkner leaned sideways to follow the ever-narrowing gap of the doorway. Before Allison could squeeze him out completely, his eyes suddenly flared in understanding. He delivered a nod, polite and knowing—neither of them wished to wake the dragon.

"I will see you this evening, Lady Allison."

"And I you, Lord Faulkner."

The name slipped out on instinct and barely over a whisper, yet, like a spell cast, it was all it took to summon her.

"Lord Faulkner! What a delightful surprise!" With Lady Weldon, the bright cooing was in earnest. "Please come in."

The handle was stolen from Allison and the door ripped wide open by her mother.

Faulkner met Allison's eyes with doomed surrender as the dragon led them both into her well-appointed lair, making about ten demands of Hayden along the way.

They were soon arranged into a triangle of misery in the drawing room, teacups in hand, and Allison with a tormentingly good view of the golden mantel clock. It read a quarter-hour to five. Harry would leave for his duties at the Gossingtons' at half past.

"Your presence was missed at the Mertons' last night, Lord Faulkner, but do not mistake me—" Lady Weldon's eyes darted to her daughter with a gleam in them. "I do so appreciate that you helped Lady Allison home. Her ankle is much better today. Fine even? *Miraculously* so."

Allison could not tell what her mother suspected but nodded along in the hope that agreement might bring an end to it.

"I am glad to hear it," said Faulkner.

They were both being their public selves. Her mother, high-spirited and effusively solicitous to those of station, and Faulkner, terse, unsmiling, and uncomfortable.

"We did have great fun last night. Lady Merton taught us all a game and I wish you could have been there. You see, we were all given blackberries and . . ."

Allison's neck nearly cracked as she whipped pleading eyes to Hayden, who stood at the ready in the room's corner.

His scarred lip wrinkled skeptically as he shrugged. What could *he* do?

Besides, Allison's mother had him running out of the room for something every two minutes after that: A better cushion for Lord Faulkner. A footstool for Lord Faulkner. More tea for Lord Faulkner. It was a wonder the viscount did not relieve himself in his breeches he'd had so much tea.

". . . It was the sort of parlor game that would foster young love, one might think."

Goodness, was Mother still on about the blackberries?

Allison caught her mother's eyes darting between herself and Faulkner.

"Sounds lovely." Allison hurried to say it, hoping to undercut her mother's meaningful pause.

Just then, Hayden returned from one of his many errands with a basket of biscuits in one hand and a neatly folded stack of . . . of robin's egg silk in the other. Allison's eyes wistfully clung to the bundle of livery as he set down the biscuits and continued his passage through the room and toward the back of the house. *Toward the mews.*

The clock on the mantel chimed. *Five o'clock.*

". . . Lady Allison's virtues and talents are numberless."

Clearly her mother had slipped onto a more direct line of conversation while Allison's mind wandered elsewhere.

"Doubtless they are," said Faulkner and Allison was sure she heard him sigh.

Lady Weldon leaned forward wielding the silver teapot at him for a seventh time. He put up a palm so hastily one might assume he were trying not to get shot. She set the vessel back down, but not before giving it a little rattle that told her it was near empty.

Hayden crossed back through the front of the house, but via the dining room, trying to dodge the next request on the countess' lips. She merely raised her voice:

"Mr. Hayd—"

"Allow me, Mother." Allison was already on her feet, chasing their interim butler to the next room. She caught up to him in the study, where he seemed prepared to be cornered.

"Pray, get me out of there," she begged.

Hayden lowered his voice to the same urgent, hissing whisper: "I can hardly extract myself!"

"If you come up with something to get *me* out of there, Lord Faulkner will go home and you will be done with it too."

"What can I do?"

"Something. Anything. Start a fire if you must—only *save* us."

Hayden's shoulders softened and he sighed at the ceiling. It was what he always did when she was overdramatic.

She returned to the settee, realizing for the first time that Lord Faulkner was perched on a chair too small for his statuesque height. A little laugh popped from her.

"Darling, is he getting the tea?"

Allison flung a palm to her forehead. "Oh dear. *That* was what I was supposed to ask. My memory, 'tis so poor of late."

Lady Weldon frowned and opened her mouth to speak, but Lord Faulkner was the quicker draw:

"You have been most gracious today, Lady Weldon, but I'd only time for a short visit." He stood. "I will see you all tonight."

"Very well." Lady Weldon's disappointed sigh disturbed the frizzy hedgehog curls above her forehead. "Lady Allison, would you see Lord Faulkner out?"

Allison was already standing and eagerly took his proffered arm. *Freedom.*

They were making their way to exit when a rush of pounding footsteps turned them back around. Hayden stood in the opposing doorway, gasping for breath.

"Forgive the disruption, my lady, but there is a small fire in the—in the—"

He froze when he saw them not in their chairs but in the archway to the entry hall. On the threshold of escape. Allison's jaw went slack as she met Hayden's eyes.

He straightened and tugged the bottom of his waistcoat. "There is a small fire in the kitchen. Which I shall go see to myself. Do not be alarmed if you smell smoke." He bowed and hastened away as quickly as he'd come.

Allison's head was still spinning from Hayden's loyalty as she bade farewell to Faulkner and hurried around the block to the mews. She'd no mind to cut through the house and risk being stopped again.

The large pair of carriage doors were open and she tossed a swift "hello" to the young groom on her way to Harry's quarters. She slowed when she saw his door ajar and snuck up to have a peek.

His back was to her and he did not yet wear his coat.

At last, a glimpse of him in the robin's egg blue. Silk pulled and puckered across his bum and thighs—across all those parts of him she wished to be better acquainted with. His shoulders rounded tightly against his waistcoat. It was a suit cut for the Harry of a year ago, the Harry who was a boy, not this Harry, the man.

The curled queue of a wig dangled down the back of his neck and his sturdy calves were sleeved in stockings rather than hid inside his usual boots. None of it fit with who Harry was—with the man she loved—but as a novelty it was a sight she would carry in happy memory to her grave.

Her cheeks tingled and she wondered whether her grin might turn itself inside out and swallow her whole.

"You're a thing of terrible beauty, do you know that, Harry?"

He spun around and ripped off the wig, leaving a rakish swoosh of blond across his forehead.

In three powerful strides, he came to her, craning over her.

Her heart flew into a faster rhythm as she imagined his lips crushing down against hers at any moment—

"Why was there a familiar landau in the street?" he grit out.

Oh.

That.

She sidestepped from where he loomed. "Lord Faulkner merely

ran an unexpected errand."

"I seem to recall you saying that his ever visiting was 'a ridiculous notion.'"

Allison thought back on the farce that had just played out in the drawing room. "In a sense, it truly was."

"Allison," he growled.

This time it was she who stomped up to him. "Harry, if you don't think I have people—taller, older, higher-ranking people than me—growling out my name in censure like that all the time, then you are mistaken. I take it from enough of them. I will not take it from you."

She watched his eyes. Watched how his blue irises twitched between narrowed lids. She'd never taken such a tone as that with him . . . with *anyone*. She waited for the escalation, dreaded that moment of learning she had ruined something precious by slipping out of her pleasing ways.

Instead, his eyes opened wider, softened.

"I swear, I did not know he would come here," she whispered.

He nodded. "I know."

Even as the spat was dodged, her unease rose to such heights that she wished to leave. "I should go inside. Be laced up into prettier stays."

His eyes followed her words to her bosom. "How could anything be more pretty than this?"

"Please, I am the flattest lady in London."

He looked as though she'd caused offense. "Do you truly believe that?"

"My mother believes it rather fervently. And Stefano used to tease me."

Harry shook his head. "What other things does your mother

say? I must know the full case in order to effectively dismantle it."

"I have thick ankles and legs. My bottom half does not particularly match my upper and I have learned to be grateful I do not have to wear breeches like *those*. I can hide my flaws beneath this pretty bell." Allison swished her yellow petticoats to make a point.

It was a moment before abashment caught up to her hasty mouth. The butterflies of a good flirt flew away and moths of shame replaced them. "I suppose that must seem a bit of a dirty trick to you. Hiding my flaws."

Allison was looking at the floor when his hand cupped her chin and lifted it. "Allison Weldon. Primrose. I have seen your legs and they tempt me like fruit in Eden. I want to put my lips to them and suck as though they could give nectar. But best of all, these legs . . ." He gestured down with his eyes. ". . . carry around on them, the most lively, shining, bright spot of a woman that I have ever known."

The same heat she'd felt in her cheeks upon her brazen inspection of Harry now flowed through her body. It came so fast. In one moment, he'd spoken of nectar as poetic flourish, and in the next, there was a real nectar slickening the cusp where her thighs met. She pressed her legs together and shifted slightly to spread it away—an exercise that only increased the runaway sensation.

She despaired when he suddenly walked away. But he took a large, shallow box from his bed and extended it toward her to be opened. "This is for you." Her arms still tingled as she lifted the paperboard lid. The permeating fragrance of every spring-blooming flower struck her as she lifted a garland so exquisite, so perfectly suited to her tastes—

"Do you like them?"

She meant to say something as she stood there, clutching the strand of blossoms to her tender heart. Why was all of this so frightening?

It was not until he settled heavily on the bed and cast his gaze outside that she realized she'd not yet thanked him. She swooped down to sit at his side.

"I love them. Thank you."

She flinched in surprise when a hand rested on her skirts.

"Tonight I will see you quite in your element, won't I?" he asked.

"Oh yes, I wager you shall. It will be elegant, but also more raucous than one might expect. The games played at these things can have some wickedness to them. We do know how to have a brilliant time."

"I will see your whole world and how you fit into it." Harry fussed with her petticoat at the knee, testing the hand of the fabric— for its softness or perhaps . . . its quality?

Allison had answered his question gaily, in that way she knew to be distinctly her own—a way dizzying to some. She was, as ever, excited by the spectacle of a lavish party. But Harry's tone had been different—a melancholy that would wilt all the flowers of her garland should it persist.

Only a moment before, his hand on her skirts had sent a shiver up her spine, but now all she could focus on was his thumb testing the silk's weave. The finest silk of Provence. A bolt of it might cost Harry a year's rent or more. She truly didn't know.

Allison picked up his hand, hoping to cease any ruminations. She met his eyes with her warmest smile.

"If there is anything afoot in the ton, I am certain it will be uncovered by you. You are brave to do this line of work, even without an assassin lurking. You are cunning and you will root out the scoundrels."

The corners of Harry's lips buckled as they tried to lift a smile. "Yes. There is plenty of work tonight. And I wonder about this Lord Faulkner . . ."

Ah yes. Faulkner. It was Allison herself who had volunteered the man as a suspect in her giddy participation, but following recent interactions, she had begun to think him harmless.

This was precisely why Harry was the investigator and she was not.

Askance through the window, Allison saw Hayden returning to the back house, but he paused and reversed course when he saw Allison and Harry inside together. Allison popped to her feet and held out the garland to Harry.

"Well, you must leave soon, but I wonder whether you might do the honor."

Allison would have to change gowns later, but here was an excuse to be close and to be touched. She would not forgo it.

Harry stood, his eyes raking over her reverently.

Again she felt that strange combination of fear and delight. She extended her arm.

He took the large ring of flowers and lowered it over her shoulder. She cocked her head to duck under it and soon the garland crossed her bodice with its ribbons cascading down one hip.

Harry cupped the side of her neck and leaned in for a deep inhale. The heat of his cheek near hers set the core of her aflame. She shut her eyes against the desire to clutch his sleeves and drag him nearer.

A hesitant knocking at the doorjamb snapped them apart. Hayden was back.

"Are you ready, footman?"

Harry scooped up his discarded wig. It was Allison's gaze he held as he responded:

"Yes. I am ready to serve."

9

Harry squinted as a reeking dishrag was swiped across his brow.

"'Tisn't fit for you to be sweating all over the place. Thank heavens it's after dark." The graying scullery maid grabbed his chin with a rough hand and put the rag back to his cheek.

Perhaps he'd not be sweating so much were they not acting out this parody in front of a kitchen hearth the size of horse's stall. Three different spits turned in its flames and Harry wished he might commit his wig to the inferno. It was dreaded itchy.

He pulled away from the filthy rag just as the maid reached up to have another go. "I think it under control. Don't you?"

The old woman was, herself, quite perspiratory. She shrugged. "Do not come whingeing to me if the butler has your name for it." She turned her attention to the long worktable beside her. "The salvers will be lined up here."

Harry stepped away from the fire's heat and fell in line with the other footmen—all looking like a clutch of robin's eggs in their blue livery.

Servants of all kinds hurried to and fro through the kitchen and its adjoining rooms. He hoped some might prove as talebearing as others he'd met through his vocation.

An elbow jabbed him in the rib. The footman at his right leaned in.

"Don't know the grounds yet, do ye? Follow me and you'll be fine."

Harry extended a hand sideways to the man for a shake. "Harry."

"Tad. You look tense. Never served at a grand thing like this, I take it?"

Harry shook his head.

"Never you mind it. Give it an hour and they'll all be so deep in cups that no mistake will go noticed. Nights like this—seems they'd be the toughest, but they're not. All the giddy idiots get lost in themselves so quick. Once the trays are all out, it's like a holiday for us."

"I find that difficult to believe, Tad."

Tad waggled his faint red eyebrows. "Got yourself a tough lord, have ye? Listen, you find me midway through the night when I'm behind a tree tupping Sarah over there. Then you'll owe me a threepenny."

Harry followed the gesture of Tad's eyes to where a young maid helped a cook.

"I've not placed a wager," said Harry.

"Fine, keep your coin. But trust I'll be winking at you when my fall is still down and the nobs don't even have a care to notice." The footman demonstrated such a wink as if Harry might not know what to watch for otherwise.

Harry cracked a smile, a smile that was snapped back into an obedient line when the harried butler came downstairs to give them strict instructions.

Minutes later, the small army of footmen were fanning out evenly across the terrace, aiming their trays of spirits at the newly arrived masses.

Harry paused before setting foot onto a manicured turf the span of St. Paul's Cathedral. He'd seen many things since becoming a Runner in London yet had no idea the manses of Hampstead could conceal their own private pleasure gardens.

The guests were like individual strokes on a canvas, little whisks of color, men and women both. Silks caught the light from ornate braziers and glittered in ever-changing hues. Some garments were so gilt, so laden with trim, that Harry could not fathom the wearer's body strong enough to bear it.

Here was another world. A world where chandeliers were hung from trees. A world fragrant with the scents of every bottle in the perfumier's shop. A world where it did not matter if one cream puff rolled away, for there were thousands more to replace it.

He'd imagined that Allison would stick out at him as though she were the only person in a beam of starlight. But here in the teeming hundreds, he'd no idea which cluster of petticoats and capes she would be found among. And it was easy to forget: she was not who he was here to find.

As he stepped down into the throngs, the song of a violin teased his ear. Even the music seemed magically conjured from nowhere. Hands heavy with rings reached out from faceless circles of revelers to take glasses from Harry's well-balanced tray.

He'd hardly made ingress into the crowd before it was time

     Daria Vernon

to fetch more refreshments from belowstairs. It happened again, and again, and again. There would be no investigating done at all if he could not break from such a cycle, but then, as sure as Tad had suggested, Harry noticed the slowing of everything.

Chatty groups settled into glowing pavilions along the path, staying near to the braziers that kept the evening chill at bay. Women lounged on laps. Lovers rubbed noses. Glasses were broken. Puddles of wine left soggy spots on the footpath. Playing cards blew away on the night breeze.

Harry was bending to pick up one such card when an unnaturally sharp laugh pierced his ear. There, in the pavilion to his left, sat Allison. Holding court from the center of a long table, she glowed like the Sun King—all in gold and festooned in the flowers he'd bought her that afternoon. She laughed again with wild eyes. A desperate beckoning.

With studied posture and a hand behind his back, he heeded her call.

"Fetch us some sweets for the table, would you please?"

Harry doubted that servants were often spoken to with such sweet smiles.

As he bowed, an older gentleman at the table added to the request with slurred speech. "More sherry too!" It was the Duke of Montagu, looking somehow gruff and merry all at once.

Wordlessly, Harry departed for the kitchen. Much of Allison's entourage was the same as at the park, including Lord Faulkner, who sat disturbingly beside her, looking dour as he toyed with the catch on his timepiece.

As Harry returned to the pavilion with a tray balanced on each hand, he realized how steady he suddenly was. He'd not felt himself for months, but now investigative focus pumped through him like a tonic, healing his tremors from all those sleepless nights.

He went around the table, dutifully leaning in with one tray, then the other, waiting for uncalloused hands to snatch away the sherry and sweetmeats. Dipping his tray between the shoulders of Allison and Faulkner, it took every drop of Harry's will not to meet his Primrose's eyes. Should he look at her, a reflexive smile would surely shatter his guise.

Faulkner did not reach for anything straight away, and once Allison had taken her sweets, Harry nudged the tray nearer the distracted man, who still fussed with his watch. At last, the thing was snapped shut and the viscount reached for a glass.

But Harry's attention was frozen on the chained fob of Lord Faulkner's timepiece. The chain was met at either end with blue enamel buttons, painted with the gold stars of Lyra. It was the watch of a seafaring man. A *specific* seafaring man. And the last that Harry had seen it, he'd had it wrapped as a garrote against its owner's throat.

A tremor charged through Harry's hand, causing the last sherry glass on his tray to rattle and dance. It was rescued by the swift hand of Faulkner, who met Harry with a raised brow. He passed the glass to his left, to his father, the cup-shot duke. The older man grumbled contentedly.

Harry knew he should lower his gaze in deference but did not. He met Faulkner's steely eyes and searched for some hidden past there, for a clue. Seconds passed before he forced himself to grit out the words, "I beg your pardon, my lord."

But Faulkner did not meet him with any challenge. Instead, an awkward and fleeting smile crossed the face of the duke's son. "Disaster averted." Then he turned his eyes down to his plate and—finding little there—dragged the tines of his fork through some gravy with feigned interest.

"Heavens young man, watch your work."

Harry was snapped upright by the familiar woman's voice behind him.

"No one wants to end the night with sherry on their silks."

He dipped his head, not chancing eye contact with Lady Weldon. "Beg pardon, Your Ladyship."

A fork clinked to its plate, followed by a different voice, most lovely. "Mother, be kind."

Harry's heart squeezed at Allison's polite defense of him. He did not look up again, but folded the empty salver beneath his arm and ducked away from the little pavilion.

He returned to the path, stretching his neck to one shoulder, then the other, trying to ease the stiffness of the submissive, dutiful posture his subterfuge called for. His stride grew purposeful—powerful—yet he was directionless.

Allison's eyes were on his back as he left. He could feel it—her questions, her fears . . . her *inevitable* solutions. Her perception left him naked, a fact that very suddenly unnerved him. It was as if she'd not only sensed that he *had* a secret but somehow knew what that secret was. She could not possibly.

He'd come to eavesdrop on the ton and perhaps find a coachman named Giddy. Instead, every wave of the Atlantic ocean had just come crashing down on his head. He was being hunted, oh yes, and it was as he suspected. He was being hunted because of the mutiny on the *Diligence* and a part in it that no one knew he played. And Allison was right about Lord Faulkner, for he possessed the timepiece of the man Harry had killed at sea.

Fears pummeled Harry like whitewater—churning his insides, filling him with an energy he struggled to contain behind his placid footman's facade.

His ill-fitting breeches suddenly pinched him in the crotch, halting him. He resisted the urge to adjust himself in the middle of a stream of revelers heading north on the garden path, yet not one took notice of him. *Like a ghost to them all. With naught on my tray, I am but a—*

A sharp whistle—a *beckoning* whistle—broke his thoughts and he turned to find the sound.

Harry wandered from the footpath until he caught the sound of a quieter, nearer whistle. He turned.

It was Tad. *Bloody Tad.* He stood in the dark with one arm on a tree and Sarah, the maid, against it. Tad winked before bending himself over Sarah to practically consume her lips with his. Her frenzied hands worked in tandem with his to lift her petticoats.

Harry pivoted away before the display became any more ardent. He resumed his fevered, aimless pace—Tad's faint chuckle fading behind.

Harry knew nothing of Lord Faulkner. Nothing at all about how this man could possess the most infamous object of Harry's past. Perhaps it had been sold, or fenced, or pawned after the mutiny? Perhaps—?

Harry put up a hand to rake fingers through his hair. Instead he found the dreaded horsehair wig and pulled away in disgust.

No. This was it. Faulkner was it. It was all happening.

Fuck.

He looked over his shoulder at where he'd come from. The canopy of Allison's dining pavilion was distant and dim. His Primrose was, at that very moment, seated next to a man with an unknown connection to the mutiny. A man who doubtless knew what Harry had done on the merchant ship, *Diligence*, nearly seven years before.

*   *   *

Lady Merton's fingers danced in the air as she stared down at her saucer of sweets.

"Oh, I do not know how to choose. Chocolate or lemon?"

Lord Merton tenderly nudged his wife's arm. "Has Lady Allison yet had one?"

The marchioness snatched her hand away from the treats and looked to Allison, all alarm. "Oh my darling, did you? They were at your behest after all."

Allison had not, in fact, had one. She'd been too busy observing Harry at his post. He'd acted strangely. Something was wrong. She felt a distracting magnetism toward the footpaths. She had to find him. Had to learn what he'd discovered.

She met the marchioness' gaze and smiled. "Apologies, I must have slipped into a waking dream." She took the lemon cake from Lady Merton's proffered plate, though her nervous stomach turned over at the sight of it.

The marchioness covered Allison's hand with hers. "I understand dreaming in places like this. Beautiful places. And to think, the fireworks have not even yet started."

Allison perked up. "There will be fireworks?"

The marchioness nodded as she pursed her lips at the rim of her glass. "So I am told. Perhaps they will use the spectacle to lure drowsy lords into a second round of sins."

At this, the duke contributed a dark and languid laugh from his end of the table.

A sigh from Lord Faulkner drew Allison's attention and she turned in time to see him pushing in his chair. "If you will all excuse me, I am going to take a stroll."

"Enjoy the grounds, son. See the sights." A bawdy, drunken

smile overtook the duke's face. The same could not be said for Faulkner, who removed himself in typically staid fashion.

Allison's mother leaned in from her end of the table, her gray eyes all hope. "Perhaps you should join him."

Now, there was the most predictable thing to ever depart her mother's lips.

"Oh yes, do!" Lady Merton agreed. "My godson would love the company. Would your son not enjoy that, Your Grace?" But Montagu was not in a conversational way and responded with a heavy-lidded attempt at a wink.

Allison looked down at the neglected lemon cake. "You know, I believe I will." If everyone wished her away from the table so badly, she would appease them and seek a roguish footman instead.

Allison never intended to catch up with Lord Faulkner but was surprised, nonetheless, to discover his lavender coattail had already vanished from the lit path.

She whipped out her fan to occupy her hands as she walked and mulled over Harry's odd behavior. He'd been rattled, surely. Did it mean he'd learned something of Faulkner? Or was there something else?

Allison chewed her lip and gazed at her hem in a way that would displease her mother. A curdled sense of guilt crept in. She'd been so cavalier about masquerading Harry as a footman, when she'd known full well that he'd anticipated a different arrangement. It had been to her a marvelous lark, beneficial to their investigation, until that one moment—the moment when he tipped his tray down to her and it was just the same as when any footman did so. A credit to Harry's performance, certainly, but too real—far too real—for Allison. Just what had she asked of him?

Deep in these thoughts, she'd stepped away from the footpath.

Looking back up, she found herself staring into an orchard at the lawn's west edge, and there was Faulkner's coattail, disappearing into it. What could he be about? Sneaking off into the trees?

Allison took one step away from the main lawn and then another, her instincts honing in on this whiff of mystery.

The orchard was lit only by waning moonlight, and as she went deeper and it felt as though the shadows might swallow her whole. She willed her eyes to adjust to the darkness, but her will had little say in it. She lost sight of Faulkner from time to time, but then the silk of his coat would suddenly reflect the moonlight, marking him a glowing wood sprite, easy to follow.

Ha! Lord Faulkner, a wood sprite, would that not be a sight?

Allison clamped a hand across her mouth, against a laugh. It reminded her of Harry's hand, of how they'd been cupped against one another on the rooftop. The memory sent a pleasant shiver through her as she continued her pursuit.

But there were no further glints of moonlight on silk. She had lost him.

She'd ventured well beyond the orchard, and here it blended into taller and taller trees—a miniature woodland.

She'd not realized how swiftly she'd been moving, and her breath strained against her stays from exertion. A cramp formed between her ribs, doubling her forward. She cast a glance behind her shoulder.

The braziers of the party now glowed so far away. What made her think such mysteries as Faulkner were hers to solve? What made her think she could do Harry's work?

She knew the answer. She wished to impress him, to convince him she might be as rugged and cunning as he. That she wasn't all Provençal silks and trays of sweets. She longed to draw a line of sameness between them at a time when their differences were glaring.

The spasm at her side deepened and she clutched at it, taking in a deeper gulp of air. *Damn.* She could not be so hasty on the way back.

She stared at her hem as she wrapped herself with her arms and waited for the stitch to pass. The ground was black, as though she stood on nothing at all. Her breaths puffed loudly, but somewhere in their rhythm, came another that was not her own.

A hand, cold and heavy settled on her shoulder.

Her throat wound up for a scream—

"Lady Allison, please!" A hissing whisper. "It is only me."

The hand pulled away.

She staggered and whirled, already knowing who stood there, inscrutable in the shadows. That voice. Faulkner.

"*Only* you?! I do not even know what that means after being frightened out of my wits."

There was something else—no, *someone* else—beyond him.

Faulkner stepped aside to reveal a young woman whose silvery gown picked up the sparse moonlight just the same as Faulkner's frock coat.

Allison caught her breath, straining to understand—was anyone in danger here?

Faulkner took several steps back, meeting the woman's side in her brighter patch of moonlight. He placed an arm around her back and she melted against his shoulder.

Allison realized she was still as frozen as cornered fox. She unhitched her muscles and straightened, ignoring her still-fading cramp.

"Lady Allison, this is Miss Stephanie Lyons."

"A pleasure," muttered Allison, certain she had never had an introduction play out like this before.

"A pleasure." Miss Lyons' voice was barely a whisper. Demure. Embarrassed.

"What are you doing out here?" asked Faulkner.

"I—" Allison's eyes followed Faulkner's hand as he slid it from Miss Lyons' waist and laced his fingers with hers. *Lovers. That is all. This is the love that his father does not approve of.*

Something else was glowing in the moonlight—Faulkner's rare smile. Looking at them side by side, Allison experienced both pity and hope. Here was a man much more complex than ever she'd expected. She suddenly wished for him to have the love he wanted. Just as she wished the same for herself.

"The truth is, I was sent after you by our dear mothers. You know how they have been. But I should not have come this far, disturbing your privacy so. Quite silly of me, really." As embarrassment crept in, Allison did not know whether it was her heart or her words rushing faster. "Perhaps, you might keep my deviation from the lawn a secret? It is a terribly poor choice I've made for my reputation, is it not?"

"Allison, wait."

She had not even realized she was backing away. Faulkner approached.

"Of course your reputation is safe, Lady Allison. We have much more reason to beg for *your* secrecy. You will keep it between us?" It took Allison aback, hearing the dreaded Lord Faulkner speak with the tremor of childlike panic.

"Oh yes, of course," Allison whispered. "Of course, that. Naturally. I would never—your secrets are safe. After all, we are friends, are we not?"

Had she truly just said that? *Well. Even villains may be in love.*

Or perhaps he *was* dangerous. Perhaps she was not so great a judge of character as she imagined. But in that moment, her romantic heart doubted he could be anything else but misunderstood.

It was clear to her now—she could not see one for a villain unless they held a knife still dripping with blood. This, again, was why she was not the investigator and Harry was.

"Yes. We are friends," said Faulkner.

She looked past him to Miss Lyons whose hair, perhaps strawberry in color, glinted for a moment in the faint light. "You make a very fine-looking pair."

"Thank you," whispered Miss Lyons. Her whisper seemed a shout in so quiet a place.

At last, it dawned on Allison to remove herself.

10

*B*OOM!

   Allison tripped and caught herself, thinking to duck out of the line of some projectile. But the orchard brightened with pink light and above her, beyond the branches, were the cascading tendrils of a spent firework.

   Her heart pounded against the palm she'd flung to her breast. She was more prepared when it came again.

   BOOM!

   Distantly, came the *oohs* and *ahhs* of guests as they awakened from drunken lolls to take in new pleasures. Allison smiled as the glow faded again. There was something nice about seeing the spectacle this way, through the branches of bloomed-out apricot trees. All alone. She propped her back against the nearest trunk.

   She pictured Faulkner and Miss Lyons still arm-in-arm in their quiet grove, watching the show as she did. *How lovely for them.*

BOOM!

BOOM!

Something brushed against her arm. A shadow at the corner of her eye—

BOOM!

She lashed out.

BOOM!

Flailed. Started to screa—

BOOM!

Harry's face shone brief and bright in the flash.

He smoothed his hands down her quaking arms, tried to calm her, but there was no calm to be had. She shoved him hard and only half-playfully.

"Does *no one* call one's name before reaching out to touch them in the dark?"

The light on Harry's face faded as the most recent firework died out of the sky. "I did announce myself," he said, "but the—"

BOOM!

This time their smiles met in the fleeting red light of the explosion. Harry cast his wig aside before the darkness came.

When the sky relit, he was nearer, his face filling her vision. The messy swoosh of hair above his brow brushed against her nose, pricking her with faint electricity. She tilted her chin up.

BOOM!

He pressed his lips to hers.

It was no whisper of a kiss like the one shared through the hack's window. This time, Harry's tongue swept across the seam of her lips in a way that implored they slip open. The gentle intrusion was indistinct—all blind sensation—and Allison parted her lips further to let him taste her and to taste him back.

Her fingers explored the cool silk of his livery—how it rippled and pulled across the taut musculature of a body not made for carrying dainty things on silver trays. He ground his hips into her, demonstrating the very strength she could feel in him as she dragged a wandering hand across his backside. The apricot's trunk scraped at the back of her neck and she fought into his kiss with a forceful thrust of her own. Her riposte only ignited them further.

BOOM!

The floral sash Harry had given her was crushed between them, releasing the fragrances of a dozen flowers into the night air.

He slid his hand around her at the spot where petticoats blossomed from her waist, before tugging her even more firmly against his need. She could feel it, that place where he was hardened for her. It bruised against her belly with each press of his hips.

Nothing but the soft sounds of rustling silk and heavy breathing filled the gaps between the rockets. The places where they touched were as hot as the fires exploding above, leaving Allison's mind ablaze with deliciously unfamiliar ideas.

She knew not if she kissed well or terribly. All she knew was that her soul slavered for a taste of this man—an instinct like none she had before experienced. An intoxication. *A drug.*

Now was not the time and here was not the place, but when else would she have him alone? Where do a Bow Street Runner and a society lady rendezvous if not surreptitiously in some orchard in the night? Some distant part of her mind thought to argue. *This is Harry. There are things we must figure out first. This should be special—*

BOOM!

Caution shattered apart.

She planted a hand in his hair and clutched a palmful of it—mussed and sweaty and—

BOOM!

She was so focused on their kiss, on all of that sensation, she'd hardly noticed how lifted she was against the tree—how her lover's knee had sunk into her skirts, keeping her on her toes. When she peeled away from his kiss for a draw of air, she noticed it all. She sharpened her eyes on where she knew his were in the dark and waited for the next illumination before delivering him a look—

BOOM!

—of lustful starvation.

The light around them went red. She watched him in certainty, in delight, as his expression turned to one of understanding—of mutual hunger—before darkness fell again.

She was delivered to her wishes as Harry shuffled her skirts upward with the hand that was not already busy feeling her.

Then he dropped to his—to his knees?

BOOM!

This she'd not expected. She took her skirts in hand to spare Harry the death by suffocation that might befall him should he exert himself beneath four petticoats. But all thoughts of such particulars evaporated at the sensation of hot breath against her inner thigh.

BOOM!

pop pop pop

Petals from her garland cascaded into Harry's tousled hair. They fell slowly, stuttering through time in the rapid explosions of light. She felt like a goddess, like a force of nature making the flowers grow—

And just then, a kiss was planted in her garden.

Pierced by ecstasy, she sank against his lips. The silken swipes of his tongue left her too limp to remain on her toes. He found her hand with his and gently pulled, encouraging her to let go, to sink down against his face as she desired, to stand somehow relaxed against this heated onslaught of—

BOOM!

Her nerves jumped as though they had no memory of the last explosion or the one before that. An ever-building tightness gnawed at her gut. It was unbearable. It was . . . Was it pleasurable? Did there exist a sort of pleasure so incapacitating?

All sensation beneath her skirts was hot and slick and blurred. She could hardly tell where she ended and Harry's face began. So she almost missed it when his finger began to explore her as devoutly as his tongue.

A fingertip slid just barely inside of her and she bore herself down, chasing the pressure, offering ingress, if only it would satisfy this unbearable need she could not appease.

Her thighs ached. Her womb tightened. Harry parted her mound with his tongue and suckled her lips. Time and again, he brushed against something that felt like the loose thread of a spool; how she longed for him to stay in that spot and unwind her.

His finger traced her entrance—something her responsive moan encouraged him to repeat. Again. And again. Between that and the chaos of his mouth on her—that loose thread of bliss . . .

"Please," she breathed. She did not plead for something from Harry, but for something from herself. *"Please."*

BOOM!

She looked up at that release of energy above her—all those arms of fire drooping into peaceful falling sparks. She held her breath. Let it out slowly. Infused it with a certain depth she'd never before tested. She tilted back her throat. Prayed Harry would not stop. Just one moment more . . .

Hot breath. Bearing down. Taking in. Dizzying pressures.

Breathe. Breathe. Breeee—

BOOM!

All went red again, but her eyes were not even open. She bit down on her hand against a wanton scream. Everything was made of sparks.

Her thighs crushed in against her lover's face and she felt him bail away from her like a man abandoning ship. Rightly so, for she was fast-sinking.

Allison removed one hand from her mouth and unclenched the other, allowing her skirts to fall like the curtain at the end of an exquisite operetta. Then she crumpled against the tree.

Reaching up to touch her pretty garland, she found only stray leaves and sparse, crushed petals. But its ruin did not displease her. How could it when the last gasps of rapture still crackled through her? She smiled, hot-faced and tired.

Harry sat on his haunches across from her, arms propped on his knees. His blue sleeve caught the moonlight as he swiped a forearm across his glistening lips and smiled back.

She'd had a million questions for him but had held them all back, because having privacy with Harry was a luxury, and having fireworks overhead was a dream.

But she could feel the questions fizzing upward, like bubbles to the surface of freshly poured champagne. *What did you learn? What of Giddy? Of your hunter? Of Faulkner? How did you find me? Why did you follow me? What did you just do to me and how—when can it happen again?*

They were all distractions from the hardest question of all, one she had only just begun to face: *How will we ever be together?*

He was silent. Something warned her he would stay that way. Perhaps he'd come and found her for the very same reason she'd dispatched with her own inhibitions: *because he'd wanted to*. Perhaps all that wondrous pleasure had hinged on their ability to push a great many things aside.

The sky was silent and hazy with smoke. They sat together in the dark with the ghosts of many unspoken words suspended between them.

"Primrose," he said, at last. And she anticipated more syllables that did not come.

Instead, she heard him shift on the grass.

"Who is that?" he whispered.

She didn't see or hear anything. She looked over her shoulder, around the apricot's trunk. Then she saw what he saw. A stealthy shadow creeping back to the path, some ten rows away in the orchard. Faulkner. Backlit by the moon and without Miss Lyons in tow.

Without the fireworks, she could hardly see Harry but avoided looking his direction anyway. "I believe it is Lord Faulkner." Her whispered, nonchalant admission felt absorbed by the night.

Harry scrambled over to her on his knees and gripped her shoulders. A gentle shake persuaded her to meet his eyes. "Faulkner?! Did you follow him out here?"

She shrugged against Harry's grip and hissed a whisper back at him. "Harry . . . I may have judged Lord Faulkner too hastily. I had no real evidence to—"

"He is dangerous, Allison. I know it now. You must stay away."

Harry's tone was unlike any he had taken with her before and she did not like it. Before she could protest, she was pulled to her feet.

"Go back. Rejoin your party. Do not leave your family's side."

Again, Allison opened her mouth to protest, but Harry had

already torn himself away, heading in Faulkner's direction. He tossed one final, "Go," over his shoulder as he went.

Harry's shadow disappeared, just as Faulkner's had, and Allison stood, dismayed.

So. This is love.

The moisture at the crux of her thighs was fast drying, but there was a heady aftereffect of her spasms she could not shake. It was her body crying for another round—a yearning it appeared would go unsatisfied.

Her fingers trailed down the front of her bodice, knocking off the last stray petals of her garland. She tore at the ribbons until it all fell at her feet, landing next to another bright thing in the moonlight—Harry's discarded wig. He'd be in a heap of trouble for its loss.

Let him be.

Nobody looked up when Allison returned to her party's table. Once more she stood at the threshold of social judgment, not caring.

Beth had once warned Allison that, were she ever to seek out a rogue as she had, then she must accustom herself to the ruin of her clothing. The adage was fast seeming true.

Allison smoothed her skirts one last time before taking her seat. Faulkner had not yet returned. A shame, for she longed to needle him with a conspiratorial wink. He would hate it, of course, but his refined look of annoyance might soothe her soul.

Clearly Harry did not share her light-hearted impression of the viscount. It made her wonder what he'd learned—what he'd been so struck by at the table.

All these thoughts competed for territory with the gentle fizzing of her body and primordial emotions that could not yet be named. She had loved fireworks her entire life but had never known them to go off inside her.

She wandered in the miasma of such thoughts until a soft hand wrapped around hers. Lady Merton, to her right.

"Allison, did you not formerly wear a floral garland?"

Allison nodded, emerging from her trance with a racing heart. "I did indeed, but it was, uh . . . wilting and I worried the sticky flowers might stain my bodice. I discarded it."

Pleased with her lie and with the fact that each end of the table was distracted by other conversations, Allison sighed with relief.

"Ah. Very smart of you." Lady Merton leaned into Allison's space, putting her lips near her ear. "But I wonder, is it true?"

A storm of blood rushed to Allison's cheeks. She did not hasten to speak though. Flustered stammers, lifelong nervous instincts—she was learning how better to control them. Was learning how to wait. How to gather her thoughts.

She shrugged. "Perhaps I shall never tell, Lady Merton." She hoped her coy and easy smile would say the rest. It was a smile the marchioness quickly mirrored.

"Wicked girl. Disallowing me any good stories."

"Need I remind you, Lady Merton, that *you* are the Oracle here?"

The marchioness laughed, a trilling joyful sound, perfect in every way, yet seemingly unpracticed.

"I hope you will call me Beatrice when in private, dear Allison."

"We have never before been in private, *Lady* Merton."

The marchioness threw back her sherry glass against her lips, but the scant drops left in its bottom refused to budge.

"Tomorrow, then," she said when the glass was lowered.

Before Allison could answer, Lady Merton turned her attention to the Weldons who sat to the other side of her husband, Lord Merton.

"Lord Weldon, Lady Weldon, I wonder if I might show your daughter some sights tomorrow afternoon. Just she and I. Would I have your trust to chaperone her for the day?"

Lady Weldon's eyes lit up. Beatrice was granted not only the approval of Allison's mother but a predictably unrestrained blessing.

"How exciting that we shall get to spend a day together." The marchioness leaned close again. "And perhaps tomorrow, I shall extract from you the truth of your *deflowering*."

The wine intended for Allison's throat was instead sputtered from her lips as she choked on the word *deflowering*.

"*Allison!* What in heavens—?"

The marchioness interrupted Lady Weldon on Allison's behalf. "'Tis my fault. I made a jest that was cruelly timed with her sip of wine."

Lady Weldon immediately came to heel, adopting the marchioness' easy smile and shrinking back into conversation with her husband and Lord Merton.

Lady Merton passed her napkin to Allison. "My apologies."

Allison wiped her lips. Her eyes watered from the sting of wine droplets that had found their way up the back of her nose. She sniffed away the rest with a wince. "I am fast learning your ways. Your timing was intended."

Lady Merton shrugged, not denying it.

A gruff voice rose from the end of the table opposite where the Weldons sat. Montagu. "Lady Allison, did you catch up to my son? How is it he is not back yet?"

"I did, Your Grace. He was very cordial, but he merely wished to walk. Alone."

The duke rolled his eyes. "Yes, of course. *Alone* is always his way, is it not? So much for the family line."

Seems unfair, thought Allison. The duke's son *did* enjoy a lady's company, just not one any seemed to approve of. She smiled at the recent memory of Lord Faulkner's fingers threaded through those of Miss Lyons.

Allison looked down the table at her mother. The countess was yet oblivious to the existence of Harry, the man she would one day officially disapprove of for her. The injury of such disapproval was a tragic object of kinship between herself and Faulkner.

Lady Merton spoke up to the duke. "He is not disinterested. He must simply make the right match."

"He is six-and-thirty," grumbled the duke.

The marchioness tilted her head in reassurance. "He will find someone, Your Grace. Someday, everything will be right." Allison had forgotten her hand was still cupped by Lady Merton's but was reminded of the fact with a gentle and meaningful squeeze.

"I suppose it will." The duke stabbed a tiny sausage with his fork but did not eat it.

Lord Merton—the oft quiet, blank canvas of a man—spoke up then. "It is my wife's way to be optimistic." He took his wife's hand—the one not around Allison's—and lifted it to his lips for a kiss.

"Yes, Lady Merton sees all," said the duke.

"'Tis true," said Lady Merton. "Lady Allison told me so. For I am the Oracle."

Allison caught Montagu cracking a smile. He finally popped the little sausage into his mouth making it hard to catch what was mumbled through his mouthful, but Allison could swear it was, *"Don't I know it."*

Harry threaded his way through the orchard in pursuit of Lord Faulkner's shadow. He tugged on his rumpled waistcoat and smoothed a hand over his hair, but for all he straightened his appearance, he could not so easily straighten his mind. His lips still tasted of Allison and he could not cease swiping his tongue between them, taking in her flavor and each little memory it offered. The habit was a poor remedy for the darker thoughts that loomed.

The timepiece. The mutiny. The stolen letter . . .

But this was good, was it not? To be on the cusp of something? For he now had a suspect in Lord Faulkner. A solution was within reach.

Yet, what good was *in reach* when Allison was in reach as well, at the hems of all this madness? She had been out there in the orchard with *him*. Alone with a dangerous man. Harry clenched his fists at the thought. *She plays with fire.*

He tasted her on his lips again and recalled her saying something. The memory was faint, for he'd not listened well through his fear-clouded mind. Had she said something in Lord Faulkner's defense? Did she now fancy herself the viscount's rescuer as well as Harry's?

He stopped walking, suddenly shot through by the vision of Allison seated at the table beside Lord Faulkner. She in her gold. He in his lavender, glittering with gilt embroidery. Allison had looked like the sun and Faulkner like the first day of spring. A complementary pair. A match.

Harry resumed his stride but was grazed by a lance of panic. What had he been thinking beneath that tree with Allison? Why had he chosen that moment to unleash all that was pent up within him?

He'd seen her step away from the footpath in all her decadence and golden beauty, with that bouncing gait he had not realized he was mad for, and suddenly Tad's recreational ideas had not seemed so outlandish. Especially with the furious energy of what he had learned pumping through him.

Up ahead, Faulkner's shadow left the orchard's edge, growing better defined as he neared the candles and braziers of the lawn.

Harry brushed off his coat sleeves and refocused.

Lord Faulkner rounded the side of the manse beneath a wisteria-draped *porte cochère*. Harry followed, keeping his back to the hedges that replaced the orchard on the west side.

In front of the manse was a vast gravel drive cluttered with the carriages—a mess of glossy black boxes trimmed in gold. It was quieter here than the gardens, the only sounds being nickering stallions and the low conversations of coachmen.

Lord Faulkner scanned the area, not appearing to know where he was headed.

Harry gained ground on him, careful to stay low and conceal himself in the labyrinth of horses and boxes.

"*Psst.*"

Harry's eyes snapped upward to a young man on the nearest carriage's driver's seat.

"Have any snuff?"

Harry's alarm faded. "'Fraid not,"

The man waved him off in a way that was not unfriendly. Harry straightened. There was no need to stalk about so carefully. Allison's choice of disguise was working to its purpose.

A sharp whistle broke into the night air, followed by, "Gideon!"

The name drew Harry to its caller like a hound and he came around the next carriage so quickly he almost staggered into the scene he wished to spy on. He drew himself back behind an empty carriage and peered through the bottom of its windows.

"There you are." Lord Faulkner addressed a tall man in gray

livery, but the man's back was to Harry.

"Yes, my lord."

"Did you see Miss Lyons back to her carriage?"

"I did, my lord. Are you wishing to depart?"

Lord Faulkner let out a lengthy sigh. "Regrettably, I must go back. My absence will not be tolerated overlong." There was a jingle as coins passed hands. "A reward for the favor."

Favor? What need had a lord to call anything by his man a favor? Unless illicit . . .

"Thank you, my lord."

The voice was middle-aged and indistinct. Too much time had gone by to say whether it was the same. He spoke more formally than the man in the garret, but Harry had put on the same sort of deferent tone for his own night of service.

But the name—it was the *name* that was damning. *Gideon. Giddy.* They had to be the same.

Harry shook his head. These were minor details now. It was the watch, the bloody watch, that tied it all together.

A scraping sound caught Harry off guard and he turned to see a stable lad, rake in the gravel, staring at him.

Harry waited to hear Faulkner's footsteps—hopefully delivering him far away—before he spoke. "Are you going to ask me for snuff? Haven't filched any. Sorry."

The lanky pubescent arched a brow.

Harry held his breath, hoping he had cut off the boy from any reckless inquisition—the sort that young ones are prone to.

The boy shook his head and returned to his chore.

Harry had spent the entirety of the night acting like he'd never been in service before, but the boy and his rake reminded Harry of his origins—reminded him what a mop had felt like in his hand at that age as he bobbed up and down on the desolate sea.

He turned back to the scene he had spied on, but Giddy—or Gideon—was gone.

Satisfied that Faulkner had returned to the lawn, Harry left the drive.

He returned to the servant's entry to see whether the heavy table had been restocked with salvers of food and drink. No sooner had he descended the steps than a hard slap connected with his cheek.

His head rang so from the sting of it that it took a moment to focus on the man whose palm had caught him. The butler.

"You are without your wig, Mr. Harper." It took Harry a moment to adjust to his alias for the evening and reply.

"My wig, sir?" Harry's hand drifted to his hair. Instead of coarse horse's hair, his fingertips discovered his own soft strands, slightly damp with sweat.

"The temporary help is never good, but this is brazen disrespect for the position. Have the Gossingtons seen you like this?"

The man didn't wait for an answer. He took Harry sternly by the arm and yanked him from the bottom step, making him stagger into the room. Several workers in the kitchen paused to gawk at the commotion.

Harry straightened as the lanky butler approached again, venom in his aged eyes.

Hold yourself together.

"You will never be welcomed back. I will see that all your future recommendations are dismissed across the city."

Harry's cheeks burned as the man loomed over him. He forced himself to lower his head in a penitence he did not feel.

"But for now," said the butler, raising his chin, "we must make use of you for the rest of the night. It falls to me that you look proper until we discard you back to the street." The butler called over his shoulder to Tad's fair maiden, whose cheeks and neck were still rosy with the rash of rough kisses. "Sarah, fetch a spare wig. Quickly, please."

Sarah disappeared, and at last the butler turned his back on Harry, storming off to another room.

From the corner of his lowered eyes, Harry noticed Tad's hesitant approach. "Mate, I—"

"Don't."

11

Exhausted and eager to retire to her chamber, Allison nearly received a face full of damask as her mother stopped a few steps ahead on the main stairs. She looked up to see her mother examining her over one shoulder, her brows knit in a familiar way.

"Heavens, dear. I only just noticed, but you look a fright."

"Do I?" asked Allison. She looked down at her bodice, stained with wine and flecked with mashed flower petals. "I'd not noticed."

Their main staircase was the width of three men but, unfortunately for Allison, so were her mother's skirts. There would be no getting around. No escape. Thankfully, her mother resumed the ascent.

The relief was impermanent. A flick of Lady Weldon's finger beckoned Allison to follow her to the dressing room.

Allison hovered in the doorway, praying to keep short whatever interview was coming.

Her mother approached and thumbed at one of her stains. "You must learn to be more steady with your drink."

Allison lowered her eyes. It helped to suppress the sting of her mother's critiques.

"It was a fun evening though, was it not?" The countess moved her hand from Allison's bodice to her cheek, brushing a lock of hair behind her ear.

Allison, surprised, peeked up. "It was."

"I regret we were so far apart at the table."

"I was three seats away."

The matriarch rolled her eyes and motioned for Allison to turn around. She did, lifting her curls to give her mother access to her necklace's ribbon for untying. Removing one another's jewelry had been a ritual of theirs on their tour of the Continent, but those days were more than a year past, what felt like a decade.

"The seating arrangement was likely for the best. You seemed to enjoy your time with Lady Merton. And with an outing together tomorrow? How grand."

Allison caught the loosened necklace in her waiting hands and turned around. Her mother's pewter eyebrows were lifted in the middle—hopeful and quivering. Allison was weak for such looks. She leaned in for an embrace.

It felt nice for a moment, being there, in her mother's arms, remembering their tour and recalling the version of her mother who could traipse through mud for miles in Tuscany, so long as it was the fashionable thing.

Allison closed her eyes to lose herself to more memories, but of course it couldn't last—

"Unfortunately, I heard the footman who came on your recommendation was an utter failure." Lady Weldon pulled away from the embrace to fuss with the removal of her own pearl earring.

"How do you mean? What did Lady Gossington say of him?"

Harry had been somewhat artless in the pavilion, surely, but not to any conspicuous degree. At least her mother did not seem to know the one who served them *was* the failed footman.

"It made its way to me at night's end. Apparently, he was dismissed after failing the very basics of keeping his livery intact." Lady Weldon tugged her earring hard, wincing when it did not come away. "You must be more careful with your recommendations. Things like this reflect poorly on one's reputation. How ever did you find him anyway?"

Allison stared once more at the polished floorboards. *Poor Harry. And it is all my fault.*

She looked up in time to see her mother deliver another gruesome and futile tug to her earlobe. "Mother, let me."

She stood on her tiptoes to examine the back of her mother's hooked earring. A curl of her wig was dreadfully tangled in it.

"You know," said the countess, "I am very pleased the two of you have bonded more."

Allison's heart skipped—she and Harry? Then her mind fell back to reality. "Lady Merton and I? Yes, tomorrow should be diverting."

The pearl earring finally released with the snap of a few hairs and Allison dropped the troublesome thing into her mother's waiting hand.

"It is a shame Lord Faulkner did not wish for company on his walk tonight. I am certain it is nothing personal, though. Did you have good conversation at the table?"

"Is that all you care about?" The words flew out at once like buckshot. "Whether or not I've been successfully foisted onto a duke's son?"

"Allison!"

Allison winced at the sing-song tone of her name.

Her father's muffled voice called out from beyond the doors to the adjoining bedchamber. "Whatever quarrel is about to be had, might you save it for the morrow?" His voice fell to a grumble. "When my head has quit its spinning?"

The countess' hands were still frozen on her other ear—on an earring she would have to extract alone.

Allison rolled her lips between her teeth. "I did not mean to speak to you like that. It is just that I have no interest in Lord Faulkner—"

"But you are so deserving of a duke. I'll not see you with some baronet or—"

"—and *he* has no interest in me either." Allison sidestepped her mother as Amelia, their lady's maid, entered. "I am very tired, Mother. Goodnight."

She did not look back as she fled the room.

Back in her bedchamber, she had a perfect view of the mews house. The lower left window was dark.

There was an undeniable weight in Allison's chest, one that left her dogged optimism with little room to breathe. Grand visions of the orchard—of panting abandon beneath rockets in the sky—mingled with that one little memory of Harry feeling the weave of her silk.

Just what had she put him through?

Harry had woken with a head splitting at its seams. He supposed all the soirée's attendees would be feeling the same. They too would hold their heads as they woke, but theirs would swim with the pain of too much drink, and their joints would ache from the pain of too much dancing. Not so for Harry. He ached not from leisure but from labor.

The cruel butler, demanding the livery back at once, had sent Harry home in rags and he'd not crawled into his humble bed until the night had gone gray with the threat of daylight. Now, as he dragged his feet toward Bow Street, it was but a scant few hours later.

Grim thoughts of the hour only served to remind Harry of Faulkner's watch, a thought which needled him with extra pain. The vision repeated itself all the way to the door of Mr. Crofty's office at the Magistrate's Court.

"Devonshire?" Harry let his question hang in the air, knowing full well that he'd asked it with the edge of offense. "Have you not heard all I've said?"

Mr. Crofty avoided his gaze, playing with a quill the same shade of gray as his thinning hair.

"You know I hold you in high esteem, Mr. Plymouth, but the magistrate can extend to you no more of his trust or time. He needs you to find the arsonist who fled to Devon. You're the only man he can spare for it."

"Can spare for an aristocrat's errand, you mean. It is a punishment, is it not? For my absence?"

Crofty readjusted his spectacles, nearly marking his face with the quill that was still in hand.

"Yes. An errand. But not punitive. You have simply been away so much, Harry, that this is what is left."

Scraps. "I am being hunted."

"I know."

"And I have just told you by whom."

Mr. Crofty's sigh was plain; Sir Wright would sign no warrants for a duke's son.

"The nobs should not enjoy such immunity from us."

Mr. Crofty pinched his nose, this time getting ink on his cheek before throwing down the quill. "I do not disagree, but do you think that targeting a member of the aristocracy will work out well for your position here?"

Harry could not fault the man for his words—he could see the work of the magistrate behind them. The knowledge, however, was a poor balm to his frustrations.

"You're right. There's so much more honor in tracking down an arsonist who burned down—what was it again? A baron's gazebo?—than in curtailing the dark activities of a nobleman's son with the power to bend the world to his will." Harry smacked imaginary dust from his hat and made a show of planting it firmly on his head. He spun toward the door.

"Six days!"

Harry stopped and turned back around.

"I can give you six more days. Only because the magistrate will be away until then. Once he is back, my power to make excuses for you dissolves. Either you are in Devon, or you are no longer a Bow Street Runner. And I will need more, much more, than vague blatherings on about a watch fob."

"And before my six days are up, will I be able to summon support?"

Crofty averted his gaze but nodded. "You will have my help."

Harry nodded and turned again to leave. "Thank you."

"Be sure to see Mr. Bowen before you go."

Harry could not possibly have heard correctly. "Mr. Bow—"

"Mr. Booker. That's what I said." Crofty wore an unnerving smile. One Harry typically only saw when his employer was deep in drink and ready to tell a joke that would receive only groans.

"Rhys is in London?"

"Rhys is in the building, Mr. Plymouth."

Harry lunged from the office, charging down the main corridor and popping his head into every open door on the first floor. He was suddenly tugged sideways from the hall.

After catching himself from a nasty fall, he looked up to see the grabber: his mentor, his friend, the nearest thing to family—Rhys Bowen—known to the Home Department by the surname of Booker—an alias to cover a disgraced name, just as the name Plymouth was for Harry.

Harry's spirit lurched back to life at the sight of his friend. "I did not know you were in London."

Rhys pulled him by the forearm into an enthusiastic hand-shake. "Of course you didn't. You were not home to receive me. I'd hoped to steal your bed for a day or two, but instead I'm in a room above a laundry yard that smells of lye all day."

Harry was eye level with the simple silver embroidery on his friend's collar. He doubted the inn was so bad. His eyes skimmed ever upward until he looked over his friend's dark head of hair. "You'd not have fit in my bed. Surely only the floor could contain you."

Rhys smiled and began walking down the hall. "The floor has suited me just fine before, as you know."

"But you cannot stay with me," said Harry.

"Why ever not?"

"There's not a bed to be had."

The jovial light faded from Rhys' eyes in response to Harry's grim tone.

"I'll explain."

"I have something to tell you as well. Shall we go to the coffee house?"

"I'd prefer an ale house. A specific one."

Harry led Rhys to *The Wise Ermine*. Its ground floor could be a tad lawless, even before midday, but upstairs there were quiet tables in nooks, buffered from the din below. He often led suspects there for illuminating chats. Now he would use it to tell Rhys the darkest secret he'd ever held. A knot formed in his gut as he got a nod from the proprietor and ascended the creaking steps beyond the bar.

Ale splashed from overfull mugs as they were slammed to their table by the barmaid, Mary—missish in appearance, but mighty in character. "Anything else I should know you'll be wanting?"

Harry lifted his mug and shook his head. "Thank you, Mary."

She departed with a shrug.

"So, who first?" asked Rhys.

"Is your news good or bad?"

"Good. Very good."

"Then please, tell me all that is good." Harry tried to wipe the hopeful desperation from his voice as he said it. Was there any good tiding in the world that could render his troubles obsolete?

Rhys took a preparatory swig of ale before leaning forward and lowering his voice. "I've had a bit of a promotion."

"Oh? What sort of promotion?"

"There is the tricky part. I cannot say much about it by its very nature, but I'm no longer formally a Runner. My scope is somewhat, ah . . . *grander* now."

"It's intelligence, isn't it? You stayed so long on the Continent during your tour with Beth. I did not understand how you got away with such a holiday, but now—"

Rhys put up a finger to cut Harry off. Mary swished past their table on her way to another.

"*Hmm.* I wonder . . ." Rhys leaned back and tipped his head to one side. "Why ever did they not pick *you* for the job?" He took a swig of ale and rolled his eyes.

Harry smiled down at his mug. A rivulet of envy was wending through his heart, but he quashed it. "I'm very happy for you."

"Oh, but that is not the good news yet."

"Oh?"

Rhys leaned in as though to share a state secret. "The good news is that we are free to have our names again, Harry."

Harry's rivulet of envy became one of dread. His limbs went cold. There was a time such news would have been a shining star, but now . . .

Harry cleared his throat. "How do you mean?"

"I mean you can discard *Harry Plymouth* and reclaim *Harry Stinton*."

Harry instinctively cast a wary eye around the room, but his friend seemed not to notice.

Rhys leaned back in his seat and shook his head. "I've hidden behind Osbourne *Rhys* Booker for more than half a decade. Now I am Rhys Bowen again, as I was intended to be. Not only to my wife, but to Bow Street."

"How?"

"When I learned my duties would be elevated, it felt too precarious a position to be in with my past hanging overhead. Mr. Crofty believes in the law but also believes in what is right, and as a friend—"

"So you exposed us as the mutineers in the very heart of the Home Department?" Harry's eyelids strained from whatever horrified expression he wore. Rhys stretched a hand across the table and placed it on his wrist.

"Harry, lad, we have been formally pardoned, given a clean slate in every possible way."

Harry pulled his hand away. "That was a tremendous risk."

"I know it must seem that way, but I've known Mr. Crofty years longer than you. It matters not to him who we were then but who we are today. He knows why we did what we did on the *Diligence*."

"God, did you also go telling him we were highway robbers?" Harry asked it mockingly but the lack of response stretched overlong.

"I'm not a fool, Harry. Our names—real or otherwise—were never connected to our later activities. Besides, we were not very *good* at highway robbery. Barely made it to the journals, as I recall."

"Oh? You would have rather made a name in the vocation? Been the next Swift Nick?" Rhys didn't respond. Only smiled to himself while picking at a splinter in the table.

Harry's legs were heavy with blood as his head grew light. Rumors were difficult to contain in London, even those originating in such secure places as the Home Department. An admission to their past crime left them wide open to blackmail, to bribery, to—

Rhys' shoulders shrugged up and down with trembles of silent laughter.

"What is funny? Nothing is funny."

"Do you not want your name back, Harry?"

"What name? Need I remind you I am a bastard? I'm not certain what my name matters to me." Harry cursed inwardly at his irritability. "I'm sorry. I'm not myself. It *is* good news, just damn poor timing. Poor and dreadfully ironic."

"Ironic? How?"

Harry went to take another nervous dram but found his cup somehow empty. He put it to his lips anyway, postponing his confession.

"I tried to tell you many months ago, in a letter I had no courage to send. And then it was lost. No. Not lost. Stolen."

Rhys crossed his arms and leaned his elbows on the table. Mirth drained from his face at Harry's tone.

"I've wanted to tell you for years. You always placed so much faith in me. I will always owe you for your generosity, but I've been a liar and a coward in the face of that generosity."

Harry paused as Mary sidled up to the table. Both he and Rhys raised a polite hand to send her away. She took Harry's cup with her, leaving him no object to occupy his shaking hands.

Harry took a deep breath. "Surely you will recall how the first officer perished in the brig during our mutiny?"

"One of the worst days of my life. We all just wanted to survive a trip across the Labrador Sea. A man's life was never an intended sacrifice, even if he was a nob who'd been handed his commission on a platter."

Harry saw the entirety of that voyage reflected in his friend's eyes. Their senile captain had been sailing the crew to their deaths. Rhys and the quartermaster had been the only ones courageous enough to put a stop to it but all had ended in misery, with the quartermaster hanged and the rest of the mutineers turned out of Bristol in exile.

"I know you blamed yourself for that officer's death. But it was not your fault." Harry summoned a stronger voice and met Rhys' eye. "It was mine."

"How do you mean?"

Harry leaned out from the nook and looked around. Satisfied with their privacy, he continued.

"I was below deck, alone, bringing the first mate his stew in the brig. He watched me, but I thought nothing of it. He had a right to be spiteful. But when I approached the bars, he opened the door straight into me—must have picked the locks or had a key still on him. I was knocked straight to the ground, him atop me. We grappled . . ."

Rhys' once warm cheeks had drained of color. His shoulders slumped. His eyes focused on the splinter he'd been picking at. The air in the nook went thick with pain, but Harry pushed on. There was no going back.

"We grappled on the floor. He had his hands 'round my neck." When I regained the advantage, I went for the same tactic. His timepiece had been cast off in the scuffle. I took it and I—its short chain became my garrote as I killed the man."

Harry had brought his voice so low, had leaned in so far, that his forehead nearly brushed with that of his friend.

Rhys pushed away and sat back, his eyes distant. Focused perhaps on the sea's horizon or the blank stare of the murdered officer.

"I'm sorry." Harry lowered his head. "I've disappointed your trust. It was my action that consigned Dewey—and quite nearly the rest of us—to the gallows."

Rhys' shoulders visibly rose and sank with heavy, deliberate breaths. He would not meet Harry's eye. He tossed a handful of coin onto the table and stood.

A curt tic of his head in the direction of the stairs bade Harry to follow him.

Rhys stayed one step ahead as they left the tavern, a chill breeze blowing off his back.

Harry followed him into the alley, where the people around them became fewer and fewer.

What form would Rhys' anger take? He would be within his rights to see Harry removed from his fragile position on Bow Street.

But the loss of employment would be nothing against the loss of their accord and Harry had already started grieving for a friend, a brother, a mentor . . .

At last, they reached a quiet place where only the sky could see them. Rhys whipped around, but as Harry firmed his jaw, prepared for his berating, he was instead pulled violently into an embrace.

Unsure what was happening, it was a moment before he responded in kind, wrapping his arms around his friend's large body, which shuddered with emotion.

"Harry. You were only a lad then. There is no shame in defending your life. We *all* mutinied in defense of our lives. We *all* did the same thing. I wish I'd known. *Of course*, I wish I'd known. I wish you'd told me, but only because it destroys me to know you've carried this for so long, alone."

Rhys pushed Harry to arm's length to look at him—to deliver a look so painfully reassuring—Harry was not sure he'd deserved such a look in all his life, but he tried his best not to break from it. It was uplifting and excruciating all at once.

Uncertain where he found the courage, he spoke again. "There's more."

Rhys nodded. "Tell me all of it."

Harry caught him up. On the attempts against his life. The ransacking of his home. The theft of the letter outlining his confession. And, most reluctantly, of Allison's recent involvement.

Rhys bit his lip, pondering the last bit. "Allison? Truly?"

Harry nodded. "I know. I should not have dragged her into this, but—"

"Does Beth know of the two of you?"

Harry noticed a poorly hidden smile dancing in Rhys' eyes.

He sighed. "I don't yet know if she has told—"

"Because if Beth knew of this and did not tell me—"

"I believe Allison's mother has restricted Beth's ability to get letters through."

Rhys put his hands on his hips, nodding in memory. "Ah yes, the eminent countess, Lady Weldon, I certainly remember that one. Bless her for demanding Beth and I wed, as though it were a punishment." Rhys laughed loudly.

Harry furrowed his brow, logic informing him they must remain focused. "If I am correct that Lord Faulkner—"

"I cannot wait to tell Beth. She will be damned delighted to hear it and then neither you nor Allison will hear the end of it."

Rhys no longer tried to school his face. His giddiness knew but a tot's restraint.

The sight of the grown man's glee brought a smile, at last, to Harry's face. "I won't, will I?"

"Nor will you hear the end of it from me."

"I'm fast aware."

"How do you feel about her?"

In love, Harry thought. But also, "Far away," he replied.

Rhys nodded. "Beth and I were far away as well, if you mean what I think you do. Our union felt impossible for a long time, but in the end, it wasn't."

"In the beginning, I thought very often of the two of you. You inspired my hope that things might work with Allison, but Beth was not a nobleman's daughter. She did not have to sacrifice her family to be with you."

"Depends on what family. As you said yourself, Beth cannot correspond freely with her cousin or see her."

"*Yes,* because of Lady Weldon, the same woman who stands like a portcullis between me and Allison."

Rhys lowered his gaze. Nothing to say to that.

"Staying in the mews, I see that elegant townhouse tower over me every day. I see it from my little window, knowing that Tallyside is unimaginably grander. And they must have properties I don't even yet know of." All of it was difficult to speak of, but there was something that made it harder yet, that left a leaden feeling in his heart. "I had so much pride in myself before I saw her world."

Rhys put a hand on Harry's shoulder.

"I am going to give you some advice. There is only one person in the world you must measure up to. It is not Allison, nor her family. Nor is it me. It is only yourself and who you were yesterday.

"You are leagues above your birth and well advanced beyond your past. That is something you innately knew when you were alone in your rooms on Dryden. You knew it when you were comfortably reading by *your* fireplace.

"You're well educated. Well employed. With loyal friends as your family." Rhys looked past one of Harry's shoulders, then the other. "Harry, I see no bastard here."

Harry's heart resisted the kind words, and for the first time in his life, he realized how cruelly he did not accept himself. His friend was right.

But it was not the sort of knowledge one could fully absorb after just one conversation. The truth itself could not, overnight, undo the erosive quality of a difficult start in life, *but* it was a thought worth keeping at the fore. "Thank you."

"Will you reclaim the name of Stinton?"

"Perhaps? I don't yet know. It seems the name has already been discovered by my hunters. Will you stay and help me?"

The answer was on Rhys' face before he spoke. "I'm afraid I must return to the Continent. I came down from the Folly and am only passing through."

Harry nodded, trying not to show his disappointment.

"But I'm not afraid for you, Harry. You're keen and determined. And, ever since I handed you the reins of our horses back at the Folly years ago, I've known you to be the capable writer of your own tale. Furthermore, you have an ally you should not discount."

"In Lady Allison?"

"Yes. Your 'Primrose,' was it?" Rhys shook genially him by the shoulder.

Warmth surged to Harry's cheeks. Why had he shared *that* amid his ramblings?

Rhys looked him up and down, shook his head, and smiled.

"The two of you are so alike."

Harry held his friend's reassurance close as they said their good-byes. Then he watched as Rhys disappeared between the buildings.

The ingrained vigilance of the past few months crept in as Harry found himself alone in the alley behind *The Wise Ermine*. He rested a hand over the spot beneath his coat where his pistol was kept, then relaxed it. No shots echoed. No blades *zinged* through the air. No voices whispered . . .

Only the wind blew through the alleyway, disturbing linens on drying lines high overhead.

Allison was right. He would catch his pursuers. His problem would be solved and it would feel like this after. It would be peaceful, and safe.

They would be together.

12

Dearest Beth,

Cousin, it has been too long, but at last I have faithful Hayden to smuggle my letters out the door. I know not how to fit recent events onto the page—there are so many—but I will do my best. To be forthcoming with you: I am in love. Or thought I was. This is precisely where I need your help. I need Beth the Bold and Beth the Wise to offer counsel. I pray that by my story's end, you will see some easy path for me, because every day that passes wilts my hopes a little more . . .

The gathers of Allison's polonaise whooshed and rustled against that of the marchioness as they walked. Sashaying with linked arms, Allison could close her eyes and imagine some of Lady Merton's elegance rubbing off on her.

"We are not far now."

Allison responded with an easy smile. She didn't care how far they were from their destination; she could promenade with the woman all day and be well.

The marchioness' blue eyes were full of anticipation and equally full of sparkle. It was difficult to remember that she was near the same age as Allison's mother—a trivia her mother oft boasted of, oblivious that it invited comparisons unfavorable to her.

Allison's mother's eyes were more gray, like the mid-morning fogs that muted the colors of the moors. They were steady and there was a reassuring stoicism about them, but they were not eyes that drew one in. There was no mischief behind them.

Allison wondered whether her own eyes possessed any such mischief today, having acquired enough secrets in the past week to fill a lifetime. That morning she had woken from a fitful slumber to find her body had a new favorite pastime: *lust*.

In social seasons past, she had flirted, she had adored, she had chastely held hands, she had rejected and been rejected . . . and she had been aware of that fluttering sensation in her stomach that was understood to be love. But the butterflies of her love for Harry had dropped to some lower place—a place where there was less room for them, where they banged around for egress, but found none without the help of Harry's hand . . . or tongue.

That morning, she had gingerly explored herself through her shift before Amelia came in to dress her, spoiling everything. She understood then the single-mindedness of a hound on a scent; she could think of little else but the chase of that Vesuvian sensation which had cracked her apart in the orchard.

Having incidentally leaned against the corner of her dressing table while being coiffed, she discovered it satisfied the urge for pressure in certain places. Thus, a new fondness for leaning against things was born and her mother nearly caught her moaning against a newel post only minutes later.

"We are here!" announced Lady Merton. With a frantic wave, she dismissed the footman that had been carrying their parasol aloft.

Allison's eyes flitted across the shop fronts, eager to land on some exciting sight, but there was nothing exciting to be seen. Instead, the two of them stood before one of the most mediocre tearooms in London. Allison forced the corners of her lips up despite her disappointment.

"Oh. How wonderful. I've not been here before." But she had.

"Allison, do not play the pleaser with me. I know you like a great many things, but it is plain on your face this tearoom is not one of them."

Allison searched for a response as her cheeks pricked from being caught out. Perhaps her proficiency in deception was not yet fully matured.

The marchioness indulged in a slow, catlike blink. When her lashes lifted, the mischief was back. "Fear not, Lady Allison. For I am taking us someplace far more exciting."

The dismissed footman returned, delivering a silk sash into his mistress' palm, before vanishing again. The marchioness led Allison around the corner of the tearoom, away from the crowds.

She clutched the silk sash to her heart and faced Allison. "Do you trust me?"

"Of course," whispered Allison, but almost immediately wished to retract her answer. She *did* trust the marchioness but knew she should not appear so guileless.

Lady Merton swirled an elegant finger in the air and Allison heeded the silent command to turn around. The rose-colored sash was held before her eyes. Its color went dark as it was pulled against her face, blotting out the daylight. Lady Merton's nimble fingers carefully tied the blindfold, mindful of Allison's upswept coiffure.

"There."

That one little word had so much approval in it that Allison's chest pressed against her stays in a prideful swell.

Allison, unseeing, felt herself an extension of the fine lady as their skirts fell once more into a pleasant tempo, side by side. It was not a long walk, but there were several giggles along the way as Lady Merton described this obstacle, or that, all which must be navigated by Allison's careful steps.

At last, they took a few steps downward and stopped. Allison breathed heavily in stillness as she heard a unique knock, a *rat-ta-ta-ta-tat*, against a heavy door. It was followed by a *clunk* and a *creak* as the door was opened.

Excitement thrummed through her, reminding her how it had felt when she'd been whisked to the rooftop by Harry—only now there was no danger and she might enjoy the strange rush completely. Yet, even as the thought crossed her mind, it darkened.

The space they were in smelled strangely small, after all, one could not pack so many scents into a place were it very grand.

Any sense of playfulness began to bleed out from the marchioness' little game of surprise. Needles of panic pricked Allison's arms, tempting her to go wild, to thrash around and find herself. The cool touch of Lady Merton's bracelet against her cheek curtailed the panic just in time. The blindfold was loosened.

Allison was not incorrect about the oppressive sense of space. They were at one end of a corridor, low-ceilinged and narrow. A young woman in a simple black round gown shut the door behind them. The loss of daylight briefly conjured remnants of panic before the flickering of sconces at the corridor's end caught Allison's eye. She moved toward the dim light—the only way to go. Her steps fell dead silent on the dark carpets that ran the hall. The faint swishing of taffeta was the only sign that Lady Merton followed at her heels.

Crimson thrills were in battle with a doomed sense of total darkness, but Allison kept her eyes directed bravely at the corridor's end. She would show no lapse in courage to the marchioness. *All will be well.*

It was clear now that the hall terminated in black drapery. Beyond it? A growing murmur. It fell to Allison to draw back the curtain. Her fingers reached out and closed around the flock of a soft and sensuous velvet. *Be brave.*

She pulled it aside.

A dim room. A few dozen eyes flicked in her direction, lit only by a smattering of candelabras, they glowed like foxes' eyes in the night.

Lady Merton stepped to her side. "Well, what do you think?"

Allison could not answer that. *What does one think when they understand nothing?*

Her eyes grazed the scene, adjusting to the darkness, seeking clues. All the fox-like eyes had lost interest and now looked elsewhere to—

Oh. To a little stage.

"It is a theater?"

"It is," confirmed Lady Merton. "Shall we take our seats?" The marchioness took Allison's hand and guided her to a divan flanked by two small tables. Ladies in black were pouring wine for them before their petticoats even brushed the cushions.

The marchioness angled herself toward Allison. "Let me explain."

"Please do, Lady Merton."

She cocked her head and pushed out her lip dramatically. "Have we not yet reached a degree of acquaintance warranting our given names?"

"You are a marchioness and I, an earl's unwed daughter. For us, I am uncertain any such degree exists."

"Damn your good breeding." The lady lifted her freshly poured wine. "And suppose I decide it can simply be another way, would you call me Beatrice?"

Allison folded her hands in her lap. "I shall call you whatever you prefer in private, *Beatrice*." Allison tried on for herself the mischievous look in the lady's eyes but did not know whether or not she achieved it. Indeed her good breeding had nearly made her choke on the name *Beatrice*. "What are we to see today?"

"Oh, a love story . . ." Beatrice looked away and shrugged, before murmuring, ". . . of sorts."

Allison's eyes were still adjusting to the dark. It was no proper theater, but a windowless space drenched in plush drapery. The patrons' overlapping whispers filled the echoless space with a general murmur. The women who tended to refreshments were all in black and as covered up as nuns.

"I've noticed a unique glow in you today, Allison."

Allison quit her observations. "I confess, it is the anticipation of our day together."

Beatrice flicked open her fan and availed herself of its breeze even though the room was cool. She lounged against the divan's scrolled arm, examining Allison. It was the least formal posture Allison had ever seen a lady take in public.

"Hmm. No. It is more than that," said Beatrice. "It is a certain ease about you, a certain light that is new. What has caused it?"

A drop of warmth slid down Allison's spine, gathering in heat and intensity. She blinked slowly as she remembered Harry's blondish mop between her thighs the night before. The thought had not strayed far since.

"Tell me, is it Lord Faulkner who causes this light?"

Allison's thoughts snapped. "Who? Oh no, not he." She nearly knocked her glass from the little side table as she flailed a hand in weak dismissal. Then she remembered that Faulkner was Beatrice's godson, a family friend. "Which is only to say, that, while he is very pleasant—"

"You owe me no explanations, my dear. Your heart is your heart. I only thought the two of you looked rather fine together, but that is not what makes a match, is it?"

Allison shook her head, relieved.

But Beatrice's fanning came to an abrupt stop and she narrowed her eyes. "I did not miss, however, that you said 'not he' implying that another holds your attention?"

She is too good at this, thought Allison.

Here was a conversation, playful and casual—the sort she wished she might share with her own mother. But such a conversation would never be possible with the great Lady Weldon.

"Perhaps." Allison shrugged coyly while taking a sip of wine, at last remembering to be mysterious.

Lady Merton smacked her fan against her lap. "Oh, Allison, do not leave me with so little."

"Well . . . he is handsome and brave. An utter poet in his love letters. What more must be known?"

This particular social season was bringing with it many lessons in self-control. Allison had ready on her tongue a hymnal's worth of Harry's praises to sing but held them back. He was a secret, one kept not just from her family but from the world.

"Well, that is something at least," said Lady Merton. "Will he be at the duke's ball on Saturday? I would love an introduction to the man deemed deserving of a jewel like you."

Allison smoothed her skirts, stalling as she thought on what to say. "Oh no, he is not—I mean—I do not believe the duke has extended him an invitation. He is new to these circles and not very long in London." In all her stammering, the more important thing struck her late. "Come to think of it, I do not know of this ball either."

Lady Merton laughed and placed a lithe hand over Allison's wrist, calming her before she made a nervous reach for her glass. "Montagu and his son are as much family to me as my own blood, I will see to your invitation and your man's as well."

Allison looked down at Lady Merton's hand, weighed down by a pearl and diamond cuff. Lady Merton's "own blood." Just who *was* Lady Merton's blood? She'd never uttered a word about her family.

"Thank you," said Allison. "For both of our invitations. It is wonderful having the support of one such as you."

"Is there any reason you should not have it? Is the man in question not of good birth?"

Ah, there it was. Allison knew nothing of Harry's family either—at least not before overhearing the word "bastard" in the mews. But Lady Merton had specifically asked about "good birth." Allison pictured Harry's deep, maritime eyes, the way his youthful body was still catching up to his broadened shoulders . . .

"He is of *perfect* birth," said Allison. "Flawless in every way. Yet . . . my family will not approve."

"That is unfortunate and serves to make me all the more curious. When I met you, Allison, I will admit I figured you naive. Now it is clear you hold secrets."

Allison's attempt to reply was cut off by the glittering *tinks* of a high-pitched bell.

She expected Beatrice to spring to ladylike attention, straight-backed and poised for the performance. Instead, the woman settled deeper into her reclining sprawl. Allison became aware of her own unflinching erectness and tested a slump against the squabs. The tufts of upholstery cradled her neck like an angel's hand and she melted.

She had prepared herself for a love story and it was, as Beatrice had said, a love story . . . of sorts. The same way that some of Thomas Rowlandson's illustrations were illustrations . . . of sorts. It was a good thing she had slumped in her seat, because surely all blood had drained from her head. Her slouched body stiffened with the rigor of shock, even as the lady beside her grew more animated.

A dairy maiden of Ancient Greece had taken to the stage and was, only minutes later, joined by a sheepherder in simulation of the very act Allison had enjoyed with Harry the night prior. Their sensual costumes were mere sheets of silk, rigged with braids and belts that seemed designed with their very inadequacy in mind. A nipple, red as wine, slipped from the peach pleats of the maiden's robe. Allison's eyes locked with it and it stared right back. Could a nipple be so crimson? So flush? Surely it had been rouged. She would never know, for the shepherd rose up to cover it with his hungry mouth.

The realization struck her cold. *None* of what she saw was simulated. She pressed her folded hands firmly into the dip of her lap. Where was there a newel post to lean on now?

The tale itself, if one might call it that, was bizarre and lewd and very often humorous, yet somehow stirringly sweet. After various separations caused by intervening demigods and a confusing conflict that rather resembled an orgy, the two lovers were together. Maiden and shepherd. With none to answer to. Grinding their half-robed hips in a bed of silk flowers on the stage . . .

Allison's mind drifted back to Harry. What would it be like to do that with him? Without any chasm between them?

The shepherd's howling rapture abruptly shredded the dream. *Harry would* not *sound like that,* Allison decided.

The curtain closed and she forgot to applaud—forgot where she even was, for that matter.

"Darling? Did I misstep in taking you here? I am very sorry you did not have fun."

Allison tested speaking through lips that had been ajar for the whole act. "Oh, but I did, Beatrice. I did." She smiled. "It was . . ."

"Enlightening?"

"Yes. Let us go with that."

Hayden held the front door as Allison passed him her Brunswick cape.

"A pleasant day, Lady Allison?" He always spoke softly to conceal informalities from the rest of the household.

"Very pleasant, yes."

"Where did you go?"

Allison passed her gloves to him and cocked her head, thinking. "You know Hayden, I am not quite certain."

"Then indeed it must have been a brilliant time."

"Did my letter make the . . . post?" Allison's voice trailed off enough that it warned Hayden not to respond.

There was a figure at the foot of the stairs.

"Mother."

"Allison." Lady Weldon did not look at her daughter but fixed cool eyes on Hayden. Her glare flicked up and down him before she finally turned to her daughter, holding out a hand. "Come tell me about your day with the marchioness."

"Perhaps at breakfast. I am dreadfully tired." Allison was already wedging past her mother. For once, she was not pursued.

She was out of her gown before the sun dipped behind the rooftops to the west. She donned her softest chemise, one of fine lawn that was like breath against the skin, and slid into bed.

For hours she stared at her canopy's brocade underside, a royal court's worth of thoughts competing for her queenly attentions. *Her mother. Lady Merton. Faulkner—friend or foe?* And of course, *Harry.* She possessed a novel's worth of thoughts on the latter.

Her correspondence with him had once flowed with the poetry of easy love, but in one another's presence, the air became harder to breathe and her mother's voice whispered disheartening opinions from faraway rooms. Lady Weldon would never accept him.

Allison counted her troubles. Her eagerness to solve Harry's problems? A flaw. Her frivolity? A flaw. Her family's rank? A flaw. Her inexperience—

Stop. She had not crawled into bed for this. There had been a purpose—a purpose inspired by Harry's humid breath upon her mound and reinforced by glimpses of anatomy at the theater. But she knew not where to start.

She squeezed her eyes shut. *Find that thread.*

She placed a hand on her stomach, letting its warmth permeate her chemise. She slid it downward, exploring the space between her hip bones. Paused. Moved lower. Into that dip between her thighs, where there was naught but a springy thicket of hair between her and—

Find that thread.

Her hand had not yet arrived where Harry's had been, but already, there was a complex pleasure spreading through her. Thoughts were a powerful thing, it seemed. She noticed her breath, just as she had in the orchard. Her fingers swirled over the fabric, across flesh that felt full of blood and vividly attuned to every gentle pressure.

How? How had she never done this before? The sensation was intoxicating, yet achieved the very opposite of any wine she had ever imbibed. Instead of dullness, there was alertness. Instead of numbness, there was crushing feeling. Instead of heaviness, there was lightness.

A concert of information passed between her fingers and her folds. *Touch here, not there. Press less, not more.* The fabric she caressed became warm, dewy—vanishing from notice.

Then she saw it up ahead, that thing she chased, that she'd only just discovered. Was this a vice? She didn't care. She followed it, pushing breath into corners of her body that she couldn't even feel before. *There . . .*

That loose thread from before.

She caught up to it, then backed away.

She had control. She could have this when she wanted to. And she *would* have it.

Her cheeks were warm and she knew they must be rosy. She felt beautiful, absolutely beautiful as she lay there with a smile so slack and contented it nearly dripped from her face.

But she had teased herself for long enough and with the flick of her wrist, she soared past the edge of bliss.

It was minutes before her sex ceased to clutch at something that was not inside it. Her limbs were happy, heavy. Her eyes refocused on the canopy in the dark.

How does anyone not do it all the time?

*   *   *

Harry stared at the trellis leading up to Allison's bedchamber. It bloomed thick with yellow climbing roses, thankfully thornless. He'd made Allison swear not to scale any trellises on his behalf, and now here he was, at the foot of her trellis in the gray light of morning.

He put a bare foot on it and it creaked terribly. It was soft and rotten, but woody vines wended through it in a dense tangle, rendering it sturdy enough—he hoped—for a climb.

He'd nearly cleared the height of the townhouse's lofty ground floor when it occurred to him what a miscalculation it all might be. What if he startled her? He'd warned her of so many dangers—barging in like this, would she not think him to be one of them?

He looked down, a direction that looked suddenly less alluring than the final step up. He put his hands on the stone lip beneath her bedchamber's window. His fingers tensed on the sill as a soft piece of trellis gave way beneath his foot. *No going back now.*

Perhaps he could gently rap on the glass until it woke her. Perhaps he could lift the latch silently and whisper her name through the crack.

He heaved himself upward, expecting to find a shallow perch on the sill. Instead, a cross breeze flicked through his hair. The window was open. Allison stood just inside, arms crossed, in only her shift, wearing a haughty glower that made him want to fall back to the garden.

"May I be of service?" she whispered.

"No." It came out as more of a grunt as he pulled himself inelegantly through the window into a heap on the parquet. He hurried to stand.

She'd not moved an inch from where her bare feet were planted. Her golden hair cascaded down one shoulder, tied loosely with a yellow ribbon.

"I was afraid I would startle you," he said.

"Harry, you made as little noise as a wolfhound chasing a rat on an old plank floor. Had you been discovered, my mother would have turned into a hydra and devoured each of your limbs with a different set of teeth. It was too intrepid of you."

Foolish, she meant. Heat spread across his skin. *A mistake. What a stupid mistake.*

Allison approached him and swatted something from his shirt-sleeve. "And now you are covered in petals from the Lady Banks'. What shall I do with you?"

He shrugged and a grin escaped him. "I know what we did the last time I was covered in rose petals."

Allison smiled and raised an eyebrow, but she took a step away from him too. "Is that what you came here for?"

What *had* he come for? He searched his head and came up empty but searched his heart and was slammed with the answer. "I came for selfish reasons and I should not have. I'm sorry." He turned back to the window, but Allison stepped forward and caught his arm.

"Selfish reasons?"

He shrugged. "Comfort, I suppose." He raised his eyes to hers and saw that they glistened more than they ought to in the moon-light.

She put herself in front of him and folded him in her arms. Her hand reached up to cradle his face as he rested a cheek against her hair. Her scent gave him hope. She never smelled of expensive orris or Bulgarian roses, just lemons, fragrant and common.

"I know your night at the Gossingtons' ended poorly and I realize it is all my fault," she whispered, still holding his head to hers.

"It's not your fault, Allison." He pulled away to smile at her.

"I was not a very good footman because I was not there to *be* a footman. I was there to find answers and I did."

Allison looked to the bed—the only place to sit apart from her stool at the dressing table. She led him there to perch on its edge.

"Tell me," she said. "What did you learn?"

"I found Giddy."

"Oh?!"

"Shhhh."

Allison covered her mouth with one hand, before whispering through her fingers. "And what of him?"

"He was being paid for a favor. By Lord Faulkner."

Allison stirred at Harry's side. He reached down to take her hand, but she did not squeeze his in return.

"What sort of favor?"

"I don't know."

"Then you have nothing. Why would a viscount have to pay for favors from a man already in his employ?"

"Allison. There is *more* than that, there was something else."

"When you were at our table? I knew something was wrong. I saw you go pale."

Of course she'd noticed. He'd spent that whole night in disguise, feeling himself quite clever, only to be seen straight through by Allison in every way.

"I saw something damning, something which ties him to me."

Her eyes grew rounder. They were so green in the daytime yet nearly black in the dark. "Tell me," she said.

"I cannot."

She shoved his shoulder roughly enough to unseat him from the lip of the bed.

"Of course you cannot," she hissed. "We are not in this together at all, are we?"

"I told you we were not from the very start." Harry's last word trailed down to a whisper as he realized he'd raised his voice. He shook his head, recalling Rhys' words of how he had an ally in Allison. "At least, I still don't—"

"*Well.*" Allison sprang to her feet. "I shall have secrets too. I shall say that I have made a friend in Lord Faulkner but will not share with you what I know of him. *Including* his secrets. *Including* what brought him to the orchard that night."

Harry's chest clenched in despair. All she had said was the word *friend*. Yet again he found himself dreading her proximity to Faulkner. This time was different though. This time, it was not solely because he found Faulkner a dangerous man.

He went to where she stood, fists balled at her sides. He stared down into her eyes—young and righteous. He wanted to rend apart any attachment she had to Faulkner. Wanted to make all of his doubts in the man her own. Wanted to commit Faulkner to the same fires that he'd flung his Primrose's letters into, but . . .

"You are justified in keeping your secrets. They are not mine." Harry could not quit his fears, but at least he could keep them from becoming hers.

She lifted her chin and nodded, looking more confident and defiant than ever he'd seen her. With naught but a thin layer of cotton between herself and the world, she was ready to take it by storm. Rhys was right. A valuable ally. He hoped he'd not yet pushed her too far.

13

There were so many things to discover, Allison found, about the
way this all worked.

Harry had just told her she had a right to her thoughts and secrets—not a sentiment she'd been much familiar with in life. Perhaps
only her cousin, Beth, had ever affirmed her as much.

She'd not expected the early victory and knew not what to do
with the remaining fury. Her blood still ran hot with frustration for
this man, yet "man" was suddenly the only part she seemed to notice.

He wore only his shirtsleeves, loose at the collar. The shirt
appeared soft from years of washing and she wished to pull herself
against it. If she'd thought that Harry in his livery was the very acme
of her attraction to him—how wrong she'd been. This shirt, roguishly undone and barely tucked into his breeches, suited him far better.
It matched the way his hair always fell forward from his short queue.
It matched the way his lip ticked up on one side but not the other

when he smiled. It matched all the things she'd wished to do to him since seeing that wicked play.

Her hand was on his chest before she'd even decided to reach out. The shirt was just as soft as she'd imagined. She slipped her hand to that spot where it was open and felt the warmth of his chest for the first time. The sparse curls beneath her touch matched the darker hair at his roots and brow, and she toyed with the little hairs, brushing them against their natural direction. How could such a small discovery make her heart pound so?

Harry put a hand over hers, halting the exploration.

She looked up into his eyes. "Go back to the bed," she demanded.

Wordless, he went.

She crossed the bedchamber without ever breaking from his gaze. Taking a key from a little bowl on the shelf, she locked the door.

The *click* of the door's bolt awoke her to a moment that had, up to then, felt a game. But she was not acting on some lark. She had a little beast inside of her that reawakened at the slightest thought of Harry. Now that he was here, perched on her counterpane, that little beast was roaring for release.

She returned to stand in front of him, hands on her hips. She didn't mind that the gesture would come across as a stern remnant of her frustrations; it was better than having Harry know she did not know what to do with her hands.

She liked having him this way, sitting, while she stood. She rarely got to loom over anyone and enjoyed the sense of command. She leaned over his face, bringing her lips within inches of his while denying him the gratification of a touch. She closed her eyes and teased him, hovering near and far, luring him into the slow chase of her lips. She knew by his breath that he followed.

"Allison? Primrose?" he whispered.

"Yes, Harry?"

"Have you done anything like this before?"

Allison smiled, thinking of her activities before she'd heard Harry trundling up the trellis. "You know that I have not."

She gave him her lips.

She'd only ever kissed him in the dark and knew not whether her eyes should be opened or closed. What she *did* know was that they approached the moment differently. Her, rough. Him, gentle. Together? A *lovely* thing.

He reached out and cupped her hip, a touch that was iron hot through her chemise. It sparked flashes of need throughout her, but his arm did not pull her nearer. Rather, it was rigid, holding her away. That one little hint of distance threatened to swallow the moment whole.

She pulled away from the kiss. "Is everything all right?"

Everything was fine. Perfectly beautiful, actually. Yet the chill of a grim mistake nagged at Harry's bones.

Did Allison even know what she looked like? Standing there with a moonlit window behind her? Her body in halo, her thin shift glowing gossamer against the light?

"There's no need to hurry anything, Allison. There will come a day when we can do everything we wish."

She smiled, or tried to. It never quite reached her lips. "Harry . . . what if there *won't* come such a day?"

The question dropped like lead between them. Neither were fools.

Allison took a step forward, nesting herself between his legs where he sat. The warmth of her hips against the seam of his breeches made him want to weep. She cupped his jaw and made him look at her.

"What if there won't come such a day?" she repeated. "What if today is all we ever have?" She grazed her fingers up over his ears, leaving a trail of tingles where her nails combed through his hair. Her eyes were both fond and sad.

Harry swallowed an emerging protest. All along, he had allowed her to carry hope for the both of them. Why should he be surprised now that her hope was running out?

He realized then that he'd not shared her burden, so wrapped up as he was in his own. She had stepped into his life—his mess—boldly, willingly. She'd extended her optimism time and time again and so often he had turned it away. It had been finite. Of course it had.

Nothing had changed between his last letter to her and the moment he found her in his ruined room. He still wanted a life with her, still wanted to find a way past his nightmares and past Lady Weldon. And he wanted, in this moment, to beg her for a game of Buoyant Belle—naming the broken thing as himself—but no, that would be selfish. She had already done what she could to put him back together, and he had not shown his gratitude.

He had loved her and had been too much the fool to say it. And now, feeling the specter of rejection overhead, he remained silent once more.

She wished for them to take what they could have, when they could have it, just as they had done in the orchard. It was not what Harry wanted, not the way it should have been between them, but he felt her slipping away and his breaking heart suddenly clung to her, claws out, grasping at every moment.

His hand tightened on her hip. He swallowed hard on his

decision.

He drew her in until her hips pressed warmly against the seam of his breeches. "We will have to be careful."

She nodded, already pulling up her chemise in the ladylike pinch of a few fingers.

Harry held his breath. Did he even know how to be sufficiently careful when he was so untried?

Allison put a knee on the bed beside his hip and he dropped back, catching himself on his elbows. She aligned herself to straddle him and took a seat upon his lap. The position scrunched her flimsy shift up 'round her waist and left her quim resting, naked and hot, against his well-worn fall.

Awareness settled over her eyes as his cock hardened beneath her, pinned by her sex. She did not flee from the sensation but shifted her hips, exploring him—

Harry jolted, delivering his rider a gentle buck.

"Did I hurt you?"

"Only in the best ways," he assured her. Indeed her squirming had aroused only the finest sensations. *Too* fine. Fine enough to finish him off before he even had a chance to touch her.

He shimmied until the two of them were farther onto the bed and pulled a cushion beneath his head. All the better to enjoy his glorious view.

Her legs, still folded at his sides, were just as he'd remembered them from when they'd dangled through his window. Strong, with calligraphic curves—a seductive mismatch from her equally lovely, but daintier parts above the waist. He stretched a hand forward, straining for naked access to the thighs that had haunted him for days.

Her virginal explorations of him transformed quickly into the grinding motions of a seasoned profligate. Wet heat suffused the crotch of his breeches, and he longed to be rid of them, but what then? Lose his seed all over her thigh within seconds? He would not.

She had apparently found the proper spot, for she released a deep croon of bliss—one far too loud for their stolen tryst.

Harry's hand propelled upward, finding a place across her warm lips. The last gasp of a severed moan puffed against his palm. He smiled at her, shaking his head in mock admonishment.

Her eyes grew large—that expression . . .

A memory stabbed him—

The look of fear when he'd first covered her mouth in his room.

But before he could snatch back his hand and unfurl a scroll of whispered apologies, her expression changed. Her gaze hooked into his and she seated her mouth even more firmly into his grip. Her eyes rolled with drunken pleasure and she moaned again, right into his palm. The vibrations of that moan traveled straight down to his trapped cock.

So he left his hand across her mouth and let her ride his painfully clad member to her heart's content.

Harry knew not a soul in the world that shared Allison's eager, almost frantic energy, so it came as a surprise when her riding slowed. She slumped against his hand and he bit off a laugh. He was willing to be a mere pedestal to her heavy head if it meant he got to feel her come all over his lap. That objective was, he realized, precisely what she was working at. She had not slowed from exhaustion, but from focus.

He put his other hand behind her head and drew their foreheads together until he could nearly kiss the back of his own hand. He followed the vibrations of moans and huffs behind his hand, used them like a treasure map of how to best roll his hips beneath her.

He looked straight into her lustful eyes.

"Come for me, Primrose," he demanded.

Another little moan trailed off behind his hand.

He moved his head aside to kiss her neck. To tug at her ear with his teeth. With each act, he knew he got nearer, warmer. He merely breathed against that spot behind her ear and she bore down so hard against him that he wondered whether he might unravel first.

"Come for me, Prim—"

She bucked atop him, commencing the same wild throes of pleasure that had toppled her in the orchard. He winced in both pain and pleasure at the chaos unfolding on his lap. Though he pressed his hand hard against her mouth, shrill squeaks of pleasure leaked out between his fingers.

"*Shhh-shh-shh*—" His shushes were cut off by the spasms of his own silent laughter as he tried to keep Allison's waves of ardor from flooding the household in a way that might go noticed by the staff.

He wrapped himself around her and rolled till he had the upper hand, straddling her as she'd just straddled him.

Her eyes twinkled with laughter, and her moans devolved into snorts of stifled mirth. As the hiccups of glee died down behind his palm, he tested the removal of it.

"Are we recovered?"

She shrugged noncommittally, but there were no more leaks of glee. Her hair, however, had escaped its plait and wavy branches of it sprawled across her pillow.

"You are spoiling me, Mr. Plymouth," she whispered.

Harry was caught off guard by the sting of his false name, by all she did not yet know of him. "I did absolutely naught," he demurred. "I merely lay there."

"And you were quite good at it."

He smiled and prayed she felt the same way about the orchard, where he'd had not one licked notion of what he was doing. He only knew he'd dreamt of tasting her and that reality was even better.

Reality struck again; he could not believe she lay beneath him, her chemise ruffled up to her ribs. Lucky fool, he.

He reached down to take a handful of that hearty spot where her thigh met her rear. A grimace briefly troubled her lips but evaporated, and he could feel her flesh soften into his kneading, appreciative grasp.

There was no more uncertainty to be seen as a serene smile spread across her face. "I cannot imagine why," she said, "but I suddenly find myself in a better state to share good news."

Good news? Did she still hold hope for them?

"It is in regard to your next appearance among the ton."

Ah. "Have I been upgraded to first footman?"

She flopped her arms to the counterpane. "Harry, we both know that *footman* does not suit you. No, this time the identity and *nom de guerre* are yours to choose . . . with the exception of a duke, of course. There are so few of them. One would know your deception in an instant."

Harry didn't know how many dukes there were. Not in England. Not in the world. "Then what is your recommendation?"

"An obscure baronetcy?"

"What about one of my own invention?"

"Even better."

"Sir Harrison Stinton," he muttered.

"Pardon?"

"Stinton."

Allison looked at the canopy, rolling the name around in her head. She looked back to him. "Stinton. I think it a lovely name."

Was it? It was his own. His mother's name. As real a name he had. And Allison thought it lovely, but would she suffer it as her own one day? Harry shook off his musings. "Where will this name get me?"

"The Duke of Montagu is hosting a ball at his Mayfair manse on Saturday."

"And Lord Faulkner will be there?"

Her precious smile fell and she nodded. "It stands to reason his son will make an appearance."

Ideas flooded him. Now *here* was something useful. This time he had a true invitation. A backstory. An excuse to go upstairs. A plan for how—

"Are you pleased?"

His calculations dispersed. "Oh, Allison," he took her hands. "Very. That ball is precisely where I should like to be. It helps very much. Thank you."

Her smile lifted only a little.

He knew how to lift it more. "Perhaps you could recommend how I might best go unrecognized after others saw me at the Gossingtons'?"

Her eyes relit as though Harry had tossed matches into them." Well, you wore a wig before, so no one knows your hair color. One might presume you a brunette due to your dark brows, so forgo the horsehair and powder." She cocked her head, assessing his face. "How do you feel about spectacles?"

Harry was sure he made the same look as whenever he found a pea in his bite of food—a disgusted one.

"Really? That awful? I thought they might look rather fetching on you."

Harry leaned down and kissed her nose. "And where does

'looking fetching' get me?"

She lifted herself just enough to free the hem of his shirt from the last spot it remained properly tucked.

"You wish to do more?" he asked, surprised.

She flopped back down and smiled. "I do. I wish to have it all."

He sucked in a breath. He could not deny her, regardless of what the future held.

He undid one button on his fall. Too slow for her, apparently, for she darted up to seize a button for herself. He caught her wrist and pinned it to the bed. She writhed beneath him, grinning and arching her hips upward beneath his taunting straddle. He approached the next button with the same deliberate languor.

"If you do not get on with it, the sun will fill this room before your seed does."

"Now there's a picture. I know you are new to this, Allison, but I do not think I could fill a bedchamber. A larder? Perhaps."

Allison gave him a good punch in the shoulder with her free arm. Then all her fire retreated and she looked surprisingly coy for one who had just come to blows.

"Harry?"

"Yes?"

"You are new to this too, are you not?"

His body cooled. It was the question he'd dreaded, yet, now in the open, it caused no harm. "I am," he whispered. "And . . ."

She reached up and stroked his cheek, the nudge of courage he needed.

". . . and I am beholden to every god of every book that this moment might be with you."

Gratitude. Optimism. He had spoken her language and a moonlit smile split across her face. Her eyes glittered with the sort of tears she forged most easily—the happy ones.

He swept down and seized her in a kiss that contained all the other promises he was yet too gutless to proclaim—those that remained dammed up behind his looming hunter, his low birth and his lost heart.

He peeled off his shirt and cast it aside, before returning to his buttons, this time with more urgency.

She wondered up at him as he worked, her lips slightly parted, just enough to imagine the tip of one of those Hyde Park strawberries pressed between them.

She surveyed all parts of him, up and down, stopping low as he finally bobbed free of his fall. Her eyes went black as her pupils lapped up the darkness to better see his waiting member.

No amount of anticipation, no amount of knowing could keep his shoulders from shivering when she finally reached out to touch him—her delicate fingers taking his pulsing cock in hand.

She did not move straight away, only held him—exploring him through the amount of pressure she applied to his encircled flesh. Harry reached for patience. The pause before their act felt like a wilderness.

He stretched long, aligning himself better over her, tearing himself briefly from the reach of her exquisite grasp.

But she could reach far enough to guide him then, to that refuge between her thighs, where his blunt, weeping tip tilted against her folds. He wrestled back the urge to plunge inside. She was warm and wet and hungry, but, even together, such qualities did little to ease the untested tightness he found himself pressed to.

She shifted down the bed toward him, moaning little invitations into the air, but he could only proceed slowly.

He leaned down to her ear. "I do not wish to hurt you."

The pitch of her moans shifted downward, toward needy disappointment.

He pushed against her, nudging and retreating, gaining little motes of progress every time.

At last, her sweet quim accepted the head of him, and this time she was not the only one from whom a sound escaped. He bit off a shuddering grunt. How he wished they were in some lea together, some dale where they might both scream until their echoes bounced from every side of every mount—

knock knock

Harry saw his confusion reflected in Allison's eyes.

knock knock knock

Then mutual terror—

The door!

Their positions on the bed dissolved in chaos—stray clothes and coverlets suddenly entwined 'round every limb.

"Lady Allison, are you well?!"

Allison was successfully clawing her way out from under him before he even had a foot on the floor. She started coughing violently. Her fit added another layer to Harry's panic until he gleaned it was her feint of choice.

"I *ach ach* am! One *ech* moment!"

She staggered into him and pointed to the armoire across the room, shoving him toward it while making her way to the door.

He hopped in and tried to shut the doors on himself, but it was near impossible from the inside. He meekly mimicked one of her coughs to get her attention, but it overlapped her own. He watched in horror as she put the key into the door. He was still exposed!

It was the relief of the century when she flung a final glance over her shoulder before turning the key.

She rushed over and clicked the doors shut, throwing him into total darkness.

A moment later, the bedchamber's door creaked open. There was a muffled conversation between Allison and a voice unknown. Her lady's maid?

"My lady, I heard painful sounds. . . am so sorry if I. . . I was only concerned for. . ."

"I only had a nightmare, Amelia. I merely choked in my panic."

"Can I bring you any water or herbs or—" The maid's question was cut short by another voice.

"What is this? Darling, are you ill?"

Harry retreated into the petticoats and frocks at his back. It was Allison's mother. The formidable Lady Weldon.

"Everything is well now, Mother. Truly. Going back to sleep is all I need." Allison punctuated the statement with an afterthought of a cough.

The door creaked again, but no click followed. It was being further opened, not shut.

"Mother, please."

Harry moved not a muscle as he heard the brisk scuffs of slippered feet across the floor.

Terrible consequences were but a mere breath away, yet all he could think of was the overpowering presence of Allison's citrus scent within the armoire and how his aching cock had been at her threshold only seconds before.

"Your window is open!" chimed Lady Weldon in alarm.

"*Ohhhh*," said Allison.

Harry rolled his eyes. Not the best actress, his Primrose.

"*That* must be the reason I had a fit. I must have caught a chill in my sleep. Now that it is sorted perhaps we can all return to bed, hmm?"

"I will see you at breakfast." Lady Weldon's voice was eerily unreadable.

"Yes, Mother."

Harry heard footsteps pass by him again, then finally a *creak* and a *click*. He breathed a breath, long held in. Seconds later, Allison eased the armoire open. From the size of her eyes, he knew her heart was pounding as forcefully as his. *Never in all his time as a Runner—*

"It seems our night has been cut short," she whispered.

He accepted a hand from her to steady him as he unfolded from the cramped space. She averted her eyes and he realized that his breeches were still peeled wide, his half-mast cock bobbing in the open. He hastened to rectify it, lest he be sent back down the splintery trellis in such a state.

"I did not re-lock the door. It would make her suspicious. You need to leave, Harry. I cannot see you until Saturday for the Montagu ball. I will relay any messages through Hayden."

Her terse words cracked open his regret over not using his time with her better. He should have shared his nascent hope with her, should have asked whether her own hopes were still intact. But they had, again, pushed their obstacles aside and chosen fleeting pleasure instead. He would not make the same mistake again. Would not leave her to wonder where his heart was, even if hers was no longer there.

But first, they had a job to finish. "On Saturday, then." He dipped his head, aiming to kiss her, but he thought better of it when her lips retained a flat sobriety.

She saw him to the window and he swung a bare leg over the sill. Struck by the gentle evening's breeze, he remembered—

"Would you be so kind as to fetch my shirt?"

Allison's mouth opened briefly in horror before she scurried to the bed and felt around for the stray article. Finding it, she tossed it right into his face.

It was time to disappear, but he took one last look at her in the moonlight. Her rumpled chemise dangled back down to her knees and still glowed in the sparse light as it had before. Knowing he'd not see her for days, he searched very hard for something right to say.

"On Saturday, you will meet Harry Stinton."

Allison wrapped her arms around herself. "He will surely be a rogue."

Stinton *was* a rogue. A mutineer. A killer. A vessel for the lies of Harry's past. When this was all over, when Allison was safe, he would have to tell her everything.

He pocketed the memory of how she looked in her moonlit chemise and disappeared from her window.

14

The run up to the Montagu ball was a long one, if five days might be called long. To Harry, it was five days without Allison. Five days of whittling his time shoveling shit in the mews. Five days of making preparations—and excuses—on Bow Street. He was, at last, on day four.

He'd not seen Allison since their night in her room, at least, not in any scenario in which he might be acknowledged. She'd passed through the garden about her business and there had, of course, been sightings of her shadow in the window, but not once had she fed him a glance. Allison—impulsive, impatient, heartsick Allison—had become the more prudent inspector between them.

Their separation, their discretion—it was torture in the aftermath of their night upstairs.

His mind oscillated between potent memories. First, of her atop him—shattering apart in pleasure. Then of her beneath him—

the sensation of his tip making warm, deliberate ingress . . .

But his mind would ruin it all with the cold recollection of his bare feet—full of trellis splinters— landing on the dewy grass. Of his bollocks, aching. Of how he'd failed to tell Allison that his fears had not vanquished his need to be with her.

So he pled that Hayden keep him busy. Thankfully the interim butler was understaffed and thrilled to delegate.

Now Harry knelt at a garden bed, trowel in hand and a borrowed, uncocked hat on his head, keeping the sun from his neck. Tending the garden had often been his lot as a boy, before he'd been dragged out to sea. It was how he earned time outside the garret in his father's house.

He rocked back onto his heels. He had already weeded the entire courtyard four times over. Had rooted out every snail making meals of the bluebells. Had plucked every dead head from every camellia shrub. Now he stared at the blurring greenery, seeking another flaw he might tackle. Something, anything, to make the shadow hurry its way 'round the sundial.

A feminine drawl suspended his search:

"I wonder whether I should not retire our previous gardener entirely. It is as beautiful as it has ever been."

Harry froze. The voice was the countess's own.

He shuffled around to face her, still kneeling.

Every sinew of instinct told him not to raise his head, not to show his face, yet to ignore her compliment might draw her memorably bombastic ire. He pulled the wide-brimmed hat from his head and tipped his chin up to her.

Her eyes were gray and gloomy, but the crow's feet at their corners deepened, revealing no dismay, no hostile recollection, only satisfaction.

"Your Ladyship, thank you, but I am—"

"Temporary." The voice came from the house's back entrance. Hayden stood as erect as the portico columns that flanked him. "Pardon, Your Ladyship. I understood the house to be understaffed. As acting butler, I took the initiative to hire extra hands for the Season. I hope I did not overstep."

Lady Weldon shook her head, emerging from some entrancement before she turned to Hayden. Harry puffed out a held breath as her gaze released him.

"No, you have done well."

Her eyes snapped back to Harry, who took the opportunity to bow his head.

"It is the best the garden has looked." With that, she pivoted on the toe of a very fine red slipper and returned indoors.

Harry replaced his hat and stabbed his trowel into the soil. "I should not be out here," he muttered.

Hayden knelt beside Harry, putting a hand on his shoulder. "Nor should you have ever been in Lady Allison's bedchamber, but that did not stop you the other night."

Harry's skin went cold under where the footman left his hand. Harry gazed at him from deep beneath his brim. "That is rather forward. I thought servants were supposed to be discreet."

Hayden laughed and looked past Harry to the door, to be sure of their privacy. "Where was discretion to be had when you nearly tore the old trellis from the bricks whilst climbing it?"

"What is it you want?"

Hayden laughed again, softer, and patted Harry's shoulder. "Worry not, my friend. This isn't blackmail. My pockets are well-lined for my station. Lady Allison sees to that." Hayden somehow spotted a sly weed and pulled its taproot straight out. "There is no threat here, only my wish that you mind her heart. Allison is a joy. She is my friend, and I would not see her hurt." Hayden's lopsided smile softened into something earnest.

"I appreciate that she has such friends. And I would not dare to hurt—"

Harry caught himself making a promise he was already uncertain he was keeping. He *had* hurt her. The bramble that lay between them and a happy union was dense and snarled—not only by their investigation, but by her mother, Lord Faulkner, Bow Street, his lack of fortune, his past . . .

Harry's eyes darted between his worries, until Hayden leaned in to catch his gaze.

"I *do* wish you well," said Hayden. "Only, please, care for her."

Harry cocked a brow at the man, wondering something. "Do you . . . have feelings for her?"

Hayden laughed, his scarred lip revealing perfect teeth. "Not as you think. I lost a baby sister when I was a boy and young Lady Allison filled that gap in my heart—the one that cried out for a little girl to irritate me with a ceaseless need for company."

Something dawned on Harry that somehow had not before. "It is a lonely life for her here?"

"I was her first friend in the world and her cousin Beth, the second."

It broke Harry's heart that he'd never thought it before. To him, she was so vivacious, so incandescent. He had thought her magnetism evident to all.

But now he could recall moments of uncertainty. Her words were often bold, yet laced with the quiver of courage. Other times she was as naturally plainspoken as they come, but such frankness was more a trait of his own class. Perhaps it was ill-welcome among her peers? Lord, he could not imagine Lady Weldon much tolerating it.

"Thank you, Mr. Hayden. For everything."

Hayden shrugged. "You may hide here as long as you need—so long as danger stays far from this house. I can help you with all of that, certainly. With Lady Allison's mother though?" He slapped Harry on the back. "Best of luck there."

Harry's eyes lingered on the building as it swallowed Hayden up. He saw it anew. Allison lived in luxury, certainly, but in no less isolation than he had known for much of his life.

Hayden had named Allison's first two friends, but it was Allison who had, the other night, named a third in Lord Faulkner.

Harry could not change what he'd learned of the man. He could not return to that scuffle in the brig and see it end differently. He could not dismiss the damning uniqueness of the watch fob in Faulkner's hand, could not excuse favors bought from a coachman called Giddy . . .

At the ball, Harry would have men outside the duke's residence. He had convinced Mr. Crofty to be there too, to receive any news from inside. With his coach fare to Devon being paid the day after, he could waste no time.

On Saturday, he would finally name his hunter in the open. He would wring the final answer from Lord Faulkner's apathetic lips: *What was your relationship to that officer in the brig?*

Harry would be vindicated in the magistrate's eyes and save himself from Devon at the eleventh hour. He would be free from all of it! And yet . . .

He grumbled a slew of curses beneath his breath and beheaded a nearby bluebell with the edge of his trowel.

Faulkner was Allison's friend and, on the night next, Harry

would be bound by history and duty to tear that friend away from her.

Allison teetered on a footstool in the drawing room as her mother and the dressmaker circled her like vultures. Madame Archambeau's perky *Circassienne* gown bobbed and rustled as she stabbed pins into the yards of purple damask that draped Allison like a Roman toga.

"The color is exquisite. Do you not think so, dear?" Her mother's eyes were more than hopeful; they were expectant. Allison shot off her usual look of displeasure. The next step of their mother-daughter dance would be the revelation that Allison never really had a choice.

Lady Weldon looked down and cleared her throat. When she looked back up, she wore an unsettling smile and turned to the dressmaker. "You know, while the violet *is* exquisite. I feel that something like a sunflower gold would better suit my daughter's complexion."

Allison had the sudden need to check her pulse or pinch herself.

Madame Archambeau gasped and tutted. "You do not worry it will make her look sallow?"

Lady Weldon shook her head and caught her daughter's eye. "Not at all. I believe it will be lovely."

"Mademoiselle?" The dressmaker's eyes pleaded with Allison to be biddable.

"I agree with my mother. The yellow will do. Perhaps with some fringe in pink?"

The roll of Madame Archambeau's eyes could be seen from her birthplace in Calais, no doubt. She left the room to retrieve another bolt of silk. The much sought-after dressmaker knew the mode, but Allison knew her heart, and suddenly, so did her mother.

She met her mother's eyes and they shared fleeting smiles. "Thank you," said Allison.

"I know you love your yellows." Lady Weldon bent to lift the silk piled at her daughter's feet and started to unravel her from the violet cocoon.

Even on the footstool, Allison barely scratched her mother's height, yet her mother seemed shrunken, studying the floor in a way wholly unlike her.

"Mother, is there anything—"

Lady Weldon's eyes snapped up.

Allison had been about to say *the matter*, but her mother again wore that strange smile. . . an almost. . . *courageous* one. Allison worried that anything, even a feather, might shatter it.

They were rescued from the moment when her father wandered in from the dining room. His eyes grew wide at the fashionable mess. "I did not realize I was disrupting important matters, please carry on with whatever this—" His face landed on Allison and he cocked his head. "Lord, what a dreadful color. Doesn't suit you at all."

Allison raised her hands, applauded, and looked around the room as though the audience were greater than her parents. "Thank you! I am pleased that we have all come to our senses about this hue."

She'd not noticed that her father had a pipe in hand until he punctuated a smug grin by popping it into the corner of his lip. He swirled his hand in a *carry-on* motion and began to leave the room when Lady Weldon caught his arm.

"Was there something you came to tell us?"

His loud *"Aha!"* nearly sent the pipe tumbling from his lip. "There was, in fact, yes." His hand fished in his waistcoat. "These invitations arrived earlier. The duke is having a ball."

Before he even had them out, Lady Weldon had rushed to receive them.

"There seems to be some confusion, though," he said.

Lady Weldon flipped back and forth between the two cards. "I should say so, Lord Weldon. We are not named."

Allison leapt down from the stool, only to nearly hang herself on the last swag of fabric still held by her mother. Recovering from an artless and frantic extraction, she remembered the self-discipline she had been working so hard at.

She folded her hands and took a breath. "Where is the confusion, Papa?"

"None where you are concerned." He passed her one of the little cards, with her name on it. "It is the other one though. 'Tis blank."

"Ah," said Allison. Feeling her mother's eyes on her, she reached for the second card as calmly as possible. "I know what this is. Lady Merton promised to procure these for me."

Lord Weldon puffed a strand of wispy hair from his forehead. His case of wigs had still not shown. "Mr. Hayden did say it was one of Lady Merton's men who delivered it, but why the blank one?"

"Perhaps it is for her chaperone?" Allison's mother stepped forward in a way that left no question as to her volunteering.

"Lady Merton will chaperone me," said Allison, striking out all hope in her mother's eyes, eyes which looked more hopeful and pitiable than ever they had. An apology bubbled up from Allison's heart, but she bit it back.

Lady Merton was no respectable overseer but would be regarded as suitable enough by those who fawned over her station. Those like her mother. More than likely, the great lady would corrupt Allison, and she was ever so ready to be corrupted.

"Of course," demurred Lady Weldon.

Allison raised an eyebrow. Since when had her mother ever demurred?

But Lady Weldon wasn't done yet. "Still, why the blank card?"

"I expressed the wish to bring a friend," said Allison.

"But dear, you have no—"

"—no friends?" Is that what you were going to say?"

"I—*no*—only that you've none in town at present."

Allison marched up until she was under her mother's nose and stared up fiercely. "I have the dearest of friends, it just happens I am not permitted to be *seen* with any of them."

Madame Archambeau reentered amid their standoff, a bolt of gold silk held triumphantly aloft. *"J'ai trouvé le jaune parfait pour—"* The woman's eyes froze wide at the sight of them.

Allison put a palm to her cheek before the tears came and pushed past her parents to get upstairs as quickly as possible.

She slammed her bedroom door.

She had *plenty* of friends. *Hayden. Beth. Faulkner. Harry, most of all Harry.* And every one of them, a secret. It was exhausting. It was . . . it was lonely.

Faulkner she might at least speak to, but not without her mother playing matchmaker and forcing their company. Lady Merton was the only one she might openly call a friend and yet she was more a mentor, was she not? More a . . . a mother figure?

Allison's real mother had been strangely soft right before she'd ripped out Allison's heart in that all too predictable way, and now Allison suspected she knew why. Had her mother grown jealous of her attachment to Lady Merton? The very attachment she'd been so unseemly in encouraging?

Allison threw herself onto the counterpane, burying her face into one of the pillows for a much-needed scream.

She still smelled Harry on her linens. She'd had him right there on the bed. A miracle in captivity. Yet even that night had been shattered apart by a knock at the door, by her mother's intrusion.

She stroked the bed linens, remembering Harry's warmth there. Her throat hitched at the memory of seeing his body for the first time. The planes of his chest. The patch of hair. The dark trail down his abdomen to—to that part of his anatomy she had longed to be lanced by. She had no lessons in such intimacy, but her body had run like clockwork toward their joining, and they had come so very close.

knock knock

Truly? The timely rapping on the door seemed designed to mock her. It was, however, far too gentle to be her mother's knocking, so she answered.

Amelia was on the other side, holding out a letter with both hands. Allison knew to poke her head out and cast a glance toward the stairs, where Hayden stood and winked at her. It would never do to have him knocking on her door, delivering smuggled correspondence directly. Allison took the letter from Amelia.

"Thank you."

Amelia smiled, curtsied, and scurried off to join Hayden.

Allison closed the door.

The crinkle of the envelope in her hands was a much-needed restorative. It was Beth's reply. Suddenly the fates seemed less mocking and more like they had heard the cries of her heart. Here was Beth's love for her. Here was her advice. Like a treasure.

15

The Duke of Montagu's manse was triple the width of the Weldons', yet there was a stifling atmosphere as nearly every member of the ton squeezed onto the duke's urban premises that evening. Allison, for her part, was wedged onto the seat of a bay window beside a pair of Season fledglings. They sang their songbird gossip at such speed it was a wonder they could breathe.

The girl nearest her was topped with a concoction of ostrich plumes that tickled Allison in the face with each dramatic whip of the girl's warbling head. Allison wriggled, trying to retake territory, but alas, her side hoops remained winged up to her elbows.

Allison's ear was clipped by the edge of a wayward fan as the girl beside her excitedly shared the story of how a baron's son bought her a cake.

I have stories too, thought Allison. *I have stories of carts crashing in the woods. Of bad men setting fire to my lover's home. Of hiding in*

his embrace on the rooftops. Of the handsomest man you saw in your life,
eating me like strawberries beneath explosions in the sky. I have some
stories.

Allison folded her hands in her lap to keep herself from retali-
ating against the errant fan. The chaste posture sent familiar feelings
rippling through her. Just the barest warmth and pressure of her
hands resting in her lap was now all it took to stoke fires in her belly.
She tightened her interlaced fingers; the impulse to let them wander
was a mighty thing.

If only she could conjure Harry—and his magical mouth—
with the mere snap of her fingers. She had expected her counterfeit
baronet to have arrived by now.

Her eyes raked the room for the hundredth time. She laughed
audibly over the thought that, only days ago, a fashionable ball had
been a thrill that worked on even her most reluctant senses. *No more.*
The air here was hot and loud. The people, hollow. All she wished
was to be in a serene meadow with Harry's head resting in her lap.
Preferably face down? She laughed again.

Perhaps she had never truly loved these functions, but merely
quaked in awe before their perceived authority. Perhaps it was why
her heart so often raced till she was ill. Perhaps it explained her
anxieties during introductions to those like the marchioness—those
mysterious luminaries of the ton. She had so long tied herself in
knots to be deemed "worthy" of these places, but for the first time
wondered, were they worthy of her?

The epiphany elicited only a passing chuff of recognition. She
flicked a spec from the rosy swag of her gown, marveling at the way
the weft shone blue at some angles. At least she did not dislike the
frocks. Of that she was certain.

"My jewel!"

Lady Merton had found her and was already outstretching her arms in delighted discovery.

Allison smiled. "Oracle!"

She stood to deliver a proper curtsy to Beatrice, ensuring that her bottom intruded into the orbit of the well-plumed storyteller.

"Such a change in you tonight, Allison! You must wear shot silk more often. I am not certain I have seen you in aught but gold."

Allison gave the marchioness a twirl, relieved at the praise. She loved her shimmering golds and sunny yellows but had realized of late that she more often wore them to spite her mother . . . who seemed suddenly not to care. Tonight she stepped outside her customs, with only a hint of yellow in the buttery silk primroses pinned to her breast.

Lady Merton scrunched her shoulders up in glee. "You are the brightest of stars, my girl. I love how you do it."

"Do what?"

Lady Merton took a long sip of wine, assessing Allison over the brim before answering. *"Shine."*

The compliment did not embarrass Allison's cheeks with color. Not this time.

She threaded her hand into the great lady's proffered arm. "Tell me, Oracle, any news of the future?"

"Well." Lady Merton patted Allison's hand as they serpentined through the crowd. "I foresee that Faulkner will *not* wed the best woman present."

"Your Ladyship, we have discussed this."

"So we have, and I can tell by your wielding of 'Ladyship' that you are not to be trifled with. However, I claim my right to flatter you, even if it be by way of passive jabs at your rejection of my son."

"You must love him very much, for you forget he is your

*god*son."

The marchioness inhaled sharply and her eyes flashed large, before settling into a pouty droop. "I suppose I do. I love him very much, but—!" She directed her pout into her wine glass. "—I propose the blunder has more to do with my being foxed."

Indeed, Allison had hardly known the woman without a bit of wine in her.

"I marvel at you," said Allison.

"Oh?"

"Tell me, how many present tonight know of your adventures to that little theater we patronized?"

Lady Merton blocked her lips with gloved fingers, preventing herself from losing any wine.

"Do not play shocked with me," said Allison. "'Tis *you* who brought me there."

"Yes! To enjoy my corruption of you, not to make you the corrupter."

Allison took a more serious tone. "Tell me."

Lady Merton shrugged and examined the crowd. "There are faces that were there that day. Faces which are always there."

"And surely the whispers get out to those who would never be seen in such a place. What then?"

Lady Merton stopped walking. "What is this about? And be honest. It is all I ask as your friend."

The word "friend" seduced the explanation from Allison like a stolen kiss. "Beatrice, I am not certain I much love the ton and the power it commands over my life. You seem to have unlocked its secrets, living as you do by your own rules, yet your name is never besmirched in the weekly satires. How?"

"Allison, my dear, you were merely born too late. Illustrations of my naked, rutting body have not made the journals for thirty years. I am old. My scandals are mummified. That is all."

Allison was dissatisfied and the all-knowing oracle read it plain on her face.

Lady Merton put a hand on her cheek. "My scandals are many. Some I delight in. Many I regret. I am true to myself purely because I cannot help it. I would not see you follow entirely in my steps. There is nothing to learn here."

Lady Merton withdrew her hand, becoming oddly fiddly for the woman Allison thought she knew. She averted her eyes as she summoned her next words. "Having not been blessed with children of my own by Lord Merton, I tend to gravitate toward the youth. I fawn. I meddle. That is how it is with Faulkner and yourself." She raised her eyes, shimmering with emotion. "Pray, do not tell your mother, but I think of you as a daughter."

Allison herself had felt the same, yet the sentiment felt suddenly too large, too overwhelming to acknowledge. "We have only known one another for days, Beatrice."

"Sometimes, 'days' is all it takes."

Lady Merton put an end to the conversation by turning to snatch a fresh glass of sherry from a passing tray. A figure beyond her shoulder drew Allison's eye.

It was Harry.

He searched the room keenly from behind brass-rimmed spectacles. His unruly queue was slicked back more tidily than usual, but rebellious hanks were still loosening over his ears. His dun waistcoat was paired with a darker coat over top—some marriage between burgundy and brown. Allison had never seen him in such an ominous shade; Hayden had chosen well for him. She had oft teased Harry with the name of "rogue," but tonight, even from behind his bookish lenses, he fair looked the part.

He had flawlessly adopted the posture of the ton. Back straight. One hand at his hip. He looked ready to tip his head at various introductions, but none would be forthcoming without someone to introduce him.

Allison took a step toward rescuing him, but Lady Merton turned back around at the same time, nearly dousing her in wine.

"Oh! I nearly ruined your gown just now!"

Allison heard her but hardly turned to look.

Lady Merton sucked a droplet of wine from her fingered glove and her alarm settled. Wisely, she craned her neck to follow Allison's line of sight. "Ahh, is he your man?" The question was packed with her usual playfulness.

But then Allison saw the corners of Beatrice's lips turn starkly downward. What was it? What was wrong? Did she recognize him from the Gossingtons'?

"I am no oracle, for I did not foresee the spectacles," she pouted. She turned her skeptical gaze on Allison. "I do hope his vision is well enough to know what a beauty you are."

Allison untensed. Perhaps it would be best to divert the foxed marchioness before going to Harry. She was about to recommend they progress to the ballroom, but—

Too late. Harry's eyes found her and an unschooled, boyish smile cracked through his baronet's veneer. He got it under control and approached them. Calm and confident. Radiating charm and wisdom and the intent to be introduced.

Allison swept toward him just as he closed the gap, on the chance he had not researched how such introductions were made among her set.

"Lady Merton, may I introduce Sir Har—"

"No, wait." The marchioness' raised hand brought them to a standstill. "Do not tell me. He is your mystery guest." Her eyes flicked up and down his body and what she saw reversed her pout. "Perhaps he should remain mysterious."

"All the better, for I have no name anyway." Harry's left eyebrow arched up over the rim of his glasses in a way that was positively knee-melting.

His swift repartee caused an astonished hand to fly to the marchioness' breast—all the better to draw Harry's attentions there, Allison supposed.

The marchioness offered her hand to Harry and he took it. To anyone else in the room, his bow would appear no different from those of the best-bred men in the country. But Allison was near enough to catch the eye contact he made with Lady Merton and recognize it as anything but courtly. She was near enough to note how his thumb purposefully stroked the back of Lady Merton's glove before releasing her. Near enough to be equally affected when Harry's eyes flicked briefly to hers with a sly smile.

A flush of pride warmed Allison's cheeks. The man was good at his profession.

"Lady Merton, I understand it is to you I owe my invitation. I have neglected these circles for too long."

The marchioness batted away his gratitude with her folded fan. "I am very close with the family, but His Grace, heaven help him, is not the best at keeping up with the rigorous social demands of a duke. I frequently impose my services on him to rectify this. Fresh blood at parties is always a boon."

Harry took a step back and his eyes flicked up and down the marchioness in a way that—judging by the laughter that trilled between her smiling teeth—utterly delighted her.

"Graceful, sharp, fashionable . . . Any nobleman worth his salt would be wise to have you as coordinator of his social calendar. Your charms must draw every interesting person in the country to your door."

Allison would have turned away and cringed at the escalation of flattery, if not for the fact that Beatrice still basked in his attentions, uncharacteristically coquettish.

"You had not told me your guest was a poet, Lady Allison."

She had, in fact, once told Beatrice exactly that.

As the marchioness cooed on about his finest qualities, Harry stole another sideways glance at Allison. The twinkle in his eye, enough to strike her dead and buried. There was something about watching him wear his ruse so deftly, about watching his talents at work, something that severed any chance at a chaste thought. She would do best keep her mouth shut till the itch ebbed, lest she cry *Touch me!* at a crowded ball.

With every dashed off glance at Allison, Harry conveyed that, regardless of what ideas the powerful marchioness was getting, it was Allison whose legs he'd be between at some later date. He knew precisely what he was doing and it consumed her.

Beatrice finally quit her lash-batting long enough to notice Allison's exclusion. "I suppose I have denied you your greetings for long enough."

Harry turned to Allison, clasping his hands behind his back as though he had to call on some restraint. "Lady Allison."

The depth of his tone left her bare. What was the origin of this silent, secret language they shared? And could she opt to speak it for the rest of her life? She was so absorbed in the easy reading of his eyes that she hardly noticed the approach of the duke behind him.

"Lady Merton, you seem to be enjoying yourself." Montagu's

words were light and jovial, but his expression unconvincing.

"Your Grace, might I introduce to you . . . oh dear, that's right, I requested not to know." Lady Merton shared a gentle laugh of abashment and turned pleading eyes to Allison, but it was Harry who stepped up and thrust a hand forward.

"Sir Harrison Stinton. You are a gracious host, Your Grace."

The duke's typically guarded brow betrayed a small twitch. He was not so drunken as at the garden party and offered his hand. Allison looked to Harry, curious to discern what he thought of Faulkner's father. Yet all his prior readability had vanished.

Montagu turned to Lady Merton. "And where is your marquess this evening?"

"He is around. Discussing the construction of his new *orangerie* or some such."

The rolling of Lady Merton's eyes did not go unnoticed by Allison. Lord Merton never seemed more than just a pleasant accessory to the older woman. What had the marquess ever done to deserve such dismissiveness?

"Then perhaps we might have a dance?" suggested the duke. "I have requested a minuet."

A minuet? It was the last thing Allison could picture the duke partaking in. He had the punching gait of a man on stilts.

Lady Merton played coy regarding the dance request and the conversation turned back to passive jabs at Lord Merton. Allison lost interest. She looked around over her shoulder. The duke's son had, as yet, not made himself known. "Pardon, Your Grace, but where is your son, Lord Faulkner, this evening?"

The duke shrugged, leveling a grumpy look at her. "I hardly know."

Allison caught Harry's eye and the fluency of their secret language returned. He needed to speak to her. *There is work to be done.*

But where does one steal a moment of secrecy in a brimming house? The question could not be thought on for long.

"I would love a minuet," relented Beatrice, at last, but it was not the duke whose arm she threaded through with her own. "However, it sounds like there is presently a reel being started. Perhaps Sir Harrison might show me to the floor?"

It was as forward as Allison had ever seen one be, but then if one were a marchioness one might do as they pleased.

The duke let out a huff of what seemed to be displeasure but was mismatched to the quick smile that overcame him. "Of course. I shall come along and beg for scraps." The duke and marchioness locked eyes, sharing a quick laugh as Beatrice angled Harry toward the ballroom.

The duke severed his laughter the moment Beatrice was out of earshot. Allison thought little of it as she glided to follow the pair, but the duke stopped her with a touch on her arm.

"Beatrice seems quite taken with Sir Harrison."

Allison was unsurprised that others used the marchioness's given name, yet there was a pang as the specialness of her own permission to do so crumbled.

"That seems a fair assessment," said Allison. "She takes easily to people; it must happen all the time."

"Do you find her to be a vulgar woman?"

Allison peeled her eyes, waiting for the rest of some jape, but the duke's dark eyes peered forth from his ruddy complexion. Perfectly still. Perfectly serious.

"No! Never." But Allison *did* find Beatrice vulgar. It was precisely the woman's allure. "I am quite fond of her."

"She feels the same of you."

Allison's embarrassment receded. "I have been fortunate to bask in her recent attention. It has been—"

"And this Sir Harrison, a friend of yours?"

The duke looked not at Allison, but beyond her, to the columned archway that led to his Palladian ballroom. His eyes squinted and flinched as though trying to spot a fox on the horizon, but Beatrice and Harry had already been swallowed by a sea of frothy gowns and coattails.

The man was so focused that Allison's delay in answering went unnoticed.

"An acquaintance, really. A friend to my cousin." Her eyes followed the duke's line of sight, and she imagined Harry somewhere amid the throng. "In many ways, I hardly know him." That part was, in so many regrettable ways, the truth.

The duke swiveled his gaze back to Allison with an intensity that was hard to bear. "How long has he been in London this season?"

"Not long at all . . . I think." The qualifier was a cautious afterthought in a conversation where she felt suddenly cornered. "I do hope, Your Grace, that I've not erred in asking the marchioness for his invitation."

The duke shook a mantle of tension from his shoulders and reset his gaze on her in a way that was less unsettling.

"The marchioness has my utmost trust when it comes to all things social. I am rotten at it." He proved as much when he nodded to an acquaintance across the room, only to miss their eye and be ignored.

Allison wished not to remain on the defensive. "You and your son enjoy a happy bond with the Mertons, do you not?" She delivered the duke her most brilliant smile, hoping that some of Harry's expert legerdemain had rubbed off on her. "Tell me, how did you all meet one another?"

She noted that the duke did not have a drink in hand and swiped one for him from a passing tray.

"I hate champagne," he muttered as the glass was halfway to his lips. He took not a sip but a swig. "Lady Merton and my late wife, Adeline, met when we toured the Continent. They became very close. Sisters almost. Our families did the Continent together each year after that—at least, until the duchess' untimely passing." The next swig left only a dram of champagne in his glass. He stared into it like an abyss. "Adeline did not survive Lord Faulkner's birth."

Allison suffered a stab of guilt at asking such a question merely to deflect attention from Harry and herself. She already knew the story. The whole of society knew the Duchess of Montagu died in childbirth in Florence.

Allison angled herself to catch the duke's lost gaze. "Well, I see how Lady Merton came to be so close with her godson. How fortunate Lord Faulkner is to have her, having never known his mother."

"*Hmph*. Yes. I suppose." The duke finished off the dram.

Allison decided to try again. "And is Lord Faulkner here? I do hope to see him."

The duke smiled a true and genuine smile. "You and every other young lady present."

Allison buried her irritation at the statement beneath a lifetime's pile of other such remarks but did not go so far as to smile.

"If you wish to be a future duchess, my son is no doubt sulking in the second study, upstairs."

Allison calmly reminded herself that killing a duke would be a hanging offense and set her mind instead to keeping him engaged. "When did you arrive in London?"

"Only the night last."

Her eyes flared and the duke caught his mistake.

"I mean the week last."

No. Not a mistake. A lie.

Before she could probe further, Montagu gave a curt nod.

"You will excuse me."

And before he'd accepted her pardon, he was gone.

The duke had been in town for a *month at the least.* Faulkner had said as much when he'd been trapped in their drawing room for the eternal tea hour.

Allison herself had run in the duke's circle for more than a week.

And people call me *a bad liar!*

No, he could not merely be bad at lying. She had caught him off his guard somehow. Unsettled him. And well he *should* be unsettled, because something wasn't right with him. Perhaps his son could illuminate what that something was.

The duke's manse had been cobbled together from multiple townhouses and the main stairs were less grand than they otherwise might have been. As Allison made her way past the landing, the flight narrowed. Bright chamomile walls shifted to a dark wheat and the din of the crowd below faded.

The upper hall was dotted by clumps of men whispering of trade and racehorses and—*orangeries?* Allison's head quirked toward Lord Merton just as he recognized her. He peeled himself away from his group of four.

"Lady Allison, I did not expect to see any of the women upstairs tonight."

It was the marquess' polite way of suggesting she was in the wrong place. He was more polite than most might be, but his remark left her acutely aware of the ambiance—of candlelit gazes that wandered away from their respective conversations to alight on her.

She smiled gently. "My lord, forgive my overhearing of your conversation, but your wife had just mentioned to me your construction of the *orangerie*—"

"And how she loathes it?"

Precisely, that. But Allison had imagined the marquess to be oblivious to the fact. Lord Merton softened her shock with a laugh.

She'd never seen him without his wife. His once blandly handsome features were suddenly brought to life by the dancing shadows. "It is all right. I know she has no love for it. My wife and I do not share many of the same passions."

His tone turned wistful, and Allison's heart ached for all of the times she had watched him fawn over Lady Merton with little attention paid him in return.

Something jolted him out of his memories. "But you, Allison. She has truly enjoyed your company. And she needs a friend. Just, pray, do not let her corrupt you too much." He looked around pointedly, to again remind her of the surrounding company.

It succeeded in pressuring Allison to come to her point. "I am looking for the second study, do you know where it is?"

He leaned forward to point the way. "Back across the top of the stairs. End of the hall."

"Thank you." Allison was half walking away as she curtsied.

"And Lady Allison?"

She stopped.

"Take care with closing any doors behind you. I would hate to be party to a ruined reputation." Lord Merton raised an empty glass to her in a lackluster toast.

She acknowledged the warning with a dip of her head and left him.

Her eyes remained down as she navigated the upper first floor. The low tones of male conversations lilted upward in intrigue as she passed. Billiards balls clicked from beyond one of the open doors. She pushed on until the corridor was quiet and dark, until she reached the last door on the right, the only one closed. A glow came from beneath.

She knocked.

"Go away."

If any words could verify she was in the right place, it was those. She let herself in despite the command.

"Faulkner. It is only me." She kept her voice soft as she gently clicked the door shut. Lord Merton's warning echoed in her mind as she turned into the room.

Two wingback chairs were framed by the fire, their backs to her. Faulkner leaned out from one of them to see her past the edge of it. "Lady Allison, if we are not more careful about being alone in the dark together, someone will force us to wed."

She invited herself to join him by the fire, taking the seat beside him. "There could be worse things than wedding a friend."

Faulkner slouched in his chair, muddling all of his body's sharp angles. His profile bloomed with the fire's amber glow. He stroked his chin and stared through the flames, as if to another world. One of his rare smiles, faint and fleeting, was detectable behind his fingers.

"But I know that neither of us wish that," hastened Allison. "So I will try to be brief."

"This sounds important." He freed his gaze from the fire's influence and turned it on her.

His eyes were so crystalline that the one nearest the fire reflected the hearth like a window to hell. She could not look away from it.

"It—it is important," she stammered. "I wonder, could you

remind me when your father arrived in London?"

"We arrived together. Mid-month last. The twelfth, if I recall."

"And your coachman, is he called Giddy? Did he bring you tonight?"

Faulkner drew up from his slouch. Every line of his face came into relief as he crinkled his perfect brow. "What is this about, Lady Allison?"

"I'm sorry." The apology, once so common to her, was eked out as a whisper. She rallied her voice and sat straight. "I swear to you I ask these things with good reason. We *are* friends, are we not?"

"Gideon is not my coachman," said Faulkner. "He is my father's man."

Allison's heart leapt; the Duke of Montagu *had* acted strangely, had been caught in a lie, yet . . .

She leaned eagerly over the arm of her chair. "Your father's man? But what of the night at Willis' Rooms and at the Gossington affair? He drove *you on* those nights, did he not?"

The chair's feet groaned against the herringbone plank as Faulkner thrust himself to standing. It startled Allison half out of her skin.

Faulkner put himself between her and the fire, looming over her like a dark tower.

"How do you know Gideon saw me to Willis' Rooms or the Gossington affair?"

Allison's mouth went too dry to swallow her sudden alarm. *A mistake. This was a mistake.*

She knew not what sort of courage was needed in the moment, only that weakness would not suffice. She dug her nails into the leather armrests.

"Gideon drove you to the Gossingtons' and you paid him for a favor not long after I ran into you in the orchard. *Why?*"

Faulkner scoffed. "And you claim to be a friend? When you are spying on me?" He pivoted one way on his heel, then the other, pacing in place before whipping back to her. The fire at his back brought no light to his eyes now. The cold pain in his voice seeped into Allison, numbing her with dread.

He leaned down, dominating her vision and blocking the fire's warmth. His breath caressed her ear. "Perhaps you came up to the library tonight because you *do* want to wed a duke's son. Tell me, is your mother just beyond those doors, waiting for the right time to burst in and catch us?"

"No!" Allison stood up, shoving at him. She teetered, eye-to-eye with the top button of his waistcoat. "She is not even here! And you would know that if you were downstairs instead of hiding in this den like a skulking badger!" She delivered another hopeless shove at his chest, finding it to be a wall.

Faulkner placed a hand to either side of her, one on each wing of the chair, encroaching until she had no choice but to fall back into her seat.

She stared up at his shadowed face, finding that abyss where his gaze was set on her. "I have no designs to wed anyone but the man I love, who is downstairs this very moment."

The abyss did not respond and she felt herself being swallowed by coldness, by the possibility she was wrong, by the possibility he was every bit as dangerous as Harry had vowed.

How stubborn she'd been. But her wrongness no longer mattered. The desired courage was not buried beneath her wounded pride but beneath the very real threat who had her cornered in a dark and distant room; somehow, she summoned it anyway:

"Why do you want Harry Plymouth dead?"

16

Harry's heels dug against the gleaming floor the way a stubborn mule's hooves might dig into mud. "I'm afraid my charms come quite unraveled outside the more sedate activities of standing and strolling, my lady."

"You do not dance?" Lady Merton cocked her head with such great offense that the baubles in her hair jangled.

"Regrettable, but true. My feet lack experience."

She looked to his feet to confirm, as though she could tell on sight. "But that is ridiculous, Sir Harrison."

He stomped his boots in place, making a show of their heaviness. "In fact, there are no feet in these boots at all. Only oak."

Lady Merton looked up, eyes twinkling. "Are you a pirate, sir?" She gave another forceful tug of his arm toward the ballroom. "If so, you will enjoy the ballroom's decor immensely. Only give it a chance."

Her voice plead, but her eyes commanded. There was no getting out of it.

Harry could pull off many affectations of the ton but dancing was not one of them—a fact that would shortly be evident. He un-dug his heels and allowed himself to be led through the ballroom's archway.

The space around them expanded into a bright white, vaulted chamber. Gilt sconces, backed by mirrors, lined the walls, but the light they flung was nothing compared to the glitter of the chandelier overhead. It dripped with crystal and long golden spikes, as though a storm of treasure had left it dripping with jewelcicles.

A stray thought flung him back to his days as a highwayman— to that deeply buried habit of assessing such objects for their worth. But his awe was not the same as it had been on the Gossingtons' lawns a week before. Something had worn off; the pangs of inferiority no longer pricked his chest. The magnificence around him was bright and loud and sparkling, but its value was empty compared to the quiet idea of his Primrose in his arms.

"'Tis a lovely room, is it not?" The marchioness' eyes were nearly level with his and were glassy with pride for the aristocracy.

"Very striking for London, I think."

"Do you find other cities more fashionable?" A hand to her throat gave away genuine affront.

"I do." Harry had never seen a ballroom in another country in all his life but assumed his character, Sir Harrison, would have. He noted, with some alarm, that he was again being dragged toward the floor. "I am not being modest, Lady Merton. The dance floor is *not* my natural habitat."

"I find that hard to believe in lieu of your preference for other great ballrooms of the world."

Damn.

"It is familiar patterns," she insisted. "Simply watch the others and you shall be fine." Lady Merton let go of him at the edge of the crowd and took a place across from him. A violin string shrieked out its first note from some unseen corner of the room, scraping Harry's nerves. A musician's toe tapped, counting them in and dancers began to bob as a rhythmic clap went up around the room.

Harry's heart thumped against his ribs with every beat and then, all of a sudden, everyone launched into a vigorous skip. He was soon passed this way and that, caught up in the butter churn of the reel. Every hand he grasped, even those of ladies half his size, forced him in some new direction.

His boots were not suited to such light-footedness and the men in slippers fairly pranced. Lady Merton came snaking down the line, returning to him. When their hands met, he heard her over the din. "You are doing well!"

And it was true. Some part of him was . . . not failing miserably. The less he thought on it, the more he improved. His eyes skimmed the crowd, searching for Allison, excited to catch her eye and delight her with his new skill.

But her flaxen pile of hair was nowhere to be seen. Had she not followed them to the room?

His head whipped toward the other end of the oblong space, checking there, but still no Primrose. He looked away. She had to be—

Wait.

His eyes flicked back to where they had just been, sticking on a piece of scenery—a vast oil painting. He'd dismissed it in his first assessment of the room, only noting it portrayed a ship. But now, from this angle, it looked to be a very specific ship.

He twisted himself from the arm of an energetic young woman and walked past her to leave the fray, getting jostled by several dancers in the process. But he continued on toward the painting, entranced.

A curdled feeling arose the nearer he came to the sprawling work of art.

Two masts. A brigantine with its sides and bowsprit painted green. A distinctive blue stripe across the top of the mainsail. The rotten feeling advanced, radiating across his chest with each new detail that came into view. The high waves gave her a snobbish tilt, an Atlantic throne from which to look down upon him. To mock him. And her name came into view:

Diligence.

A hand on his shoulder startled him to turn.

"Do you like it?" The words were light, but Lady Merton's expression, hard to read.

"It seems I am woefully undereducated when it comes to my host. Does the duke have ties to the sea?"

Lady Merton shrugged, arms crossed in front of her. "I am sure it is only decoration. Do not think too hard on it." Her eyes flicked from the painting to him. "Thank you for the dance, Sir Harrison." She gave him the curtest of curtsies and left him for better, more attentive partners.

Caesar, the enigmatic Duke of Montagu, had a painting of the *Diligence* at the heart of his London manse. It was the very vessel Harry and Rhys had sparked mutiny upon. Where Harry had his fatal encounter with the officer who'd possessed Faulkner's watch fob. It could be no coincidence. Lord Faulkner was not the only danger here.

Harry spun around, again seeking Allison and again finding her absent. When last he'd seen her, she'd been following him and

Lady Merton alongside the duke . . . who was equally absent. The fact fell like lead into Harry's stomach.

Harry abandoned the manners of his character, the baronet, covering the ground floor at an unbecoming pace as he scoured it for any sign of Allison. Ascending the stairs to the first floor, he barged in on several games of whist and cast wary eyes toward every masculine conversation.

The eastern corridor was bereft of such chats. He followed down it like a rabbit's hole, feeling how the light waned and how his dread grew. And at its very end, he heard it—

Allison's voice. Muffled and tearful. Speaking Faulkner's name.

It took everything in him to open the door like a man rather than a beast.

Entering silently, he could not have prepared himself—

There they stood, in silhouette before the fire, Faulkner's arms wrapped warmly around Allison's small and sobbing body.

"Get away from her."

Allison and Faulkner separated abruptly. Harry clicked the door shut behind him.

The scene of the two of them settled over him like a fog. *They had been embracing.*

He locked eyes with Faulkner, straining to focus on the more appropriate source of anger. *Dangerous, the man is dangerous.*

Harry drew the pistol he'd concealed in his coat, leveling it at Faulkner and cocking it full.

"Harry?"

It broke Harry's heart how soothingly Allison squeaked out his name—as though she were approaching a wounded dog, an unpredictable stray. He could not bear to throw a look her way, but her gaze was evident on him as it always was.

"This man is dangerous, Allison."

"He's not."

The words burned against him. Didn't she know how badly he needed her out of harm's way?

"That can be determined by the court, in the meantime just—"

"It *has* been determined. Will you not listen to—"

"Please." Harry's voice cracked as he finally dared to catch her eye. He had never made a greater plea in all his life. Had never wanted anything more than for her to be *away*. He blinked against the sting of salt forming in his eyes.

Allison's soft and perfect lips fell open, and the look she gave him left splinters in his soul. She did not speak another word as she backed up several paces, stopping against a wall of bookshelves.

The fist of fear that had been gripping Harry's heart finally eased off. He returned his attention to Faulkner.

"Lord Faulkner, would you have a seat?"

The duke's son did not resist the request, stoically taking the nearest chair.

Harry placed himself between the viscount and the fire. "Does the name Harry Stinton mean anything to you?"

The man looked to his left, to where Allison stood by the shadowy shelves.

"You will not look at her. You will look at me," ordered Harry.

Lord Faulkner did as he was bade.

"I do not know a Harry Stinton nor a Harry Plymouth."

Now it was Harry's eyes who shot to Allison at the betrayal of his alias, the one she thought to be the truer name. It looked, for a moment, like she would hold her secrets, but such was not Allison's way.

"Why should the alias of Sir Harrison Stinton mean anything

to him? Or to anyone else?"

"No. Not *Sir Harrison* Stinton, Allison. Just . . . Stinton. Harry Stinton."

Harry could feel the whole story welling up inside of him. He felt cruel the pressure of it, the overwhelming volume and realized, for the first time, the breadth of the things he'd not yet told her.

She approached him, disregarding her exile to the corner. "Your name is a lie, isn't it?"

He faced her as front-on as he could bear but was rendered mute.

"Tell me," she pressed. "Had we married, what name would I have *truly* been taking?"

Harry forgot about the pistol in his hand. Forgot about Faulkner. The fog closed in until the only person near enough to see was Allison. Until the only clear thing was her pain.

"*Stinton,*" he said. "You would have been a Stinton."

The beauty of her transparency, of his intimate knowledge of her—it all slipped away behind a visage gone perfectly unreadable, matured beyond recognition.

"I promise, I will tell you all of it, but first—" He turned back to Faulkner, glad to abandon her silence. "Where did you get your watch, my lord? The one with the celestial fob."

Faulkner eyed the barrel of Harry's pistol, before calmly reaching for his waist. He unclipped the fob in question, laying it in Harry's waiting hand. "A gift from my father. Said it had been in my mother's family for a very long time. Made by a master horologist in Bavaria."

"Your *late* mother?"

"I see you've noticed the absence of a duchess. Or perhaps you did your research at the Home Department?"

Harry didn't look to Allison this time. Betrayal turned to irritation. Just how much had she told the man?

Harry's thumb glided over the delicate chains that made up the fob's length—not so delicate that they could not leave a fatal impression against a man's neck. He tested its strength, tugging it taut between one fist and his pistol hand.

Faulkner's brow pinched. "Mind you," he said. "I *do* have a fondness for it."

Harry relinquished the heirloom. He was no longer here for Faulkner alone. "It is clear you've been made aware of my profession and perhaps even aware what you are suspected of." He paused, daring Allison to defend herself, continuing when she did not. "But I have just seen something downstairs which complicates my suspicions. Something which broadens them."

"And what did you see?"

"A ship. In the ballroom. What do you know of that ship?"

Lord Faulkner's eyes flickered, perplexed. "The *Diligence*? She is a fictional ship. Or so my father has always said."

"Strange, that," said Harry. "Because I have sailed her."

Harry felt Allison's skirts brush the backs of his knees as she crossed behind him. She went around and planted herself in the other wingback chair, crossing her hands and tilting her chin up with rapt attention. Ready for a story. Ready for answers.

No story came, because it was Faulkner who spoke up first. "I do not know what the ship means, but it is clear enough you believe it ties my father into this. Do you think him, a *duke*, to be your tormentor?"

Harry re-leveled the faltering wrist that held his weapon. "I am afraid I have not absolved you yet."

"And I am afraid I do not know my father over-well. He is a

distant man. So you will gain more ground asking me about some-thing I have knowledge on: *myself.*"

"Gladly. What favor did you ask of Gideon—or *Giddy*—at the Gossingtons'?"

"Gideon is my father's man. Not mine."

Allison cut in. "We covered this before you arrived, Harry. It is how I know Lord Faulkner is innocent."

"*Innocent?!*" Harry's irritation at last got the better of him and he spun toward her, forgetting his pistol hand. "You are *not* a part of—"

His right arm was caught at the elbow by Faulkner before the pistol could swing in a regrettable direction. Harry looked down to the hand grasping his arm, then onward to the pistol, heartbroken by his folly.

Lord Faulkner's cautious voice came from behind. "Friend, she has had enough fright for one evening, and I regret I was the cause of it. Please do not repeat my furious mistakes."

Harry brought the pistol back to half-cocked and Faulkner released him.

Still bent toward her, he met Allison's eyes. Her wide, glassy, brave eyes.

"I'm sorry." He barely whispered it as he straightened, but Allison nodded with as much forgiveness as she could muster and far more than he deserved.

Harry let the pistol hang limp at his side before replacing it in his coat. It was clear it was not needed. Faulkner had upset Allison. Then had comforted her. *That* was what Harry had seen on his arrival.

He reached up to rake a hand through his hair and bumped against his forgotten spectacles. He removed them and tossed them gently onto the mantel behind him.

It was again Lord Faulkner who opted to curb the silence. "The favor I asked of Gideon that night was that he might drive home my betrothed after a surreptitious rendezvous. Something my circle would be in arms about, but not a crime where Bow Street is concerned."

"It's true, Harry. I came upon them beyond the orchard that night, before you found me." Allison's voice was clear and calm and assured.

"Your Lady Allison is a ruthless interrogator," said Faulkner. "Perhaps Bow Street could use a lady Runner."

No wonder Allison had found a friend in the viscount. Here was someone who validated all the parts of her that Harry had failed to.

He reached down through his self-hatred to rally a weak smile for her alongside the compliment she much deserved. "I think you would be splendid at it."

Perhaps it was wishful thinking, but he thought he saw the firm set of her lips gentle some.

She was no longer the flighty girl he'd met in the stables in Bartswell. Nor was she his playful, lovesick correspondent. She'd not lost her lightness, nor shed her passion for gowns and pretty things, but there were passions in her he'd not before been mindful enough to see. A pursuit of wisdom. A zeal for justice. An eye for the truth.

And he had been punishing her for all such traits out of fear. The fear for her life, the fear of his inferiority, and—only just dawning on him now—his fear of being loved.

The veil lifted. He *believed* her. Lord Faulkner was not their man.

Harry turned to the viscount. "You say this Gideon is employed by your father. Is it true he goes by Giddy?"

"Sometimes. Yes."

Harry paced, about to dash off a new and urgent theory when the viscount continued.

"While I have no deep well of love for my father . . . I do not yet follow how the evidence against him is substantial?"

Allison stood up and, this time, she had all of Harry's attention.

"I know why you used your original name tonight. You were using it as bait, were you not? It would lure reactions from anyone who knew of the mutiny."

"Such was my intention, but the duke did not flinch."

Allison darted a look to Lord Faulkner. "I believe, in fact, that he did."

Faulkner shifted in his chair. She had *both* their attentions.

"Faulkner, when I first came upstairs, it was to ask you about your father. After I was frightened, I—well, I did not get to finish. And then Harry came." She turned to Harry. "After Lady Merton stole you off to dance, the duke held me back. His questions on you became suspiciously pressing. I became the questioner and caught him in a lie, a lie about his time of arrival in London. He tried to make it sound more recent than it was."

Her tone waxed apologetic as she returned her gaze to Faulkner. He did not meet her eyes, only stared into the fire.

Allison reached for Harry's arm. "Your ploy worked. He recognized the name."

Harry straightened, adopting a cold, professional air. This was it. "I am going to find him. Interrogate him. My men are waiting on the street. I expect an arrest." He directed the words at Faulkner, but the stoic viscount did not turn his eyes from the fire.

Allison's hand tightened on Harry's arm, holding him from leaving. "Will you not summon your men first?"

"Not yet." There was so much fire in him that he almost missed the worry in Allison's eyes. "Allison, Primrose, this is the end. Please understand. I just need to see my hunter's eyes."

She put her hands on his chest as he made to leave.

"Do not go anywhere alone," he whispered.

She nodded toward the silent viscount, implying she would stay. Harry lifted her hand, holding the warm back of it to his cheek. *Almost done. It is almost done.*

A moment later, he was back in the corridor with the study's door shut behind him. He checked the pistol in his coat, still half-cocked. Somewhere in this house was the man who ordered him stabbed, who set fire to his home, who tormented him for months and wished him dead.

A wind built at his back, propelling him across the upper floor in urgent strides. He turned his head at every whisper, flung open every doorway. He ignored the subsequent astonishment, the curses and the stodgy, *"I say!"*s. He was no longer Sir Harrison. He was Harry Stinton, a Bow Street Runner with retribution to satisfy.

His mind barely registered the scenes he burst in on. The shadowy games of piquet and four-ball—tall stacks of gold on the table felt. The hushed briberies exchanged and called "business." A duke's home, it seemed, was as much a den of iniquity than any chosen alley of St. Giles.

He flung curt questions toward baffled guests. "The duke?" "Where is the duke?"

None answered. Montagu's grim jowls were nowhere to be seen.

Perhaps the duke had returned to the festivities on the ground floor, hiding himself in plain sight amid a sea of his people? Or had he absconded entirely? If Allison was correct—and Harry found it likely—then the duke knew *who Harry was.*

The walkway that wrapped the top of the stairwell was more populated. Harry summoned some prudence, slowing his pace. He caught sight of a man from Allison's party at Hyde Park and from the Gossington fête, but it was not the duke. Lord Merton, was it? Careful not to meet his eye, he maneuvered past the man's group to check the next door.

He opened it carefully, finding no scene, only darkness. He let himself in, leaving the door cracked. The air was stale. As his eyes adjusted to the dark, he found himself in an intimate boudoir. Had the duchess been alive, he might have entered on a gaggle of feminine companions taking brief refuge from the din downstairs. Instead, it had the untouched feeling of a place long sat silent. He followed the edge of the small room, passing a table of perfume bottles whose oils had gone dark and gummed to the sides. The candles on the mantel were pristine but for one that had gone brittle with age and shattered. The dent in the chaise longue left the eerie impression that it had not been warm for decades.

The far corner of the room was obscured by an embossed Spanish dressing screen. Harry approached it, patting for his pistol as he went. But before his hand could slip past his coat, he heard the room's door click shut.

He turned.

The door's click was followed by the *shhhing* of a drawn sword.

"Harry Stinton. Here you are at last. Or is it Harry Plymouth?"

There it was. The long-anticipated voice of his hunter, Montagu. He'd not recognized it during their brief re-introduction, but this new, more menacing tone fell perfectly in character with the one he'd heard from his roof.

"Your Grace." Harry kept his palm against his lapel where he'd been about to reach for his weapon. Until his senses grew better adjusted to the dark, he dared not draw it against a brandished sword.

He could see the duke's shadow moving now, wending his way around the seating area in the center of the intimate room. The sword glinted faintly in the ambient light that bled through the room's cracks. It was outstretched, closing a good fraction of the distance between them before the duke was even near.

Harry's hand flinched toward his pistol.

"*Ah-ah!* Whatever you reach for . . . do not."

Harry returned his hand to neutral, refusing to remove it from his chest entirely, as the épée's tip came into striking distance of his heart.

After weeks spent in anticipation of this moment, he found himself without the upper hand. A future with Allison was fading into the void, not because of their differences, but because his life might soon be ended. Perhaps there was a comfort in that—knowing she would be safe, that she could pursue all the grand destinies he saw in her.

He only had to know first . . .

"*Why, Your Grace?* What was your relation to that officer on the *Diligence?*"

A smile, gallingly self-satisfied, lifted the man's sagging cheeks. "I had not the faintest personal attachment to that man. I *did*, however—"

The room's door flung open, casting a wide swath of light across them. "What in God's—?" Lord Merton's stunned question was lost in the ensuing chaos.

The duke panicked and lunged. Harry turned sideways, catching a gash across his stomach. He recovered swiftly enough to fling a porcelain urn at the duke as he fled. It exploded by the duke's ear as he barreled toward the door. He led with his sword hand, shocking Lord Merton with a stab to the shoulder as he fought past.

Harry tore into the hall, pistol drawn, but the duke was not on the stairs below. *But how? He had only just—*

Brunt force slammed into Harry's wounded abdomen. The duke had appeared out of nowhere from the crossing corridor. He wrapped two thick, powerful fists on Harry's collar and delivered another knee to his gut, before using his grip to fling Harry toward the stairs.

Harry's thoughts rattled loose in a commotion of gasps and shouts and the sounds of his own head cracking against the steps. His body skidded and reeled until he thudded flat onto the corner landing, grateful that his spins had not sent him the rest of the way down.

He flexed his hand. The pistol was no longer in it. The duke's solid, war-worn heels thudded down the steps above. Harry fixed his reeling vision on the duke's hands for long enough to see that the pistol was not there either. Small blessing.

Harry shut his eyes. *The spins must stop.*

There was a pause in Montagu's heavy stomps. "Off of me! I am a duke! I will do as I please!"

The dooming steps resumed. *Neared.*

Harry opened his eyes to steadier vision, but every other body part cried out for the grave.

The boots arrived to share the landing with him.

He could not see it, but was somehow aware of the tip of Montagu's sword hovering over his middle.

His mind went white with every shallow, aching breath. The world was fading, but a plea broke through—

"Harry!"

Allison.

Harry twisted, jerking from the sword's path and winding himself for another spasmodic motion that kicked the boots from under Montagu. The duke landed on his stomach below the landing. His limbs sought purchase as he thudded and slid. Unlike Harry, he recovered like a demon, scuttling up toward the landing on hands and feet. His sword, never lost from his grip, clanked against the spindles. Harry scanned again for his pistol. *Nothing.*

A sharp whistle broke through the din, drawing his attention upward. Lord Merton stood on the upper half and tossed Harry's pistol the very moment they locked eyes. It landed in his grip, fully cocked—

"Caesar!"

Harry fired.

An invisible punch behind the smoke sent the duke careening back from whence he came—pitching in a violent tumble until he flattened, prone, on his entry hall's marble compass inlay.

17

Allison's eyes traced the staircase below her to the crowd on the ground floor. Half the women had dropped—some fainting genuinely, others politely, others dramatically. But she was no fainter. No. She was forced to see all of the red. The crimson on Harry's dun waistcoat advanced like a blotch of ink. Lord Merton sat upon a step, clutching a sleeve run down with blood. And the duke. *The duke.* Sputtering. Face down in so much of his own cardinal fluid it was a wonder he still tried to get one hand under himself to rise. The man had proved an ox-like fortitude, but he would not be rising far.

Someone's sleeve brushed her shoulder. She looked up to see Faulkner's stone profile. A pall of horror and pity fell over her. He did not deserve this.

Faulkner did not rush down the stairs though, nor did he cry out his father's name. Merely stood. Staring. This man who might, at any moment, on the turn of a final breath, ascend to the dukedom.

Faulkner left Allison too mortified to move—to run down to Harry's side. If the duke were to die, it would be on Harry's hands. And it would be fair. But Allison did not expect justice to be a consolation to her friend.

One of the women still standing was Lady Merton. She stood where she had during the altercation, near the foot of the stairs. Allison recalled the name *"Caesar!"* cried out as the trigger was pulled, and it had been her, the marchioness, calling it. She looked now as stone-faced as Allison had ever seen her—a hollow look that echoed that of Faulkner's.

Harry carefully backed down the stairs. The hushed crowd was repelled as he—a possible duke killer—arrived at the foot of the stairs. He avoided the struggling duke and rested his back against the nearest wall, clutching his wound. Allison could hold herself back no longer. She picked up her hem and rushed down the stairs, knowing she would be forever judged for not pausing to assess the duke's condition first.

A stranger jostled past her to do what she had not and took a knee beside the duke. There came a sudden cascade of action as though everyone awoke from their stupors all at once. Several in the entry hall fled straight through the front door, and a footman could hardly open it in time to accommodate the rush.

The din swelled as word spread from room to room that their host had been shot. Chaos broke out in the ballroom. Cries rose up: "Is he dead?" "Arrest the murderer!" "Don't let him leave!"

But Harry wasn't going anywhere. He stared forward in a daze until Allison placed herself between him and whatever distant memories he'd been staring at.

She put a hand to his cheek, keeping her eyes up. She did not want to see the extent of his wound. Dreaded even a glimpse. Harry's focus shifted nearer, to her.

"Harry," she breathed. "How bad is it?"

"Just grazing the muscle . . . I think, but . . . breathing is agony."

His labored words said as much.

"It matters to me only that you *are* breathing."

Harry weakly lifted a hand to her shoulder. "I promise then . . . that I shall not stop doing it." He turned his stricken eyes to the floor. "But the duke—"

"Still breathing, also." Allison placed her skirts in the way of Harry's sight of the duke. *He did not need to see the blood.*

Two noblemen suddenly manhandled her out of their way. Each took one of Harry's arms. He did not resist them but opened his mouth to speak. One of the men shut him up with a strike to his slashed abdomen.

He wheezed.

"Stop! He's done nothing wrong!"

One of the men cast a piercing glare at her over his shoulder. "I would not defend the possible murderer of a duke too loudly were I you. Your pretty mouth will see you arrested alongside him."

"But *he* is the one here to make arrests. He works for Bow Street and the duke is a—"

"Would-be murderer himself."

Allison looked around to see who had interjected and found a weary Lord Merton, holding his bloodied shoulder.

The stranger ignored Lord Merton and rolled his eyes at Allison. He and his companion turned Harry toward the door, but Lord Merton hurried to put himself in their way.

"Whether or not the man represents Bow Street, I don't know, but he acted in his defense. The duke attacked him in the boudoir. I witnessed it."

Another voice joined, its steadiness broken by a subtle hitch of sorrow. "He *is* a Runner," said Lord Faulkner. "Let him go."

An earl's daughter could not convince them, a marquess could not convince them, but the duke's son himself? The men threw Harry away from them like refuse. He resumed his agonizing lean against the wall.

Allison found the courage to look into her friend's eyes. She rested a hand on his forearm. "Faulkner," she whispered. "I am so— this was not how things were supposed to—"

He stepped coolly out of reach. "I hope his crimes were deserving of this."

Faulkner's father had been rolled to his back and the men who had come to his aid pressed makeshift bandages against him to staunch the furious bleed.

Faulkner pivoted away from the sight, disappearing somewhere upstream as ball-goers flooded toward the front door—all of them careful to keep their hems from the blood and equally careful to gawp at the horrific scene on their way out.

Lord Merton had joined Harry at his "leaning wall." They looked like two soldiers lined up for the medic. Lord Merton was once more absolved of any notion of blandness. His eyes were weary and wistful, betraying a depth Allison had not before noticed. She followed his gaze past the entry to where they rested on his wife, the marchioness.

Lady Merton had been forced aside by the schooling throngs and now stood beside the stairs, gripping the spindles for support with white knuckles. Her own gaze was cast down at the duke in uniquely frigid horror.

Allison turned her eyes back to Lord Merton.

"Thank you for your testimony."

The dignified man looked down at her and smiled weakly.

"And," she continued nervously, "for your other assistance."

"Ah, yes. How many do you suppose saw me?"

Allison had no idea how many people saw Lord Merton toss the pistol but supposed it was greater than a few. Perhaps Lady Merton herself had seen it? Perhaps that was why she stared at the duke on the floor rather than coming to the side of her own, injured husband.

"Is there anything I can do? Fetch something for your arm?" asked Allison.

The marquess shook his head. "It is superficial. I'm sure." He nodded his head in Harry's direction. "He shall need more stitching than I."

Lord Merton caught the arm of a young footman scurrying around the corner. "A chair for this man." He nodded again toward Harry and the young servant changed course.

The men surrounding the duke found an old door to roll him onto, to take him upstairs to bed. The duke's groans sparked a new wave of agitation through the remaining crowd. A dandy with a striped waistcoat stepped forward, jabbing his finger toward their little congregation. "Dukes do not get cut down. I will see you all hanged."

Lord Merton stepped toward the man, threateningly. "Do you think shrieking lies in a courtroom will fetch you the title you've pined for, Mr. Bally?" Mr. Bally's eyes went wide with indignation as several snorts of laughter escaped at his expense. He backed off from Lord Merton, but other men were nearing, *daring the marquess to challenge them.*

Allison pressed close to Harry and whispered. "I do not know if Lord Merton's word against theirs will be enough."

"It will be all right. But we need to get my men in here."

His men! "Should they not have barged in at the sound of a pistol?" Allison turned furious eyes on Harry, as though he could account for their shortcomings.

"I don't rightly know." He looked over his right shoulder toward the open door, still crammed with people. "Allison, you should distance yourself from me. Go home," he begged.

Unbidden, her eyes chanced a look at his abdomen, at last confronting the dark split across his waistcoat. She shook her head. "I cannot possibly."

"You must." He didn't deliver his words to her so much as to Lord Merton who, understanding his meaning, pulled Allison away.

"But he needs help!"

Lord Merton surprised her with a one-armed embrace. He lowered his voice soothingly. "I will fetch my doctor for us and we will be stitched up. In the meantime, he is right. You should go." He drew away.

"But—"

"Please, entrust me with his care."

Allison shivered with uncertainty.

Harry nodded to her, reassuring, pleading. "Primrose, please."

"Husband."

Allison turned, startled to see Lady Merton right behind her, not a lick of tears in her eyes. The marchioness reached past her to stroke her husband's arm below its injury.

"Is it very awful?"

"I'll survive."

"Ghastly business." Lady Merton set her eyes on Allison. "And your guest . . ." Her eyes moved to Harry. "Will he live, Lady Allison?"

It did not go missed that the honorific had been tacked back onto her name. "He will."

Lady Merton gave her a smile, but it was a half-dead thing, listing to one side and empty of light.

"We should all leave," suggested Lord Merton. But when he did, his wife's tender stroking fell abruptly away.

"I will stay," she said. "The duke is our friend. I will not leave him to languish alone with doctors and opinionated nobs. He must have someone to advocate for him. To comfort him."

The marchioness' words were true enough, but *comfort* was the very last trait that she presently exuded.

"You're right of course. Stay with him. I know your constitution can handle whatever comes." The bland formality of Lord Merton was back. He watched his wife as her skirts swished up the stairs, following the men who carried the duke.

The marquess looked back to Allison and her fears must have read plain as day—

"I promise you, Harry will be fine."

"Where will you take him?"

"Back to my home. He will be very comfortable. I've an excellent doctor."

The young footman returned with an ornate dining chair and Harry fell into it with all the burdensome weight of the night.

Their eyes met. She knelt in front of him.

He took her hand with the one that was not bloodied. She was surprised to see a smile, one which fought against his intermittent winces.

"Buoyant Belle," he said.

Allison could not believe it. "You truly wish me to tell you the merits of this moment? *This* moment? With a duke's blood right behind me and yours right in front? Even *my* optimism has its limits."

"Then I will take a turn at the game. I will be your Buoyant Beau. As perhaps I once was."

Allison remembered the Harry of old. Uncertain in his inexperience yet ever moving toward the bolder path. Always smiling, always joking, even in moments too grim for lightness. Here it was, his playfulness emerging in the darkest moment yet.

He stroked his thumb across her hand. Light and soft. She wished for privacy, but the eyes of the ton still burned at her back. Every second she held his hand was another notch of scandal the nobility would carve into their rod.

"Very well," she said. "This moment, Buoyant Beau, tell me the beauty of this wretched moment."

"In this moment, I am no longer a hunted man. The threat is gone. You are safe and we are free."

Free. The word left her even more aware of the distressed stragglers at her back, itching to see Harry hanged for what they could not understand. *How free* would she feel once dangerous gossip pumped like blood through the journals at dawn?

Her heart demanded she give him a parting kiss, but her mind denied it on behalf of the two dozen angry sets of eyes that burned into her back.

She was still trying to convince herself to let go of Harry's hand when another shot was heard beyond the manse's open door.

Harry—ever understanding of her instincts—pushed her back, rallying past his pain to put himself in the door ahead of her. But he could not keep her from following.

The cool night air was like a first breath after being steeped in the humid crush of chaos, but Allison had no time to linger on the relief of it.

Faint echoes rose from the streets. "He's getting away!"

Allison could not see the *he* that anyone referred to, but a small group of men crouched in the street using nearby carriages for cover. Two of them abandoned their posts to take chase into the fog.

Another young man in common clothes shook his head and spotted Harry on the stoop. He jogged urgently toward them. "Apologies. We lost him."

"Lost *who?*" bit out Harry.

Allison stole a sideways glance at Harry. She was stunned to see him standing tall despite the wound he still clutched at.

She noticed the man's wide eyes drift to Harry's wound, before smartly ignoring it. "A man firing from the corner," he answered.

Harry's eyes shot to Allison's. "Did you—?"

"I heard nothing, but the din inside the house was terrible."

"Surely you both heard the *first* shot," insisted the man.

"I *shot* the first shot." Irritation leeched into Harry's voice.

The man let his eyes assess Harry's wound at last. "Then you are not shot?"

"I am not."

"What happened inside?"

"I shot a duke is what happened."

The stranger's face lost all tension and color. "You—"

"I shot the damned Duke of Montagu."

Allison escaped from the stress of their conversation by watching the men reorganize in the streets. Another was walking toward them. An older fellow. A more administrative sort. She knew him. Had seen him at Tallyside. Had met him at Bartswell, but she could not place a name—

"Crofty," said Harry.

Ah, yes. Mr. Crofty. The chief magistrate's man.

Harry met his superior's eye. "I'm afraid it was as I suspected but I—"

"I already overheard." Mr. Crofty was as calm as his younger associate was worried. He released a blustery sigh, as though the shooting of a duke were just some mere nasty business. "After the shot went off inside, we mobilized to enter, but someone was watching and shot at us, protecting the manse."

Allison's heart raced, but her mind raced faster, eager to put all the pieces together. The duke had already been shot so he could not have done it. Every other known person was accounted for in the entry until—

"Giddy," said Harry.

"Oh. Yes, of course. Giddy. I knew that." Allison was nervously smoothing her skirts when she felt eyes on her and realized she had mumbled her insecurities aloud.

"Who is *Giddy*?" asked Crofty.

"Giddy is the duke's valet, coachman, and apparent lackey for all things dubious."

"He was the man we overheard in Harry's apartment with the duke on the night they tried to burn it." Allison smiled, pleased with her contribution.

Crofty smiled politely at her and his spectacles caught the reflection of the nearest street lamp as he adjusted them. "I do recall that story, yes. Only Harry told me he was *alone*."

A nervous hiccup escaped her. She pinged from one thought to the next, hoping to find one that could smooth over her misstep. Instead all she uttered was, "Oh."

Harry let out a loud sigh beside her.

Crofty leaned in to see Allison more closely. "I recall you from somewhere."

"Bartswell, sir," said Harry. "But we should not just be standing here with our loose end fleeing."

"Plimpton and Cowry gave chase and they are fleet-footed," said Crofty. "We'll have the man in a cell by morning. *If* all is as you say with the duke."

"You still don't trust me?"

"I always trust you, Harry, but that trust is not always enough to surpass my fears of men more powerful than us."

The night suddenly felt darker. The fog, nearer. The complementary "Lady" in front of Allison's name was not title enough to be of any help to Harry. She lived in the world of these "more powerful," yet was not one herself. What good were any trappings of the ton if she still could not come to the aid of one she loved? If she could not contribute to justice? She was but a paste jewel—regal in appearance only.

Free. Even if Harry were not dragged to a prison, they would never *be free.*

Harry was bending again beneath the weight of the night and his injury. Allison was not tall enough, nor strong enough, nor common enough for him to lean on, yet she put an arm behind his back anyway.

"You need to get help soon," she whispered.

He did not respond with words but by giving her some of his weight instead.

Mr. Crofty put a hand on Harry's shoulder. "I hope you have evidence, Mr. Plymouth, because this mess will not be undone on your word alone."

They had more than Harry's word. They had the duke's man on the run. They had a ruined apartment on Dryden. A small scar on Harry's back and now a larger one across his front. Even the duke's own son had raised no formal objections!

Allison looked up from Mayfair's streetlamps toward the stars. Just what did it take to bring down the mighty?

18

. . . I've no doubt, dear cousin, that you will find your way through this dark forest. You must have presumed how thrilled I would be at this news of you and Harry? If you did not, then have I been a failure at showing you my true self?

It is true you have a more difficult task ahead than I. You are trapped in the web of the nobility, whereas I was not. It may take time to find passage in this range of mountains between yourself and Harry, but it will be there. Trust in it.

Your friend eternally,
Eager to learn the outcome,
Beth

That morning, Allison had dressed herself in hope. Amelia helped her into her brightest yellow polonaise, gathering up her train with its hidden ribbons until her hips were as puffed as clouds. Then she'd sat down to her dressing table, pinning ribbons and roses at her breast. But the tired girl in the mirror was mismatched to her confident colors, and no dousing of citrus oils could conceal the scent of sorrow.

Lord Merton had taken Harry home with him, giving every reassurance Allison had pled for. Yet the night had rendered her helpless and alone as she was packed neatly into a sedan chair and sent home.

She'd not slept much, preferring instead to watch the window in the mews house from her own, but Harry's candle was never lit.

Was he all right? Was his wound deeper than it appeared? Was he dead? Arrested? How fared the duke?

For most of her time in London, Harry had not wished her a part of his mess. But she *was* a part of it. She'd grown intimately involved and now it was all happening elsewhere, without her—perhaps the darkest moments yet.

She was the first downstairs, with hours to torment herself over the uncertain fate of the night. She was pacing the darkened drawing room when she heard Hayden whistling *The Valiant Lady* as he made his rounds outside to open the shutters. A wedge of daylight cut across the medallion rug as the first shutter clacked open. Hayden caught her eye through one of the lower panes of glass and nodded her way before resuming his work and his tune.

The words to the song—Allison could not recall them fully, but remembered a verse:

> *'Twas in the spring-time of the year*
> *There was a press begun;*

And all their full intention was
To press a farmer's son.
They pressed him, sent him out
Far o'er the raging sea
Where I'm sure
He will no more
Keep my daughter company!

The other window opened, bathing the room in morning light. Hayden's whistling faded, but the verse clung to Allison as she paced, repeating it to herself in mumbled soprano.

She forewent breakfast when offered, resulting in her mother returning every ten minutes or so—a cup of chocolate in one hand, a roll in the other—urging her daughter to take one or both. Allison waved her off each time. She had not breathed a word to her parents about the past night's events. What in heaven would she have said? *My commoner lover dueled with the duke and won?*

When answers finally came, she was on the wrong side of the house to see their approach. Hayden's voice caught her quite off guard as he announced visitors.

She rushed to the window, pressing her cheek flat against it to see whether she could catch a sideways look at who was on their stoop. Two indistinct coattails were all she could make out.

She drew back, catching Hayden's quick, sharp glance in her direction as he opened the door. She heard the fleet yet dignified cadence of her parents' footsteps as they came. She wished to join them at the door, to be the first to hear the news but remained rooted to her spot.

The archway to the entry hall became a proscenium and her parents arrived on the stage. Her mother, leading.

Allison pressed both hands over her stomach. Had she taken

breakfast, she might have retched.

There were low murmurs from the door before Hayden turned to make his formal announcement. "Mr. Crofty, Assistant to the Chief Magistrate, and Mr. Stinton, also of the Magistrate's Court."

Allison's knees threatened to buckle when the name *Plymouth* did not come. Then she heard the voices at the door more clearly—heard *his* voice. Strong and clear. The sweetest sound in all the world. *Stinton. Of course.* With a clearer mind she may have remembered straight away his other name. His *real* name.

Her sigh of relief was breathed inward rather than out and she shuddered, but her locked knees held.

Several more murmurs were exchanged—"investigation . . . last night . . . Bow Street . . ."—before the earl and countess led their visitors inside. Lady Weldon stopped short, startled, apparently, by Allison's stealthy presence in the drawing room.

"Oh."

Allison anticipated a shooing gesture, the sort one might use if they wished a spaniel to vacate their favorite chair, but none came.

Mr. Weldon stepped forward for introductions that he could not have known were unnecessary. "Mr. Stinton, Mr. Crofty. My daughter, Lady Allison."

Allison was vaguely aware of Crofty's bow as he clutched a tricorn to his chest, but her mind could not spare much time for him. She stared instead at Harry. Gone was his pallor of the night before. Gone was the stain across his waistcoat. Gone were any silk or spectacles. It was just him—a few tiny moth holes in his dove wool coat.

His eyes once more communicated to her in their secret language, just as the night before. Only now, she could not understand him; the flood of meaning behind them was too great. Overwhelming. There was far too much to be said. So as his deep blue eyes reached out to her across the room, she could only understand it as a feeling—a feeling she would *never* forget.

"Lady Allison." Harry dipped his head, limiting movement to above his shoulders. The light, wispy hairs around his face fell forward, out of his queue as they always did.

"Mr. Stinton." She dipped her head. Catching herself staring at him overlong, she turned to her mother who . . . who *also* stared at the Bow Street Runner.

Lady Weldon did not even pull her gaze away to address her daughter. "Lady Allison, these gentlemen apparently need a word with you. They are from Bow Street."

Allison nodded, testing several crinkled expressions, uncertain how to disguise what she already knew.

Her father stood protectively nearby, arms crossed. "Perhaps you gentleman might first elaborate on what this is about?"

Mr. Crofty stepped forward, gesturing to the settee. The earl reluctantly went to it but did not sit.

Mr. Crofty wrung his hands in silent distress, revealing the night's outcome to Allison before he even uttered a word. "I regret to tell you the Duke of Montagu is dead."

Allison lurched forward, reacting to her mother's light-headed sway before her father could. But it was Harry who reached Lady Weldon first, catching her arms before she went completely limp. Allison and Harry helped her to the settee while Lord Weldon fluffed a cushion to place beneath her head.

Hayden swept from his post in the archway to fetch a pitcher across the room and wet a kerchief. He passed the cloth to Lord Weldon whose knees cracked as he lowered himself beside his wife's face.

Allison's heart broke as her father turned his confused, pleading eyes to her. "Just what happened last night?"

"Father, I—"

Mr. Crofty came to her rescue, raising a palm that pled for silence. "I am afraid, Lord Weldon, that I am here to ask questions more than give answers, but I *will* share with you the basics as my associate escorts Lady Allison to Bow Street for questioning as a witness."

"She cannot . . . go with him . . . alone." Lady Weldon raised a weak finger in Harry's direction.

Ah yes, *propriety*, the smelling salts of society mothers the world over.

Lord Weldon calmed his wife with soothing shushes. "This sounds important, darling." Lord Weldon looked up at Harry. "I am sure the Bow Street men know good judgment and," he looked specifically at Harry, "discretion."

Harry did naught but nod at her father and Allison could sense his mortification at the irony.

Harry stepped aside and gestured to the entry hall. "Lady Allison?"

Allison bent to put a hand on her mother's clammy wrist. "I will not be long." Then she went to Harry, doing her best to pretend him a stranger. "Mr. Stinton. If you would kindly lead the way."

Allison walked slightly ahead of Harry, at her natural energetic clip, and he had to lengthen his stride to keep pace. The bright morning sun bounced from her golden hair and right into his very soul. He took a deep breath and suddenly it felt easier, even against his stitches.

She had been right all along. Their problem *was* solvable. The duke was found out and was gone. His lackey was still at large but with no surviving pocket to pay him. Harry was no longer a hunted man. His nightmare was ended. He could reach out and touch Allison without tainting her with some curse—without the fear that whoever wished to harm him might see her as the perfect conduit by which to do so. The very notion stung behind his sternum—a reminder of just how grave things might have been.

He once worried he had forgotten his love for her, but that was the furthest from the truth. His distance was never for a lack of love. Rather, love had fueled it. With love came fear, came worry, came visions of futures without that person in the world . . .

But now. Now he could be with her. Now—

Allison halted and spun round. He grabbed her shoulders to catch himself from tripping full into her.

Her eyes, looking more green than ever in the morning light, were tinged with fear.

"How are you, Harry? I mean your injury, how is it? Do not lie to me."

"Lord Merton's physician patched us up well. You needn't worry on my behalf. Not anymore."

"But—"

"It's not deep, I promise. I am merely stiff." With Allison suddenly pressed against him, he became aware of an incidental *double-entendre*.

He reached for her face, but just as in the dressmaker's shop, she pulled away. "When we reach Bow Street, will you tell me every-thing?"

"Of course. So much happened last night after we—"

"No. Not about the duke or any of that. About *you*. About Mr. *Stinton*."

She stabbed out the syllables of his surname—his *real* surname.

He owed her. He owed her all of it.

He *had* been taking her to Bow Street but not on any formality. He'd merely made professional excuses to be alone with her, and Crofty, doubtless wise to it, had allowed him. But the answers Harry owed her—he could not peel open his tender history at the Home Department, not with his peers on the other sides of thin walls. "I will tell you," he said. "But not at Bow Street."

"Where then?" She lowered her gaze to the pavement. "Because it cannot be here either."

Yes, they needed the sort of privacy reserved for talk of mutinies and cruel childhoods, but he knew that wasn't what she meant. She looked around herself consciously; she still cared about being seen on the street with him, a common man. He forced the painful thought aside. Today was too important.

"We will go to Dryden. To my home."

The rest of their walk passed in silence, and silence, it seemed, was like salt on his throbbing wound. The four flights of stairs to the garret proved torturous, just as they had earlier that morning.

By the time he closed the door and caught his breath, Allison was deep into the little apartment, carefully navigating piles of massacred books. It was not unlike the way he'd found her less than a fortnight before.

From the night of their first meeting in Bartswell, he thought he'd recognize her anywhere, from any angle. But after a year of having only dreams for memories—not so much as a miniature to remember her face by—she had caught him off guard. His investigative mind had looked her over like a checklist. Flaxen hair? Yes. Short stature? Yes. A proclivity for all things golden? Evident in the rich, gold silk of her gown. Yet he still had not dared believe it, even upon hearing her voice.

Their convergence in London had so far been brief, yet felt as a lifetime.

Again she stood with her back to him, again in her signature hue. The moment felt like an opportunity, like a chance to do something over. Do it better. But before he could step forward, she turned around, just as she had that day. The sight of her filled his heart, stunning him into a bashful glance aside.

"Did you sleep here last night?"

"'Sleep' would be overstating it—a morning nap, more like—but yes, I came here after parting ways with Lord Merton."

Allison wandered to the deflated mattress. The mere breeze from her skirts displaced some of the down and wool that Harry had tried to pile into something comfortable.

She knelt to chase some of the feathers with her hands, before stuffing them back into the mattress' gashes. "I am very grateful all *your* feathers didn't come out last night. That you do not resemble this mattress."

Harry smiled. "Me too, Primrose."

She continued to fuss with the feathers, which floated away as fast as she could re-stuff them. She paused with her hand in the mattress and looked up at him, a sparkle of tears at the corners of her eyes. "Harry?"

"Yes?"

"Would you let me see it?"

"See what?"

"Your wound."

He wasn't prepared for the question and had no answer ready before she hurried to explain—

"I worry that my fears for you cannot be allayed until I see it with my own eyes."

He looked down at his clothed waist. "I'm not sure it will give you the peace of mind you seek." But he was already walking over to her, already shirking his coat. He yanked the hem of his shirt from his breeches.

A fresh white bandage was wrapped thrice around him. He untucked the tail and unwound it, letting his shirt fall just as the bandage dropped away. He tossed it aside before Allison could see its angry stain.

She knelt on the pallet as he stood before her. She hooked a thumb beneath his shirt's hem and drew the linen gently up. To his surprise, she did not flinch, but a long, soft exhale washed over his navel. She studied the wound in detail. It was shallow but reached nearly from one side to the other and was still prone to bleeding in the middle. Was this truly the peace of mind she needed?

She kissed a spot below the wound. Soft though the touch was, it burned him. Not for proximity to his wound but to his breeches.

"Does it hurt?"

It did. A little. A *lot*. But Harry found himself shaking his head in denial as she guided him down to join her. A pouf of feathers and straw ballooned into the air as his knees clumsily landed, and he groaned.

"You're lying," said Allison. "It *does* hurt you." He held his shirt up for her as she painted his upper hips with an affectionate stroke of her fingernails. She drew her lower lip between her teeth in concentration.

Harry pulled his hem higher, but the stitches pulled taut as his arms raised, eliciting another groan. Allison's soft hands brushed against his as she took the painful task away from him. His shirt-sleeves were cast to the floor.

She leveled a stern glare at him, one which reinforced—correctly—her insistence he was in pain. But beyond the teasing lecture in her eyes, he saw what he hoped was still love and tried to convey something of his own. *We can be together now, Allison. We* should *be together now.* He buttressed his thoughts with courage; when would be the time to utter them? He could no longer leave her to guess.

Yet he was so very drunk on the imbibement of her presence and loathe to lose her. The marigold poufs of her polonaise were pushed clear up to her elbows by the way she sat. The soft dip between her small breasts was garnished with a spray of fresh, peachy roses at the neckline. She remained the frilliest woman he had ever known, yet he now knew her to also be the most quietly serious. It seemed less paradoxical the longer he knew her. After all, the sun was light and bright and pretty to paint, yet owned such sober tasks as bringing crops to flourish.

A loose ringlet of blonde spilled forth from her hair's crisscrossing ribbons. It danced about with every slight motion as she trailed light touches around his injury, brooding over it. That loose curl taunted Harry—dared him to spring like a cat. He reached up and caught it.

Allison's lips grimaced, but her eyes smiled.

He gently pulled until her face was brought near his. "We are safe now," he whispered. But his words didn't seem to gentle the tension in her shoulders. "Do you hear me, Primrose? *Safe.*"

She sat back on her heels and the silky lock slid from his pinch. "Your men found Giddy then?"

"Not yet, but they will. And what motive has he now his master is dead? He would not risk the Runners' wrath with his pay cut off. I do not even care if he flees. Let him. It is done."

"But he tried to kill you."

Harry pushed a hand into her hair. "Allison, you were right in the beginning. That it would be resolved. That it would not keep us apart." There were so many words to follow but—

Her eyes drifted back to his injury. "We should re-bandage you."

It was an evasion of his reassurances, of the long and difficult conversation that was incoming, the one *she* had asked for. Yet, his throbbing wound cried out for that rebandaging, and his throbbing heart pled for one last tender moment.

"There are fresh strips of linen in the pouch there." He pointed to a bag slung over the splintered foot of his capsized bed frame.

She resettled on her knees in front of him with a fresh roll of gauze. He raised his arms as much as he could muster. Each time she leaned in he could smell the roses at her breast, tinged, of course, with her usual lemon. She looped it around him once, twice, three times, biting her lip as she worked. Then she tucked the tail in neatly at his side. The gentle hug of the bandage soothed his throbbing pain.

A little *hmm* of a moan escaped her as her fingers left their work. That one little sound saw his patience burn down.

He kissed her, feeling for himself the lip she'd just made red and swollen with her vice of concentration. It was his turn to bite. His turn to intrude upon her mouth and taste the warmth of her tongue. So much of his prior gentleness had been caution—caution and fear. Fear was death. Fear was a graveyard for love and passion. But all his passions were reanimated as he held her now. All his pains forgotten as they fought one another for dominance of the kiss.

Allison pulled out of the depths to take a gasp of air, before re-sealing her lips to his. Her one hand still explored him and an errant finger bumped against a stitch through the gauze, but the pain—fast and sharp as lightning—was absorbed into his pleasure.

"Primrose." He did not expect it to be moaned.

"Did I hurt you?!"

He put his forehead to hers and lowered his voice to a rumble. "You hurt me beautifully."

He held onto her for support as he shifted and lowered his back to the sorry mattress. She did not follow as he'd hoped. It left her lips far too far away from him, and he, on instinct, tightened his stomach to raise his head. *Disastrous.* His eyes slammed shut against a wave of pain that did not vanish so quickly.

"*That* did not hurt you beautifully," she said.

"No."

"What can I do?"

"Come down to me again."

Allison leaned down over his face, but he did not dare strain himself to close the gap.

"Do you dislike when I am far away?" she asked.

"I dislike it rather much!" He suppressed a laugh, dodging more of the un-beautiful sort of pain. "Please, my love."

Harry had not noticed his own words before seeing the change in Allison—a fleeting gloom across her sea-green eyes. She heaved herself to stand.

"I should not whinge about comforts when, well . . ." She gestured to his bandage. "But it is less than comfortable down there, leaning over you like that."

Harry smiled. "It was only a little wish. I am just grateful you are here with me. You needn't join me on this shabby—" He shut his mouth when he realized what she was doing.

Allison was pulling pins from her gown and distributing them in a chipped cup she'd retrieved amid the wreckage. Her garment remained remarkably un-slack until the ninth pin *tinked* against the pottery. Her compere front fell open, revealing a pink set of stays with silvery-blue bows tied at the straps.

His breath picked up its pace. All night he had been forgiving of his wounded body—grateful just to be alive. But now? Now he cursed it. The need to make up for his inconsistent affections was driving his patience to its limit. How could he take her in his present state? How would he get her round his cock when he could hardly sit up? He didn't know how. But he *would*. He would make love to her. No one—and no wound—would stop him.

As these internal avowals tapered off, he returned to the sacred vision looming at the foot of the mattress. She shot a coy look over her shoulder as she shrugged out of her safflower frock. Nimble fingers went to work at the ties of her peachy petticoats.

Blood surged to Harry's loins at the thought of seeing her legs again. The petticoats dropped away. Then her pockets. Until there she was: rumpled white shift, pink stays, and a pair of familiar embroidered garters hugging her clocked silk stockings to those beautiful calves.

At last—*at bloody last!*—she extended her hands to help him sit up again. He did so with a grown.

She knelt with him on the sorry bedding, giving him her back so that a ladder of spiral lacing faced him. "Would you, kindly?" she asked.

His knuckles skimmed her spine as he went to undo the lacing. The memory of retying her garter resurfaced. He had stolen a needless brush against her bare skin that night. Now he had to steal nothing—would be given *everything*. Apart, perhaps, from what he truly wanted.

"Allison?"

"Hmm?"

"Do you not wish to talk first?"

He felt her lungs fill with a sigh as he continued to pluck her laces.

"This morning, I—" Her voice caught.

He scooted himself nearer, to wrap an arm around her shoulders from behind.

Her voice caught as he hugged her to him. "I—whether Plymouth or Stinton—I did not know whether I had lost you. Sometimes—or often—I just need the dream to be real for a moment."

She had called it a dream. Meaning it was wonderous, but also that it was not real. He longed to show her that it could be, but he understood. He understood why she barreled forth with their stolen moments and why he kept doing the same. He squeezed her tighter, even as his injury protested.

She sniffed and reached behind herself, between them, to pull the final lace from the eyelet. "I wish to finish what was started in my room that night, Harry. Because when you needed comfort, I needed it also. And I need it again now."

Her stays fell away, revealing the crumpled linen beneath, slightly damp with perspiration.

He traced her spine through the linen with his finger. *One more time. Just one more time.* "Help me to my feet?"

Without hesitation, she stood and took his arm. He groaned like an over-burdened ship as his abdomen crunched forward.

He looked around the room, confused for a moment by its ruined state, forgetting that anything else existed or happened outside of Allison. A common symptom of her company.

He had an idea, but—*damn*—was there not a single surface left unscathed? His clerk's desk still lay on its side in a pool of dried ink. His seats by the mantel were still shattered and singed. There was, however, the dormer's sill—not the one obstructed by his inky desk but that nearer the door.

"Harry, what is it?" Allison's face wore the elements of mild concern. Raised brows, lips gently ajar. And she stood so innocently against him, as though he could not feel the heat of her through every inch of her shift.

He guided her to the deep sill of the dormer window.

"I cannot do the bed, Primrose, if a 'bed' it may even be called. I can hardly move when I am down there. I—"

"I could do the moving *for* you." She rubbed against him with intent, her melancholy gone, her spark relit.

Harry had to wet his lips before he could speak. "That *had* crossed my mind." He put his hands around her waist and hopped her up onto the sill. "But I have waited far too long for this and I mean to participate."

He tilted her chin up to him, her lips still flushed from their kiss. Her cheeks and nose were faintly golden and sprinkled with freckles only revealed to those privileged to be so near.

"I have waited to steal this moment," she whispered.

Harry shook his head and did not release her chin. He had to see into her eyes. Had to make her understand. "No, Allison. I will steal no more moments with you. I want for the *moments* to steal *me*. I want to be locked into a moment with you that lasts until the ends of our days."

19

Allison's vision blurred. Harry wanted her. Not for a moment but forever. His vow gave a name to the uneasiness she'd felt as he'd offered the very answers she sought. Answers had the potential to break everything, everything that was already so fragile.

Her hand clenched, recalling the fist she'd made around the handle of the knife each time she'd carved a notch into the casement back at Tallyside. *Twelve. Forty. Sixty-three.* And finally—*eighty-seven days*—the day they left for London. *Harry and I will unite and elope, and all our dreams will come to pass . . .*

Such girlish dreams. She was no longer a girl.

And Harry? He stood in front of her now, with light and life back in his eyes. His shoulders squared and heaving up and down with each anticipatory breath. His arms, sculpted with ropes of strength, were slightly apart from him. A diamond patch of hair darkened his sternum and trailed down over his chiseled middle, briefly disrupted by a stripe of stark white gauze. A rod was hugged tight to him by his breeches. He was no longer a boy.

She had no answer to his beautiful vow. She wanted a lifetime also, but her hopes for it had never been stolen by his hunter but by her reality. If she were with him—if she *dared*—would she ever see her family again? See Tallyside? Would her parents and brother Stefano move through the world as though she'd never existed? Her mother, always holding the household in her tidal pull, made it seem as such.

Harry descended into Allison's vision for another kiss, perhaps hoping to snatch her from the celestial outpost of her thoughts.

Alas. It worked.

Half-formed notions about Harry's past shriveled and disappeared into the ether the very moment she felt his cock against her thigh. Her mind made one final, feeble protest as her body took over—

But there are questions I must—

Shh, shh, shh.

And she trusted her body. After all, Harry was so much finer to rub against than a newel post. She peeled her chemise off and cast it away. "I *need* you, Harry. I have always needed you."

A shiver traveled over her as he took several steps back, as though struck by something. His dark blue eyes slid over her.

Am I enough? she wondered. The thought was habit but held no meaning. For the first time, it sloughed away, inconsequential. She lifted her chin and arched her spine, letting the morning sun heat her back, and Harry's gaze, her front.

She had seen awe before. She'd seen it on her tour, in the eyes of those walking the ruins of Paestum or craning their necks to the Pantheon's dome. She saw such awe in Harry's eyes now.

She could sense his breath as though she breathed it herself, and she noticed the very moment it quickened—the moment he was going to come forth and take her.

It was a wonder he did not lose a button, so quickly he freed himself from his fall. His hands went 'round her, grabbing the cheeks of her rear. He tugged her to the very lip of the sill and leveled her hips with his rearing erection.

A sudden and bullish kiss forced her head against the window's rail and Harry's tongue laved into her mouth, bringing with it the suggestion of everywhere else he had put it. His cock slid up against her folds as he tested for himself what she already knew: her absolute need and readiness to have him.

She tilted her hips to him and clawed at his shoulders, beckoning for nearness as she sank against the window. He responded by bending over her before a flinch sent him back upright. Allison's usual apologies formed but dissipated; he could handle himself. As could she. This moment, this *culmination*, it was a grand and messy thing. Its risks. Its uncertainties. The messiness suited them.

"Legs. Up," he commanded. He peeled his breeches lower and clapped a hand against the flesh of his hip, showing where he wished her to be.

Allison had her ankles hooked behind him in an instant. Obedience had never felt so right.

She rubbed against him, understanding a sort of suspense previously unknown to her.

He allowed his cock to slide against her one last time, before reangling himself for a thrust.

"Harry. Look at me."

"Yes, Primrose?" Perhaps he enjoyed obedience as much as she. She gave her head a sideways toss that unseated several pins in her hair, loosening it.

"You were directed to question me, were you not?"

"I was."

Her eyes flicked down to where their bodies were so near to joining. "So, question me."

He tipped his chin down devilishly and looked at her from under his shadowed brow, through stray golden hairs. He plunged into her, stealing her breath.

She watched as his eyes filled with so much bliss they rolled back. Then she allowed her own eyes to do the same as she was wedged apart by his heat for the very first time.

She felt too full to speak, yet—

"Question me," she begged.

He reached behind her, threaded his fingers into her hair and made a fist, controlling her gaze. He drew out of her slowly and plunged again.

"Where were you last night?" he asked.

"At a ball. Watching a Bow Street Runner at work."

"What else were you doing?"

"I was—"

Her breath was stolen again by another prying stroke.

"I was helping him."

Harry leaned low to her ear and let out his words in a whispery growl. "Yes, you were. You were helping him so much."

She shuddered as his hot breath washed over her ear.

Another long stroke—one which nearly abandoned her before intruding again.

"And what did you see last night?"

She locked her eyes with his. "I saw the man I love released from his nightmares."

He slammed into her.

The word *love* had fallen from her lips like a dried leaf from a tree. Natural and easy. The first time any vows from her letters had been spoken aloud.

She could not tell whether he caught that leaf before it blew away. Had he, he said nothing. They always said nothing.

He thrust into her again. And again. His path more slickened with every stroke.

She groaned, shifting herself upward so as not to lose her shallow perch.

"What else do you know?" he croaked.

"I know nothing else."

The grip in her hair tightened, bearing her neck to the gentle scrape of his teeth as he spoke against her skin. "Do you know how beautiful you are?"

"I . . ."

He nipped her neck. *"Do you?"*

Not an inquiry. An *interrogation.*

"I do," she breathed.

"And do you know how clever you are? How wise?"

She said nothing.

The teasing ministrations against her neck ceased. His eyes hovered over hers. He did not release her hair, but his stormy eyes went calm. *"Do you?* Do you know what I think of you?"

Allison shook her head against his grip, stunned into silence.

"I think you are clever, Primrose. Cleverer than I . . . and wiser too. I should have been gladder for your aid." He released her hair and smoothed his hand downward to cradle her neck. "I am in love with you, Primrose."

No. Nothing was supposed to interrupt them this time, but

emotions—*tears*—were surging upward to batter down the door. She would not have it. "I know," she said. "I know I am clever." She tilted her head sideways to keep a tear from spilling. *It was everyone else who had not known.*

Her hands darted out, a quick and playful shove at Harry's chest—like a puppy begging to return to tug-of-war. *Please,* thought Allison. *Please, let us not. Let the questions not return. I am clever, yes, but wise? No.* Another shove. She grinned as he batted her hands away like flies and smiled at her. The sweet pumping of his hips resumed. *Nothing about this is wise.*

Harry had feared the moment shattered, but his sage Primrose had sucked them back into the dream with her play. She had not quite said it back, but had uttered *"the man I love"* in a wayward slip. For him, it was enough.

The grip of her body around his cock was the sort of acceptance he had never in his hard life fathomed. It nearly broke him that anyone could trust him so. Never had he taken a woman, nor she, a man, but between them the act came easy, their fumbles never thought on overlong. He listened to her body, to her low croons and gentle spasms, to the tightening and loosening of her grip on his arms. He seated himself right up to her, pumping hard and fast, leveraging himself with a grip on the casement.

Her plush flesh was trapped between their pubic bones as they ground together, and he could tell the grinding brought her pleasure. The window rattled with their rhythm.

Fears that he would lose his seed too soon dissolved into the humid air. His body craved their act far too much to shorten it. He slowed down, drawing in and out of her in long, almost arduous strokes.

"Harry," she breathed, as he pulled out to the very edge of her. "Please. Please."

The rim of her hugged him the tightest. He smiled at her needy torment.

"Please."

His cock finally answered the plea, driving into her so hard and fast that her head bumped against the sash, cracking one of the panes.

"Allison!" He hastened to cradle her head, but a smile on her face eased his worries. "I'm so sorry," he said, trying not to laugh.

She nodded, panting and nude and exhausted. "I'm fine."

But she let her legs go slack behind him and dangle to the floor. She impressed him with limberness as she placed a foot against his hip and shoved him away.

He staggered back, left to teeter in his half-drawn breeches and aching bandage, his throbbing cock, suddenly bereft of its cozy lodgings. Perhaps he should have withdrawn and come sooner after all.

Allison looked over her shoulder and undid the latch on the sash, hoisting it upward. A cool breeze rushed in and Harry's whole body went taut as he saw the effect of the air on her nipples. She looked out over London, as comfortable with her nakedness as the bawds down the street.

Harry stroked himself, wondering what came next.

She put both hands to one side and twisted her body, before ducking her head under the window rail and leaving her backside dangling at him. She looked coyly over her shoulder. "Harry. I want you to—"

"To question you?" He stepped forward.

Her grin glowed in the sun. "Yes. That."

But he had no more questions for her as he speared back into her soft quim. As he cushioned his thrusts with her buttocks. As he lived out the fantasy he'd had from the *first* time he'd seen her legs dangling from one of his windows.

Every sound she made, loud or soft, echoed across the rooftops of Covent Garden as they seized a new rhythm together. He traced her back with his fingers, musing on how he would soon paint it with his come.

He gripped her hips and drove faster.

Her stockinged feet sought futile purchase against the wall in a struggle for leverage. "I am slipping—I cannot—would you—?"

He pulled her one leg up and freed it from garter and stocking, then the other. But still she could not brace herself, could not find a way to hold herself against him, so, like a good lad, he took up the cause. He took a small, but decisive step forward, pinning her more tightly to the sill. She shrieked an exuberant, *"Yes!"*

Her high-pitched sounds ebbed into moans as he explored the white flesh of her backside, kneading it by bruising handfuls.

He folded forward, but a cruel pain sliced across his belly. He pushed past it this time. He had to be nearer. Had to seal himself against her and feel her heat.

He shaped himself over her back, not allowing her to feel him wince. Her feminine grunts filled the morning air as his shoulders joined hers outside the window.

The rooftop. Where she'd first been pressed against him.

He braced a hand on the gentle roof slope, trying not to crush her as he suckled the back of her neck. The curve of her back changed beneath him as she pressed her stomach against the sill with a moan. Her soft hips pushed up into him—a beckoning tilt that drew him deeper inside.

He noticed his own rasping breaths as they puffed into the

morning air. He was lost, utterly lost to her. Not only to the coating heat of her quim, but to every word they'd ever spoken, every choice they'd ever made, every mistake they'd ever shared—even if this, right now, was one of them.

He trailed lower with his bites, but Allison reached behind her shoulder, seizing a fistful of hair at the back of his head. Harry sucked air through his teeth at the sweet pain of her grip. She leveraged it to force his lips back to her nape, where she clearly wanted them. He gladly reburied his nose in her luxurious, lemony mane—a scent a man could live off of.

Her grunts were shrinking into something tight and quiet as she held him against her, as she pushed against him. Her fluid back was tensing . . .

Harry fought her forceful grip to nudge nearer to her ear, whispering, "My Primrose."

The walls of her flesh suddenly clenched around his cock in rolling spasms and she cried out to all of London, startling a flock of doves from the parapet. But the birds were not the only caught by surprise—

As her cries woke Dryden's late sleepers, Harry's own body responded—her spasms milking from him the finest feeling he knew, finer than he'd ever felt it.

The prudent instinct to pull away was fought not only by Allison's ardent, cutthroat grip, but by her cries. "Stay! Do not dare leave me!" And so he spilled into her with a year of pent-up longing, weak against her, against everything that existed beyond his little room on Dryden.

After, he lay sealed to her back, spent and panting. Looking out over the rooftops, London seemed sucked dry of sound. Nothing else mattered but the whistle of the breeze and the gentle coos of Allison's recovery. Her hand in his hair went slack and she shivered beneath him.

He kissed the back of her neck and solemnly backed away. *Why? Why had she not let him go?*

He raked a hand through his hair, finding it disheveled. He longed for a future, yes, but what if she returned one day only because she was with child? How would it feel for that to be the tie between them?

She still dangled with her feet several inches above the floor, her rear end, splotched with the pink marks of his grip. She rolled onto her back, lackadaisical, and ducked beneath the sash.

He watched as she calmly shrugged back into her shift and examined her surroundings. She picked up his broken wash stand and propped it against the wall on its three remaining legs. Was she setting his place to rights? Or herself?

He swallowed around a lump of fear. "I have been a coward," he said.

She paused her tidying.

Harry buttoned his fall and hobbled toward her, his pain made suddenly worse by his grief. "I'm a bastard, Allison. I was born a bastard. I grew up in a garret much smaller and darker than this one and was pressed into sailing before I came of age. Stinton is the name I once went by, yet I have no claim to it. No more than Plymouth. It does nothing to complete me. Such is my reluctance to share it." He reached out for her and rested a regretful hand against the slope of her neck, stroking his thumb there. "I should not have made you wait for that. We came here because you wanted answers. They should have spilled from my lips straight away. Before we ever—" He looked to the window, where they had just been.

Allison looked to it too and shook her head. "No. Do not

express regret for that. For any of it. I had as much a part, and I will own it." She shifted to catch Harry's eye. "It will be a happy memory, come whatever may."

He tried to lift a smile for her, but previous fears intruded. He held them back, searching for one of the many other threads that called for explanation. "This whole dreaded affair, Allison. The duke . . ." Harry looked for the words, realizing even *he* had not finished piecing it together. "It has to do with the mutiny."

Her brows crinkled. "But did you not already serve your punishment for the mutiny by exile? In your years as a poorly-fed highwayman?"

Harry dropped his hand from her shoulder. "I played a darker part in it than even Rhys knew, though he knows now."

Allison did not shrink in apprehension nor retreat from his angst. She stepped nearer, resting a light hand on his chest as he pushed on.

"I believe I once told you of an officer who perished in the brig? Whose death saw our quartermaster hanged?"

"You did."

"His death was by my hand. He attacked me. We grappled. I won. I took his life. The duke was avenging him."

"But *why?*"

"I don't yet know. But a painting of our ship, the *Diligence,* looms over his ballroom and he stole a letter wherein I confess to the officer's killing. And Faulkner's watch fob . . ." He waited for Allison's comforting hand to fall away at the name of her friend, but it did not. "It belonged to the officer. I used its chain against his neck."

Allison lowered her gaze.

"My best guess is that the officer was of the duke's blood. A bastard like me."

Her hand left his chest to cradle his jaw. He fought her as she turned his face to meet her eyes.

"A bastard like you . . ." she trailed off into a whisper.

"A garret dweller."

"But, Harry, you have *made* your name, whatever it is. You have made a life of these ashes." Her eyes glittered with the tears he could not spill for himself.

He looked past her shoulder at the ruin of his room and scoffed. "A life."

She looked too and swept suddenly past him. "We will put it back together, your room. Another solvable problem."

Nothing solves the past, he wished to say. But it comforted him to see her flit about in his space, being so very solution-minded. So very *her.* She took ruined books, one by one, opened them up, shoved pages back into their tattered maws. Then set them neatly on the shelf behind.

She picked up shards of his pitcher. Gathered legs of furniture like firewood. She placed everything into neat little stacks.

She knelt at his toppled desk, preparing to sweep papers into her arms, but paused.

Harry noticed a sudden cloud fall over her eyes. "What is it?"

"It is nothing." She shook away the troubled expression. Tearing a paper from the dried ink stain, she crumpled it into a ball and tossed it aside. Harry's eyes followed it; it didn't leave the room looking any worse. Nothing could.

"I have wanted to show you this place for so long. I had hoped it might look better."

"What was it like before?"

"Well, all of those books? You have placed them precisely where they ought to be. It's the very vision of the past."

She glanced behind her at her work. A large tome she'd placed as a bookend flopped down with a *plonk* causing the whole shelf to come off its nail. It spilled its contents so near to Allison's feet she had to leap back.

"Perfection," said Harry.

He made his way back to his shabby pallet and stared at it. Allison detected his conundrum.

"Let me help." She hurried over and, with no small donation of her strength, helped him to lie down.

He sighed with relief as the thinly cushioned floor welcomed his back. "Help me off with my boots? I've not been a moment without them since Lord Merton's physician helped me on with fresh clothes."

The air felt so fine against his calves as she peeled the first boot away and then the next. His heel thudded rather hard to the floor.

"Harry?"

"Yes?"

"What is this?"

He lifted his chin to see a tiny piece of paper pinched in her grip.

"It is written in my hand," she said, confused.

The remaining sweat of their lovemaking suddenly rendered him cold, but he didn't try to stop her from reading the scrap as she settled on her heels.

"Hands . . .wishes redeemed . . . no poet, but . . . days in the sun." She murmured it to herself, then traced the burnt edges of the vellum until a little trail of soot was on her finger.

She met Harry's eyes. "You told me our letters were gone. You did not say you'd *burned* them."

"I'm so sorry. I panicked when—"

"I remember this one," she said. "It was something like 'all nights come to an end, and we will have our days in the sun.'" She sighed and looked up at him. "We did not yet know how dark the night would be, did we?"

Harry shook his head where he lay. "Do you think we ever will?"

"What?"

"Have our days in the sun?"

Her brows lifted in a way that revealed honest curiosity. "I do not know." A mote of hope. "Do you?"

"I do."

She gave no clue as to how his answer left her. Never before had he felt so tethered to another. They were one another's anchors, tied at the heart. If one sank, so did they both. Her *"I don't know"* might one day soon drag him to the depths. He accepted that and all the pain it might bring.

He'd wasted so much time being grief-stricken at their differences. And then he had seen Rhys. *"The two of you are so very much alike,"* his friend had said. And they were, weren't they? They both loved a puzzle. They loved to prove themselves. They were determined and loyal. Cautious. Protective not only of one another but of themselves. Of their wounds. To a fault.

Something yet remained unsaid.

"This was my first real home, Allison. Believe it or not, this bed was once quite comfortable. The hearth could heat the whole place in short time. Its light was perfect to read by, even when it left me sweating."

"Would you ever read in the nude?" she asked. She playfully grabbed his ankle and shook it.

"Sometimes."

The seriousness of his answer brought her voice down to match his earnest tone. "I sometimes do as well."

What a lovely thing to picture. But Harry wasn't done. "The splinters you gathered up by the fireplace? They were two chairs, once upholstered in burgundy. Finest things I owned. A gift from a grateful carpenter."

"Grateful how?"

"I brought his boy home from a kidnapper."

She shook her head, smiling, shaping her lips once more in disbelief around that phrase, *a bastard like you* . . . "You are good at your work," she said.

"You're good at my work too."

She smiled. "Oh?"

"I got in a rut thinking Faulkner was our man. I'd not have gotten out of it if not for you."

"Well, nor would you have gotten *into* it."

Harry wondered whether she referred to her own early suspicions about Faulkner, or if she had perhaps caught the whiff of Harry's envy.

She dragged one of her petticoats near; their time was running short.

"Will you not return to the mews, then?" she asked.

He shook his head. "No, your mother knows my face quite well after this morning."

"I told you, she pays no attention to those outside the peerage."

"It is easy to underestimate people, Allison." Yes. *Easy.* Just as *he* had once underestimated *her*.

Allison's shoulders shimmied at his remark—something she did, he'd noticed, when she bristled at something.

"It's not the only reason I won't be returning, though." He

looked around his apartment as she pulled a petticoat on overhead. He saw beyond the splinters to his once orderly bookshelves, to his chairs by the fire, the surface of his little desk bathed in golden sun . . .

"This is my home, Allison. I love it here."

She stopped herself before the next petticoat, giving the apartment her shy attention. Could she see in it what he saw?

"This humble home is the one I'd hoped to bring you to." Her focus snapped back to him and the gathering of courage became a harder thing. He patted the pallet. "I imagined this as our marriage bed." He huffed a quiet laugh before looking to the window. "Sometimes the sunset makes the whole room turn strange with rosy light. I'd hoped to see that with you and bathe in it."

He nodded in the direction of the far window. "I have had you there. But I've wanted you there, by the fire, and in the bed too. I've wanted to make love to you every day in this place. I've wanted to hang the kettle in the hearth and prepare your tea. I've longed to sit in those now splintered chairs and steal glances at you over the top of my novel. I've longed for you to steal glances back." How he wished he could more easily rise up and take her hand. "Primrose, this is not only my home. It is all I have to offer as *our* home. I have to be as honest as I can about what life with me would look like."

She nodded slowly, seriously. Harry knew her well enough to know the smile she wore was a brave one, summoned over top of much uncertainty.

"I can imagine how lovely it must have been before," she said. "Truly, I can." She stroked his leg for a few seconds, then pulled the second petticoat overhead and stood to tie its ribbons.

"You have to go," sighed Harry, unable to keep the disappointment from his words.

"I'm sorry, but if my 'questioning' goes on much longer, my mother will demand my father take her to Bow Street. And they will not find me there, will they?"

Allison helped him to his feet before she left, so that he could help her back on with her feminine trappings. He handed her pins from the broken mug as she put the last details in order. As the pins in the mug grew fewer, a lonely shadow in his heart grew greater. He handed her the last one and committed the sight of her to memory as she placed it.

She took his hand and kissed his cheek. "Please be careful, at least until Giddy is found."

Harry knew better than to give her any reassurance about Giddy when all he could account for was himself. "I will," he promised.

She turned to leave, but he squeezed her hand before it slipped away. He pulled her back.

"If this was another stolen moment, Primrose, then let it be the last."

She looked up at him, her eyes stark. He lost himself in them, perhaps for a final time. She nodded once, almost imperceptible.

And then she was gone, taking with her an essence that suddenly felt essential to any place feeling a home.

20

Back at home, Allison encountered her father's harried complaints on her behalf—*"How dare they traumatize a young lady like that, asking you to recount murder!"*—and found her mother only half-recovered from her spell, too dazed to notice Allison leaving the house again, alone.

Allison had neither desired Hayden's escort nor wished to call a hack. She chose anguish as her company, keeping her eyes down to conceal tears from passersby. The baskets of fruits and meats, made up hastily by the kitchen staff, were fit for the king yet felt paltry in her white-knuckled grip. One for Faulkner. One for Beatrice and Lord Merton. *Her condolences.*

But the death of a vengeful duke was not the thing in this world for which she was most sorry, despite what the black ribbon around her sleeve told others.

No, what she was most sorry for was the reckless batting of her lashes at Harry one year ago in Bartswell—sorry for the lack of reins she'd kept on her flirtation. She was sorry for not sparing his kind, young heart from a path that led them both to dead ends.

She had approached *him*. *She* had encouraged *him*. *She* had brought up marriage in their letters. And when the weeks drew out beyond his last letter without another? It was *she* who entitled herself to heartbreak.

How could she be so selfish as to feel that heartbreak again, when all Harry had asked was that she *decide*?

He'd caught her noticing something as she tidied his room. She had rediscovered the smudged *Dear Primrose* at the top of a blank letter, only this time, that letter had been in two pieces. Harry's pain was such that he must have torn it when he returned home from Lord Merton's. *She, Primrose, was the cause of his distress.*

Her certainty, her optimism—she had won at luring him past his demons. But somewhere their hearts had crossed, and it was she who suffered demons now.

What would it have been like if, ten days earlier, she'd not found him a broken man, but happy by his hearth instead? Their missing letters, a dreadful misunderstanding? Why, she'd have skipped the ball at Willis' for the altar! Why could she have not found him thus? Found him when her heart was still pounding with rebellious zeal? When she'd not yet been burdened by so many cruel realities—by hunters lurking and differences looming?

Had it been so, they would now be wed. They would be in his un-splintered chairs, reading his un-tattered books, before retreating to his sensible bed to do unsensible things. Things such as they had just done. Allison rubbed her arms to soothe the frisson that flew across them at the thought. Her womb still ached from their act— their lawless, incredible act.

He had, as always, been more judicious than she, trying to bail away. Yet she had kept him there, not wishing to part with even a second of an act they may never share again. Perhaps she was still as naive as she had always been, but she could picture herself with no other than him. She could not picture her heartache ever cooling over, building some new love atop the old. And certainly not with some titled toff as was permitted by her class.

No. It would either be Harry or no one at all. In the haze of finding the latter more possible, she had abandoned herself to the moment. Had done as she wished.

And *he* had called her on it. *No more stolen moments.*

The sweet memory of him inside of her was still so fresh. The fullness. The nearness. *Who would reject such a chance at happiness even if it could not last?* The thought made her want to smile and cry at once.

The morning had gone serious, just as she had asked for, and just as she had dreaded. Now she had to decide. For his sake, and, she realized, for her own.

Allison turned the corner. *There, ahead, was* Lord Faulkner's townhouse. Much smaller than his father's but with a facade twice as elegant.

She wiped her eyes and straightened, moving both baskets to one hand in order to lift the brass knocker. *Clack clack.*

The glossy black door cracked open. An elderly butler filled the gap.

"The Duke of Montagu is not taking visitors at present, my lady."

The Duke of Montagu. The title almost staggered her.

The butler was already closing the door.

"Wait."

He paused, and she thrust the handle of one of her baskets at him.

"Would you please see that the duke gets this?"

The butler opened the door enough to take the basket before shutting it just inches from Allison's face. Faulkner's new title still vibrated on her tongue. She did not like it.

Turning back to the street, she spied Miss Stephanie Lyons approaching with a female companion. Miss Lyons' creamy complexion glowed with a smile until she spotted Allison and schooled her lips into a shape more somber.

"Lady Allison," she said in greeting as they passed.

"Miss Lyons. Oh, I am afraid he is not taking visitors at—"

But as soon as Miss Lyons' companion knocked, they were whisked discreetly inside.

Faulkner made an exception for his betrothed, because of course he did.

Allison rallied herself not to be hurt, but she was no fool as to the connection she held to his father's death. She swallowed a lump in her throat as she counted one of her few friendships deceased. She braced herself to possibly lose another.

The walk to Charles Street was not long enough to cleanse self-loathing from her face but perhaps it might be interpreted as grief.

The door of Lord and Lady Merton's home was opened reassuringly wide to her by . . . Lady Merton herself.

"Lady Allison." Beatrice whisked Allison's basket to a sideboard in the entry, before turning to regard her from the doorway to the drawing room. "You look positively . . ." Her sharp eyes flicked up and down Allison's yellow polonaise, ". . . sunny."

Allison felt the shame of not changing into something more

somber than her hopeful little morning frock before noticing that Lady Merton might be one to talk. The marchioness donned a lurid shade of red. She had foregone a fichu and her plunging neckline threatened to spill a nipple. The only marks of grief on her were a black mourning ribbon and the downturn of her heavily stained lips.

Her comment seemed a sign that their friendship was not long to last, until she suddenly opened her arms wide. "Darling, come."

Relief washed over Allison, luring her swiftly into Lady Merton's waiting arms. She could not tell a soul about her morning with Harry, least of all the marchioness, but could let her tears of confusion fall here, let them be mistaken for mourning.

To her surprise, though, no tears came. Wrapped in Beatrice's long and slender arms, Allison had anticipated comfort and safety—a maternal reassurance—yet, *nothing*. For all the woman's vibrance, her embrace was strangely limp, her arms, passively draped.

"It was a *dreeeadful* thing to see last night." Beatrice's drawl washed over Allison's ear with hot, gin-tinged breath. "I fear I shall never forget the sight."

Allison slipped out from the woman's drooping embrace and let herself be led to the drawing room's settee. Spotting the silver set on the tea table, Allison hasted to pour a cup for the marchioness. It was as much to help the marchioness sober up as it was to help Allison put off the inevitable.

She passed off the tea and poured a cup for herself, staring at it as she gathered courage. "Beatrice," she whispered, praying the moniker was still acceptable, "I am very sorry for the loss of your friend."

Lady Merton shifted herself to lounge the way she had at the bawdy play, but nothing felt as it had that day.

"It is a pity . . ." said the marchioness.

Allison nodded along somberly—

". . . about you and Lord Faulkner."

Allison's tea cup clicked indelicately back to the saucer. *About . . . what?*

"I know the two of you do not suit, but it makes me sadder, knowing what I know now."

"What you . . . know now?" Allison repeated the words in disbelief. How had their conversation started here, of all places, on *this* day?

"That Caesar was not long for this earth. That the marital demands of Faulkner's title would swoop down upon him so soon."

Oh. Allison set aside her teacup and tested a hand on the marchioness' knee. "Last night, did you stay very long at—"

"Was I there when he passed?"

Allison drew her lip between her teeth and nodded.

"Yes, dear. I saw him from this world. Held his hand. Heard his last wishes. Railed against his impotent physician. Scribbled down his last words. After all, he had no duchess to do so." She looked past Allison with icy eyes and swigged her tea like more gin. Her eyes nearly startled Allison from her seat when they flicked back to her. "Bow Street men visited my house this morning. Not your man, but others. I do not blame you for bringing him into Montagu's home, if that is what you worry."

It was *precisely* what she had worried. Allison's shoulders relaxed.

"No, I don't blame you at all." Beatrice's face changed, as it so often did, but for the first time, Allison saw her eyes glass over with raw emotion. A tear spilled. Allison took a bracing breath. Of all Beatrice's fickle expressions, this was the most trustworthy. The most frighteningly real.

The woman put a cool hand to Allison's cheek. "You are as a daughter to me."

The words clanged to the floor like a tin bowl. And Allison didn't know why.

She removed Lady Merton's hand from her face and held it. "That is still the kindest thing of you to say. You have fast become a mentor and friend and . . ." Allison wished to return the sentiment, to call her "like a mother" but could not.

"I forgive you all of it." Beatrice sighed and looked to the ceiling as if she could see heaven beyond it. Her gaze returned to Allison with fewer tears. "I do hope you see now, though, that the man who holds your affection merely used you to his ends."

"Pardon, but my—?"

"Your Runner. He needed to get his spying eyes into the den of the well-heeled to do his deed."

"His—his *deed?*" Allison shook her head in disbelief. Her love for Harry—what had it to do with anyone else? With her mother? With the marchioness? It should have—*could* have—been this precious thing had no one else existed.

Lady Merton sat up sharply taking both of Allison's hands desperately in her own. "He is beneath you in every manner. Promise me you will cast him forever from your thoughts."

The marchioness' shivering eyes drew her in, a Gorgon stare threatening to turn Allison to stone.

"No," said Allison.

"Pardon?"

"No."

The marchioness slammed their held hands to the seat in a tantrum. "Allison! Please!"

"I will address my affections in whatever manner I please!"

Lady Merton's face went a darker hue. Her trembling grip, unrelenting, almost painful.

"Lie down," commanded Allison, calmly as she could muster. "Do not be ill over it. We can talk. I will stay."

Beatrice did as Allison bade, too racked with distress to oppose her.

Allison looked around the room helplessly. *Where is a footman? Lord Merton, for that matter?* Before she could stand to give Beatrice space, the marchioness' feet were kicked up over her lap. Allison sighed and rested her hands on Lady Merton's skirts, smoothing them as she sought a change of subject.

"Tell me something of the late duke. A fond memory perhaps? You shared many summers on the Continent, with Montagu and his duchess, did you not?"

"We did."

"Tell me of those days."

"The Duchess of Montagu. Her name was Adeline. She was my dearest friend."

Brilliant. Now she is reminded of not one dead friend but two. Allison cursed herself for the clumsy segue, yet Beatrice's voice steadied.

"The duke always let the same large cottage on a tributary of the Seine. In my first summer there, Adeline insisted we set up easels on the water at dawn and paint." Lady Merton looked down past her chin at Allison. "I was not so fond of being up at dawn. She made me sit there with her each morning until, at last, I rendered an adequate watercolor of the stream. I had never suffered so sedate a hobby in all my life to that point, but, bless her, I enjoyed it.

"It was my *last* summer there, though, which I will never forget. It was somehow more grotesque than last night."

The summer she spoke of, no doubt, was when the duchess

died giving birth to Faulkner. Details of her passing were not scarce. Allison avoided Beatrice's eyes, wishing again she'd not made mention of the past. She continued to absently stroke the marchioness' skirts, soothing herself as much as Beatrice.

"I'd always thought Adeline very fortunate in her husband. He indulged her hobbies and her desire for travel. He told riveting war stories and looked every part the hero then. He kept her smartly apart from his affairs, letting her see nothing but the man who doted . . ."

Allison was only half-listening to the merits of Montagu—a man she loathed—when her unfocused eyes were caught by something on the wall across the room. It was a plaque with an angled sword mounted on it. Her vision sharpened, drawn by the curious fact that, judging by two empty pins, there ought to have been another weapon crossed with it. Her eyes landed on the sword's decorative hilt, admiring its beauty—

". . . but that summer, I saw Montagu for what he *really* was."

—its *familiar* beauty. A checkered inlay of nacre and lapis. Just the same as the dagger dropped, then taken back, by Harry's hunter.

The air felt thin. A sense of imminent danger. *This wasn't over, none of this was over.*

Beatrice had stopped talking, and Allison realized, somehow, through her panic, that she'd been cued for a reply. "And what *was* Montagu?" asked Allison.

"A murderer. Just as your Runner claims. And just as your Runner is himself."

The house was still. Excruciatingly silent. Lady Merton's legs, so heavy across Allison's lap. She had no self-govern over what she uttered next:

"And what are *you*, Lady Merton?"

There it was in Lady Merton's eyes again. That horrible sense of the truth. She raised up on her elbows and answered with no drop of frailty. "A vengeful mother."

Allison shoved at Beatrice's legs, but they were dead weight.

"*Stay,*" commanded Beatrice.

"No!" Allison shoved again, extracting herself enough to lurch from the settee, turning and running straight into a gray wool waistcoat, or was it a granite wall? Her eyes scanned upward with feeble hope. *The footman? Lord Merton?* She knew such hopes were foolish even before she saw the face.

She'd seen it once before and only from very far away, but as all the pieces fell together, she knew—*Giddy.*

She stepped back and the giant of a man did not pursue her. He merely made a display of the pistol in his hand as he crossed his wrists and addressed his mistress.

"Your Ladyship."

Lady Merton straightened and took a sip of tea as though everything were genial.

Allison was in reach of her own cup on the tea table. She took it and flung its tepid contents at the woman's face. The marchioness did not even flinch as she blinked tea from one eye.

"*Lord Merton!*" Allison directed her scream to the ceiling as though he might be in an upstairs study, somehow unaware.

"He is not here." Lady Merton took a kerchief proffered by Giddy and daubed her cheek. "My husband is doubtless at the Magistrate's Court helping to sully the name of the dead."

"Why are you doing this, Beatrice?"

The woman stood to look down at her. "You cannot call me that anymore. I gave you a chance. I gave you an opportunity to renounce him. I would have found another way to hurt him."

"I thought I was as a daughter to you."

"You were!" The anguish in Beatrice's scream bordered on unendurable as the cracks in her facade opened wide. "You asked me to share my memories of Caesar? Of the Continent? Then I will tell you. The duke was not a friend but a lover, willing to do anything for me."

A memory lanced through Allison—Lady Merton screaming the duke's given name right before the shot rang out.

Allison's eyes burned. She was in some purgatory where she cried yet shed no tears. All attempts at emotion were rendered struck from likelihood, even as all became clear. She could do nothing now but be like Harry. Listen. Investigate. *A vengeful mother who . . . who, what?*

Then it hit her. She met Lady Merton's eye. "The officer killed on the *Diligence* all those years ago—he was your son."

"He was."

"With the Duke of Mont—"

"No."

Lady Merton gestured at a chair with a quick nod and Giddy responded, grabbing Allison's arm. She was flung roughly into the seat.

"Perhaps you have heard certain *things* about me over the years. I promise you would have heard much more had you been alive in my youth. I was not born to this lavish world, but I had a penchant for facade, and the madams of London could see that. Do you catch my meaning?"

The past weeks had been a whirlwind education in worldliness. Prior to them, she may not have understood, but now? "I do."

"I found my way to the ton as a mistress, with master after master until I met the duke. That officer in the brig? He had a name. My *son* had a name. Jonathan. He was born many trysts ago, but when I begged the duke to buy him a rank—to elevate him—he did it for me. And then your pathetic little deck swab cut him down."

"Harry was attacked."

"And right he should have been for mutinying!" Beatrice's wrath came and went. She folded her hands politely at her waist. Allison recognized it—this tendency toward facade. It came with the territory as a woman of their set. It was the very illusion Allison once strived for and often failed at. She was too guileless, too earnest, and suddenly—in the face of her opposite—was very glad for who she was.

"I loved Caesar. He did not bear me Jonathan, but he bore me another."

Allison searched her mind. Where had the marchioness hidden a second son? Then she realized, *in plain sight.*

"Faulkner?"

"Yes."

"Adeline was not with child when we arrived that final summer. She could not bear any. It was *I* who arrived with the duke's child in me. I've always had a strong stomach for the sea, but I was sick many times crossing the channel that year, so I knew quite early. I was not worried, though. Lord Merton had asked for my hand a year before—never even having had me in his bed—can you imagine? I decided I would simply turn back to London and marry him."

"You do not treat your husband very well."

The marchioness waved the comment off. "He was too dull to notice."

No, not too dull, thought Allison. *Too in love.* "What of the duke that summer?"

"My error was in ever telling him my condition." Lady Merton examined her own hands as though they would spark the memory.

"He came back to me, that first night on the Seine after I'd told him I was leaving. His hands were swollen and red from strain. He told me he had done it, killed his wife—my *friend*—to marry me." She scoffed. "He earnestly thought that would please me."

"It pleased you enough to remain his mistress." Allison's words drew a cold glare from Giddy, but the marchioness merely shrugged.

"Because of what Caesar had done, there was the chance to have my child raised as heir to a dukedom. It was enough for me to stay and bear Faulkner in secrecy. The story back in England would be that Adeline had died in birth somewhere in Florence and the duke would return with his kin alone."

"So Lord Faulkner is illegitimate. A bastard."

Lady Merton put an astonished hand to her breast. "How crude a term, Lady Allison. I did not see you as one to use it."

"I suppose I do not see the shame in the word."

"You, perhaps not, but the ton? I cannot have them destroy him."

Lady Merton did not elaborate on what that meant for Allison, but the implication was clear; she was not intended to live with such knowledge. She took a deep breath. "If you were still willing to stomach the duke after his deed, why not marry him?"

"He offered for me many times over my confinement on the Continent, but I could not so much as touch him after Adeline. Grief and anger drove my stubbornness to accept Lord Merton instead. I was getting older. I needed security. I needed to be in the same circles that my son would be raised in but never too close." The marchioness bent down to be level with Allison. "There is some part of me, dear, that is a husk. I have been such a great pretender for so long that I cannot often tell when I am pretending."

"I find that very sad," said Allison.

"As do I." The regret in Beatrice's voice was real. "It took a decade to forgive the duke enough to return to his bed. Life grew dull once youth and beauty faded, but youth was always something I could seize with him. Caesar would forever look at me the same way he did when we were young. It is a powerful thing, that."

Allison imagined so. She could picture it with Harry. Holding hands in old age and seeing the past in one another's eyes.

The marchioness forgot her wistfulness and raised an eyebrow. "What gave me away?"

"You've a dagger missing, though I suspect it is not far." Allison glared at Giddy who glared right back.

"Well, well. Aren't we keen, *Primrose*?"

Keener than the woman knew, for Allison's mind came to life with memories. The name *Primrose* gave away more yet.

"You went to Harry's home last night. Why?"

Allison waited for the marchioness to deny it.

But the marchioness shrugged and answered, flatly. "Tormenting him was no longer enough, not once he killed Caesar. I went to kill him."

Allison nodded, her suspicions correct. "You heard him call me Primrose last night. It was *you* who tore the letter with my name on it." Allison *tsked*. "You must keep better hold on your emotions."

The marchioness smiled slyly. "And why were *you* in his rooms this morning?"

Allison did not hesitate. "To be rutted by him on the window-sill."

The marchioness took a long, bracing breath, her eyes flickering from one expression to the next. There was indignation, surely. But also, the barest hint of pride? Allison did not wait for her to express either.

"So, all this time, you knew where Harry lived? Knew his real name? Why did you not flinch when he showed at the ball?"

"Lady Allison, I did not, prior to last night, sully myself with such business. I told the duke a year ago that I wanted my boy avenged. I did not need to know what contacts he made or what journals he scoured for his clues. He knew better than to bring me anything but proofs of that revenge . . . the final being proof of death. Such is how I have always had my needs met. All Caesar had handed to me by that point was a letter signed simply, 'Harry,' which confessed to Jonathan's slaying." The marchioness frowned. "A letter which I have since lost.

"So you see, I knew very little before last night. Caesar gave me all I needed from his deathbed, including his surnames, both old and new. And then he died. Leaving another soul to be avenged. I summoned Giddy to take me to the address straight away.

"Unfortunately, while I was in your Runner's stinking garret, he was *here*—beneath my very roof—being patched up alongside my guileless husband."

"And now you will lure him back," said Allison. "Using me to do so. And all for some poorly perceived wrong."

"There is nothing flawed with my perception. Mr. Stinton killed my son and I will—"

Allison stood up, forcing Lady Merton back. "But there *is* something wrong with your perception! You admitted it yourself. You have been a pretender for so long that you understand nothing!"

Giddy took a step forward in the periphery, but Allison could not stop herself.

"You challenge me for loving a murderer, yet the details of *your* lover's deeds are far more dooming. He murdered an innocent woman. *Your friend.* But what is a friend to you, I wonder? You call me friend—a *daughter*—one day and use me as bait the same. You are a scarecrow, stuffed not with straw but with contradictions, *Your Ladyship*." Allison spat the noble address with venom.

"Do not call me that!"

"Another contradiction!" Allison shot a quick look at Giddy, daring him to move, before looking back to Beatrice. "You wish for me to use your given name? You told me only moments ago that I could not. Which is it? You loved a friend but seized on the advantage of her murder. You loved a duke but would not wed him. You hated that duke but would not disown him. You are a lost soul, incomplete."

Allison smoothed her skirts and waited. She was, as ever, no gambler. She had no face for cards and her steadiness was no facade. Yet she wondered how long her heart could hold constant beneath the cutting gaze of the marchioness.

"Giddy." Lady Merton threw a look over her shoulder at him. He straightened with military readiness.

Fear came then, but Allison still did not waver.

"I *understood* Caesar," said Lady Merton. "To this day, I understand the dissonance that causes a man to kill for love."

Giddy stepped behind Allison and took her shoulders in a bruising grasp.

"More than one thing may be possible at once, Lady Allison. You are too young to see that yet." Lady Merton gestured to one side with an open palm, and stared at it was a heavy-lidded gaze. "I truly am fond of you." Then she raised her other hand and her eyes drifted to it, considering. "But I also have revenge to fulfill. If you cannot denounce your lover, I see no other way. I am sorry for it."

Allison met the woman's allegedly sorry eyes. "Perhaps you are right about the complexity of things. Because I am sorry too, yet I am also grateful to witness the tragedy of you. I once dreaded I was on the same path. The path to losing myself, to denying my heart's desires. Now I see you and that fear is gone. I gain clarity. Know myself a little better. My love for Harry does not waver in the face of whatever you think you are going to do. To me. Or to him."

Lady Merton gestured to Giddy. "Downstairs with her."

"I pity you," said Allison. "'Tis an empty place your soul inhabits."

But the marchioness did not answer again.

21

Allison's blindfold was the very same sash Lady Merton had used before their trip to the "theater." Only this time, it was poorly tied. Allison could make out the lap of her skirt beyond her nose, as well as the slow movement of a sliver of daylight across the cellar's dirt floor. Time did not pass quickly.

Allison had thought herself to see others so well, yet here she had been flinging herself at the affections of a ruthless schemer.

Lady Merton was undeniably skillful in her manipulations, though, to admit it left a bitter taste. The woman had built a reputation from nothing, walking the rope between scandal and elegance with such flawless balance that murders and affairs went unearthed for decades. Poor Lord Merton. And Faulkner too.

Deceit, Allison decided, was not made up solely of lies. It existed in the ever-changing expressions of Lady Merton as she searched for a look that suited her ends. It was in her politely folded hands and icy tones. It was in the denial of who she loved.

Allison had spent so much of her young womanhood straining to delight those around her. She had, for years, stood on the steps of Willis' Rooms, bracing herself to perform, to *win* at something nebulous. But she no longer wished to win. What was to be won without love?

donk

donk

donk

Someone knocked on the front door, right overhead.

Allison screamed, or tried to, but a gag blotted out her cries. She heard the door being opened. Heard Giddy greet someone with muffled words and then—

"Lady Weldon to see Lady Merton, please."

Allison's eyes grew. *No.* She screamed harder, more futilely, into the rag. *Mother! Do not come in!*

Their conversation faded as Lady Weldon was led deeper into the marchioness' lair. Allison hung on the faint echo of every step and murmur above until, many minutes later, she heard her mother again . . .

Leaving.

Harry grunted as his knee thudded to the floor. He could not help but continue the tidying Allison had started. How else was he to keep his mind from wandering to her, from wondering if she would ever come back through his door? His final words to her were an attempt to guard his heart, but it was far too late to not be ruined by the loss of her.

He finished collecting the stationery where Allison had started, leaving it in a neat little pile. He uncrumpled the paper she had earlier thrown. It was half of his attempted letter, with *Primrose* at the top. He did not remember her tearing it that morning.

An urgent *KNOCK KNOCK* shot him upright. His heart jumped and he dropped the note. If his injury protested his haste to stand, he hardly noticed. He was too eager to reach the door—to welcome Allison's return. It *had* to be her.

"One moment!"

He nearly slipped on the scattered book pages as he tore open the door, banging it into the fallen bookcase.

His smile died.

The grand Countess Weldon stood at his door.

Her gray eyes assessed him, tracing him up and down in what could only be disapproval. Not awaiting an invitation, she pushed past him into the destroyed apartment. In the middle of the room, she turned. "I remember you."

He lowered his eyes.

"I noticed you as a failed footman, then as a successful gardener. And this morning you were a Bow Street Runner bringing ill news to my door. I thought I was going mad." She approached, tipping her chin up to better glare at him from beneath a luxuriously-brimmed hat. "But I suspect I also know you from somewhere else. From a year ago. From the stables in Bartswell. Is that true?"

"Yes, Your Ladysh—"

"So which of these things are you, *really*?"

He met her eyes.

"A Runner."

"And are you also my daughter's lover?"

The question flew into his stomach like a punch. "I—"

"Do not lie to me." She raised a finger in warning.

He met her eyes, expecting to see ire. Instead he saw pain. So he summoned humility rather than courage. "Yes, Your Ladyship."

Her lips tightened. "I appreciate your honesty. It means I can trust you for the rest of it."

And what *was the rest of it?* The demand for marriage? Or for banishment?

"How did you find me?" he asked.

"You mean apart from seeing this address on the incoming post dozens of times at Tallyside? I will grant, putting *Lady Harriet* on the front of your letters had me long fooled into thinking Allison had found a new and proper friendship."

The canniness of the countess' deduction left him raw. Unease outpaced his curiosity, and he inquired no further.

Lady Weldon looked to the windows and squinted in the late day sun that poured through. "You are the last person I wished to come to but the only I feel can help."

"I don't understand."

"Allison is in danger."

If the last words from Lady Weldon had been a punch, *this* was a cannonball. Harry's vision flashed white as he absorbed what the countess had said. He recovered. "Where is she right now?"

"With the marchioness, Lady Merton."

"How do you believe her in danger? I thought the marchioness was a friend?"

"Allison left to bring condolences to Lord Faulkner and the Mertons and has not returned all afternoon."

Harry swallowed, suddenly wondering what Lady Weldon had worked out about Allison's earlier delay for 'questioning.'"

"After recovering from my bout of shock, I felt it my duty to pay Lady Merton my condolences and perhaps find my daughter there."

"And how *was* Lady Merton?"

"Fine?" Lady Weldon strolled to the far window.

"Careful," said Harry. "There is broken glass."

The elegant woman retracted her foot like an owl pulling up a talon. "Do you live like this, always?"

Harry didn't mean to, but a laugh escaped. "No, Your Ladyship. I do not. The duke did this."

"Why ever for?" Her gray eyes were truly lost. Her words, dusted with a subtle and instinctive defense of the duke

"Vengefulness. For something very long ago."

Her eyes brimmed with questions, but her lips curled between her teeth, keeping them back. A habit not unlike that of her daughter.

"Please," begged Harry. "Tell me of the danger."

Lady Weldon's eyes popped wide, slapped awake by his question.

"Lady Merton did not seem distressed when I arrived, nor was she her usual playful self. There was a coldness about her that set me ill at ease."

"And was Allison there?"

"No. But . . ."

"But?"

"Her basket was." Lady Weldon looked around, apparently needing a place to sit. Realizing there was none, she continued. "The basket she had brought for consolation was untouched on the sideboard in the—"

"Could Allison not have dropped it off and left?"

Lady Weldon delivered him an impatient look; he would do well not to interrupt. "I spoke to the marchioness and, of course, asked after Allison. Lady Merton claimed she had never arrived at all." Lady Weldon suddenly and vigorously shook her head, on the verge of some emotion. "I do not understand why she would lie. Perhaps . . . perhaps . . ." There was a detectable tremble in the countess' clasped hands. It traveled up her arms until her shoulders heaved up and down in an outburst of sobs.

Harry risked impertinence, sweeping forward to hold her. The moment she was in his arms, her body sagged.

"Perhaps I only *want* to believe she is in danger. I pushed her toward connection with Lady Merton and it worked. She looks more to the marchioness now for advice than she does to me. I wonder whether she's not simply run off to live under Beatrice's roof, quietly abandoning me."

Harry almost said, *Allison would never—*, but wouldn't she? Abandonment would be precisely what the countess would face if Allison showed herself again at Harry's door. Lady Weldon sniffed loudly and pushed against Harry to right herself. He dropped his arms and stepped back, recovering the propriety that was surely on her mind.

He averted his gaze as Lady Weldon whipped out a kerchief to blow her nose. His eyes landed on the desk. On the pile of stationery. On the unrumpled half of his blank letter.

"I am probably hysterical," sniffed the countess. "My daughter is likely fine and—"

"No," said Harry.

Lady Weldon met his eyes, all hope.

"I don't believe she is."

Something wasn't right. Allison had noticed something earlier, and perhaps it was the same thing he had. His letter torn in two. Someone had been there.

Harry plucked a long wooden box from the bookcase and opened it. Lady Weldon gasped softly when he pulled his pistol from it.

"You were right to come, Lady Weldon. Take me to the marchioness."

The whole of Charles Street was in shadow as the day grew late. The summer breeze carried a brisk chill as it squeezed through streets and mews of Mayfair. Hayden and Lady Weldon had seen Harry to the nearest corner, where he'd instructed that they wait in the carriage. It took many vows of reassurance to convince the protective footman that Harry should go to the house alone.

The ground floor windows of the Merton residence were shuttered, but the amber flicker of a candle in the drawing room seeped through the cracks.

Harry went around back to the mews. He waited for a gap between passersby before stealing inside through the stable. He detected little in the way of servants' activity as he passed through.

The home of the marquessate did not have much of a garden. The house was too grand and extended too far back.

He stalked across the little yard and knelt near the corner of a window to peek over its sill. A grand dining room. Not a soul within. He hurried low past the back entrance to the windows on the other side, looking in one, then the next. He was about to proceed to the last when movement caught his eye. A tall, broad-shouldered man in gray livery passed through the downstairs hall. A butler? He disappeared so suddenly through a door that Harry was unsure whether what he thought he'd seen was real—a pistol in the butler's hand. When did butlers carry pistols?

Harry retraced his steps, hoping to follow the man through the other windows. But there was no more sign of him. He looked to the upstairs windows. *Dark.* Then he looked down. A narrow, grated window at his toes was gray with soot. The kitchens.

He lowered himself to the ground with a wince and put an ear to the obscured portal. The murmur of a lady's voice came straight away. The marchioness. He strained to catch her words, but they eluded him. A plodding baritone cut in. "What now, Your Ladyship?" The dutiful, resonant voice had a faint familiarity—one Harry had not quite remembered from the rooftops but knew from the Gossingtons' drive. *Here was Giddy.*

Harry's breath quickened. Any doubts that Allison was in danger were scattered to the winds. They had her. They had her because they wanted *him*. A wave of fury crashed over him, soaking his good senses. How could he have missed this? He heaved himself upward and drew his pistol from its place at his waist.

But suddenly, the voices were louder and more clear. He pressed his back to the wall just as the servant's door on the opposite end of the yard was opened. He inched himself sideways behind the foliage of a topiary shrub.

"And how do we lure him after that?" Giddy's baritone rumbled clearly from the open door.

"We will lure him with her disappearance, of course. The investigator shall investigate. There is nothing suspect in that."

"Will he not be wary of you? After last night?"

"He does not know what Montagu was to me. Now go, reassure Andrews and the cook that they may rest until tomorrow. Let them think me gracious in my grief." The sturdy thuds of Gideon's steps headed for the mews house.

"And Giddy—" The marchioness' hiss turned him back round. "Find me immediately if my husband returns from Bow Street. Remember, I am *ill* with grief, and that is why the house is empty."

Harry watched through the leaves as Gideon nodded to his

mistress and dragged himself to the mews.

The kitchen door banged shut.

He does not know what Caesar was to me . . .

It was not hard to guess at; *lover* was the suspicion. But the marchioness' connection to the *Diligence*, to the mutiny? Yet unknown. The answers lay inside the house.

If the woman or her lackey had disturbed a single ribbon on Allison's gown or so much as a hair on her head, they would pay for it the rest of their lives.

Harry hurried quietly back past the house's garden entrance, to the lower servant's door. He pressed an ear to it. No sound. He pulled away and aimed his attention toward any sounds from within. A door on the ground floor was shut somewhere. Light steps resumed on wooden flooring, at a dignified pace, before being deadened by a carpet.

Satisfied the marchioness had made her way upstairs, Harry eased open the cellar door.

He stepped into a darkened kitchen. Half chopped vegetables rested eerily *in situ* beside a knife on the work table. The scent of rosemary hanging up to dry almost salvaged the place from its sense of doom, but against the deathly silence, it was not enough.

Harry crossed through a small archway into a cask-filled antechamber of the storerooms. He gently pushed open one door and found a closet full of grain sacks. He opened the next on racks of wine and crates of brandy. He tightened his grip on his pistol as he opened the third . . .

And there she was. Her figure blended with her chair in shadow. The eerie shape was branded into his very soul. Here it was—all his nightmares come to pass. But then she moved, turning her blindfolded face in profile as though she felt him there.

He rushed to her, tearing the blindfold from her eyes and the wad of cloth from her jaw. He crushed his lips to hers as soon as they were freed. The rag had left a fusty taste; he kissed her even harder with a vow to destroy whoever had put it there.

His lips finally, reluctantly let go of the kiss. Her face nudged forward, as though she needed the lost kiss even more than he.

"Harry." An urgent whisper. "She's still here."

"I know. She's upstairs."

"And Giddy?"

"In the rear house."

He rocked back on his heels to study her binds. Her skirts puckered between each tightened ring of rope. But he spotted one of the knots. A poor one. Clearly Giddy had never been a sailor. He set to work.

"What is her part in this?" he whispered. "Were the two of them lovers? She and Caesar?"

Allison wriggled as the binds grew slack. "They were."

"And what of the mutiny? Did she tell you the connection there?"

"The officer was her son."

"They had a son?"

"They . . ." Allison wrested one arm from the slack rope and stared at the angry red burn it had left against her forearm. Harry saw it too but could not bear to look at it overlong. Allison met his eyes. "He was only her son. But they had another, together." She paused her wriggling. "They had Lord Faulkner."

The knot between Harry's fingers tumbled from his grip. "But he—"

"He does not know. He's never known." Allison shook her head as the final knot came free.

"He is a bastard?" asked Harry.

She helped Harry to slough away the remaining rope. And he helped her to stand.

"Illegitimate. Not a duke," she answered.

Lingering resentment toward Faulkner fell away like the rope to Allison's feet. Guilt took its place. The target of Harry's envy—and he could admit it was envy now—had always been a bastard, same as he. The man was about to fall from the highest of heights.

Harry refocused on the present, squeezing her hand to keep her with him. "Did Lady Merton say what she was doing? How long can we expect her to be upstairs?"

"She only came down briefly to fetch Giddy. The only other thing I heard was a visitor an hour or more ago, overhead. My mother."

"I know. She is why I am here."

Allison's hand went limp in his. "What?"

"She came to me to find you. She saw your basket on the sideboard and knew something wasn't right."

The color drained from Allison's face. "But how—?"

"Suffice to say that I know where you get your investigative skills from." The light-hearted words did nothing to bring her focus back around.

"Harry." Her voice held a new fear—not of the woman holding her captive but of what her mother's knowledge of them must mean.

Harry shook her arm to rouse her, then took her by the hand. "Later, Primrose. We must get out of here first."

Allison tried to ground herself with the feel of Harry's hand around hers. *Mother had gone to—*

No. She shook her head. Harry was right. They had to get out.

The light through the sooty windows was almost gone, but she did her best to point them toward the servant's stairs she'd been earlier dragged down by Giddy.

Harry had just placed a foot on the first riser when steps were heard behind the door at the top. Allison had only just registered the sound when Harry pushed her urgently away.

She caught her balance and rushed to tuck herself against the stony wall of the staircase's rise, the only place in the barren quarters where she might go to hide.

The footsteps were too indelicate to be that of Beatrice.

Allison hissed a whisper at Harry just as the door's hardware rattled. "He will have a pistol."

She heard the ready *click* of Harry's hammer in the dark.

A dull band of light slipped past Giddy's shadow into the space below. By it, Allison could see a sliver of Harry where he pressed himself to the wall, ready to pounce or charge. She held her breath.

"I've something for you to eat," called Giddy, almost gently, into the dark.

Cutlery rattled against a tray; he could not have a readied pistol *and* a tray. Allison locked eyes on Harry's shadow. Did he understand as she did?

Giddy's heel clopped onto the first stone step, then another—the tray's rattle punctuating each stage of the descent. Then a hesitation, a noticing of something not right—

There was a dull click in the dark, a misfire, and Harry rushed the stairs so fast that the explosive clash of the tray seemed instant. Allison shielded her head as its contents spilled overside of the steps. She prayed Giddy himself would not land atop her as a teacup shattered at her feet.

"Lady Mer—!" Giddy's shout was stifled.

There was a metallic slap as the tray was weaponized against a body, but Allison could not discern whose. It clanged down the steps in a racket, and Harry and Giddy came tumbling down after.

Allison winced as their reeling bodies slammed into the stone wall at the base of the steps.

It was a helpless feeling, seeing Harry grapple with a man of such size. To catch only hopeless glimpses of their bloodsport as they rolled through the streak of light from above—a four-armed monster.

Allison heard the *shing* of the silver tray as it was recovered from the slate floor and held her breath—

CLANG!

Giddy's unconscious face flopped into the slash of light.

Harry appeared in the light too, looking down at his work. A dark line of blood ran from the corner of his lip.

A pistol's hammer clicked and, for a moment, Allison's mind fooled her into thinking it Harry's, but his misfired pistol had been abandoned in the fight.

"Do not move."

Harry straightened at the foot of the stairs, gazing stoically toward the new shadow darkening the door above. Lady Merton.

Relief over Giddy dissolved, replaced by the same helplessness as before.

Allison heard the rustle of Beatrice's taffeta skirts brushing the wall on the other side of the steps. It brought back the pleasure of their day out together—the companionable sound of their skirts swishing in unison. How wrong Allison had been about her.

Her thoughts returned to the present. To the skirt. The crimson hem hung over the edge of the steps on Allison's side as Beatrice made her slow descent.

Allison reached up, balled her fist around a handful of silk and dropped her entire weight.

Lady Merton's scream was cut off by the sound of a pistol's aimless report. Beatrice's angular body landed partly atop Allison in a jagged heap. Clawing hands tore at Allison's clothes, searching for a limb to attack. Allison struck out her leg violently, and a piercing shriek informed her that the strike landed true.

She tried to scramble away, just as footsteps rushed toward them. The heavy red blur of the marchioness was pulled off her.

"Be still," said Harry. "In the name of the king, you are under arrest."

Allison felt around herself, trying not to trip on her own hem as she stood.

Harry held the marchioness' arms behind her at the foot of the stairs near Giddy's unconscious form. He beckoned Allison hither with a nod.

There were no kisses or embraces this time, just lucid urgency. Harry gestured with his foot to where his pistol had fallen. "Pick it up, pull the hammer back, and keep it trained on Giddy until I have her secure." At her hesitation, he smiled. "We are together in this."

She lifted the pistol and stepped quickly back as though Beatrice could somehow snatch it from her with a mere look. But the marchioness seemed emptied of vigor and venom. Tears streaked her face, glowing amber by the scant light. The once faint lines of her face now seemed starkly furrowed.

"You will have nothing left. Nothing at all." The marchioness tossed a weak nod over her shoulder at the man who held her.

If I wed Harry, she means.

Lady Merton slumped in Harry's grip, and Allison lowered herself to the woman's eyes. "Tell me again, Lady Merton, *who* has nothing left? You corrupted me in many good ways, but you shall not corrupt me in the bad. I will not make your mistakes, and I've a whole life ahead of me."

22

Lord Merton hung his head and Harry caught a glimpse of Lady Merton beyond his shoulder in the drawing room. She sat, hands tied, in a chair under rigorous interrogation by Mr. Crofty. The marquess had been at the Magistrate's Court and had followed the Bow Street men when they were summoned to a disturbance at his own home. Harry did not envy what the marquess found on his arrival.

"It has been a long time coming." Merton's words were flat and unaffected.

"Do you mean you knew about her affair with the duke?" asked Harry.

"My mind knew, even as my heart rejected it. There is some buried part of me that understood what I was doing when I threw you the pistol on the stairs last night. Certainly, I saw Montagu attack you and I wanted to help, yet . . . there were underlying instincts in my action—instincts which would see me to hell."

"Do not be hard on yourself. You saved my life."

"There is more, though." The marquess slumped against the mantelpiece as the fire gently crackled. "I regret I had more information than even I was aware."

"How is that?"

Lord Merton borrowed a candelabra from the mantel and beckoned Harry to follow with a nod of his head. He walked past his arrested wife with nary a glance in her direction. They stepped over Giddy, slumped half-conscious in the dining room's archway, tied hand and foot.

At the dining table, Mr. Hayden and Allison ministered a soothing herbal tea to Lady Weldon—a scene Harry avoided as studiously as Merton avoided the eyes of his wife. Harry had not had a moment alone with Allison since Hayden and her mother had burst in two hours earlier, having heard the errant gunshot.

The marquess led Harry to the rear of the ground floor, not far from the cellar door. He reached a hand behind the frame of a mundane watercolor landscape and regarded it while he felt for something.

"My wife painted this, once upon a time." Lord Merton's wistfulness lasted scarcely a second before he pulled something from behind the frame.

A little folded letter. One Harry had not seen for months. One that had left him sweating in his sleep, dreading the exposure of his deed. His stolen letter to Rhys.

Harry stepped back and studied the marquess with narrowed eyes.

"I understand your distrust, Mr. Stinton. But this is not blackmail." He presented the letter to Harry. "It is yours."

Harry took it. "You have read it?"

"I have. I found it secreted away in my wife's jewelry box and thought I had come across a love note. But the contents puzzled me. Only now do I fully understand. Your secret is safe. However . . ." Lord Merton cast his eyes toward the murmurs filling the house. "Perhaps it needn't be?"

The marquess was fetched back to the drawing room by Mr. Crofty for more questioning, and Harry's mind wandered on his words. He flipped the small letter over and over in his hands. Lord Merton was right. The theft of the letter—once so consequential, so deadly—had been rendered null. Harry's act was in the open now, even to Mr. Crofty. All had reassured him that he'd only done what he had to survive.

Harry was caught off guard as a tall, elegant shadow came into the corner of his vision, stopping before drawing too near.

"You are adept at your profession."

Harry offered Lady Weldon an earnest shrug. "I'd have known nothing today if not for you, Your Ladyship. I see where your daughter gets her cleverness."

"We are not much alike, she and I."

"I once thought I was very different from her also." The words were out before Harry could recognize them as unwise.

"Pardon, but you *are* very different from her." A shiver drew Lady Weldon more erect, her hackles raised. "You will never come to her again. Do you understand?"

"I will never go to her again," agreed Harry. An easy promise. He had already told Allison as much. He would not go to her again. She must come to him. He could subject himself no longer to the uncertainty. Never again would he see her, *touch* her, only to not know whether he would again.

Lady Weldon nodded, seemingly satisfied with his answer. Yet she did not depart.

"For now, though, we are departing and I wonder whether you might use a comfortable ride back to Dryden?"

Harry could not school the astonishment from his face. He stared at her, agog, unsure whether his open jaw could be discerned by her in the low light.

Her shadow shifted uneasily. "I am grateful to you, Mr. Stinton. You found her safe. I wish to show my gratitude by delivering you home if you are ready. The other men from Bow Street have just taken Lady Merton and that dreadful valet away."

Harry pocketed the letter. And his heart clenched around the thought of one last carriage ride with his Primrose. "I accept."

Allison would never forget her last sight of the marchioness. Lady Merton had cast one final, pleading look over her shoulder—one of plain betrayal. Allison shook her head from time to time as though she could fling off the memory like water, but she knew it would take time to fade.

It was not much easier to remain in the present, where she sat knee-to-knee with Harry in the carriage, her mother crushed against her side.

It was past ten and the oil lamps of St. Giles did not glitter as Mayfair's did. There was so much to share with Harry, so much to cry and embrace over, yet they were trapped as they so often were. Gagged in proper, performative silence. She could not even see enough of his eyes in the dark to share their private, silent language.

The coachman cried *"ho!"* and they rolled to a stop at Eight Dryden.

Harry's knees brushed her skirts as he made his way out of the carriage. His boots hit the ground outside with a heavy slap and he turned, his eyes catching a glint of amber light from the carriage lantern.

Allison poured her heart into the look she gave him. There were no words that could contain it all, she thought—that was, until *he* said them.

"Tonight you look just as you did a year ago in Bartswell." He smiled as though seeing her for the first time. "Goodnight, Primrose."

And then Lady Weldon reached across her lap to pull shut the door, and Harry's lopsided smile was erased from the night.

Allison's father met them in the street with a lantern and she was led, like a child, into her own home. The front door clicked shut behind her and her mother brushed past, heading straight to the drawing room's settee.

The entry hall was warm with light from the sconces. Allison stared down at her yellow polonaise. The sunny frock, selected in a bout of hope, was filthy. Destroyed.

She remembered once more Beth's words about dalliances with roguish men, and what it did for one's wardrobe. *So it is.*

And that was what Harry had meant by invoking that night in Bartswell. He'd meant that adventure—or *mis*adventure—rather suited her. That was how he had fallen in love. By catching her in her least dazzling, yet most dynamic hour.

Allison was snapped from her thoughts by the realization she was in her father's embrace.

"All is well," he said, stroking her hair. But he pulled away with eyes of fear, eyes

betraying his own need for reassurance. He patted her shoulder and drifted upstairs.

A small and pitiful sound drifted to Allison's ears. She turned toward the drawing room. Her normally straight-backed mother was hunched over, a shuddering pile of moiré silk, weeping into her palms.

Allison stepped into the room, cautious that a more terrible side of her mother might awaken at any moment. Yet, even as she sat down alongside her, her mother's weeping did not change.

"Mama?" She'd not called her that in years.

Her mother gasped at the sound of the word and wept harder. "I . . . I thought . . . I thought I'd lost you."

Allison rested a hand on her mother's trembling back. She had never seen her this way before.

"I am rescued, Mama. All is well." Her own words were about as believable as when her father had uttered them a minute earlier.

Her mother lifted her swollen face from her palms, delivering a look of pure anguish before shaking her head.

"No, Allison. Before that . . . I was losing you to Lady Merton long before she took you."

The confession dropped like bricks into Allison's heart.

"But you *wished* for me to spend time with her, before we— before we knew her true character."

"I *did*. And it was for selfish reasons. And then, I *did not*. And it was also for selfish reasons." Her mother sniffed loudly and dropped her face back to her palms.

Allison had never seen her so small, so broken down. She could hardly bear to keep a hand on her mother's back, to feel the cata-strophic pain ripple through her.

"I am sorry that I do not . . . understand you better." The words were muffled by her mother's hands yet were perhaps the clearest thing ever spoken between them.

"I fear I am guilty of the same," whispered Allison. Truly not knowing this side of her mother who wept so earnestly.

"Yet still, I cannot . . ." Lady Weldon raised her eyes to Allison's. She did not finish her words. In cowardice, she waited for her daughter to understand.

And Allison *did* understand and removed her hand from her mother's back. "You will still not allow me to wed, as you see it, beneath me. Is that it?"

Her mother's eyes answered again, heavy with the toll of stubbornness.

Allison drew a long, slow breath. "Mother, I have been unfair. I was searching for all the ways you sought to hold me back—and they are many—but I failed at times to understand your affection. I can see now, some places where it was missed."

"I know I am not warm. 'Tis not strange that it was missed."

"Why do you push me so hard?"

"Toward great things?" Lady Weldon unwound, sitting taller. "I was blessed with great comforts Allison, but not great friends. It seemed I could not be accepted as myself. When I married your father, when I became a countess, it drew company to me like bees to nectar. I shined beneath it. I *found* myself."

She placed a hand on Allison's cheek. "Do not misunderstand me. I notice in you the possibility to be far more popular than I. I never wanted you to feel alone as I did, not for one second of your life."

"But I do not need the ton's adoration to feel loved. For me, it takes only a few." *Harry, Beth, Rhys, Hayden, Faulkner . . .* Her loneliest moments happened among greater numbers, when she had to hide her friendships in front of those she once exhausted herself to appease. She looked around. So many of those lonesome moments happened here, in her own home.

"I am glad you found yourself back then, Mother." Allison gently removed her mother's hand from her face and stood. She imagined a short silk ribbon tied between them and prepared herself to cut it. "I have found myself too."

Her mother's gray eyes swam in tears, waiting for whatever came next.

"If ever you wake up," said Allison, "and I am not here, it will not change that you are my mother, and I, your daughter. My mind is set on that."

Her mother choked on a sob.

"My mind will never change and my heart will be ready at a moment's notice, but I suspect you are not there yet."

Speechlessly, Lady Weldon shook her head.

"I love you." Allison bent down and kissed her mother's hair. The countess' pungent perfumes had faded, leaving behind only faint lavender and sweat. Allison held the scent in mind as she left the room.

Her mother's good intentions were muddied by ancient self-doubts. Allison could not wait forever for her mother's doubts to heal.

The sight of the garret's slanted beams grew tiresome, but how else was Harry to spend his time? His wound reminded him of its existence the very moment he left the Weldons' carriage and he could hardly move.

Now it begins, he thought. *Each day from here will feel a little less like waiting, a little more like moving on . . .*

The melancholy would improve once he had tools in hand, once he was able to right his bed and sand his stained floor. He would occupy himself in remaking his home. A vision of Allison flashed before him at the notion of "home."

Back at the Merton residence, Harry had been in the middle of detaining Giddy when a rush of frantic knocking disrupted the quiet. It was Mr. Hayden who barged in before any came to answer. Allison's mother was close behind and screamed Allison's name upon seeing her safe. They had heard the gunfire from the corner and could wait no longer.

Harry knew no mother of his own, so it was with almost academic curiosity that he observed their reunion. Lady Weldon's embrace of her daughter was tight enough to smother a fire, regardless of their feuds. And their tears had flowed freely like gin in St. Giles.

He could not imagine her leaving her mother then. Could not imagine her choosing him . . .

> *hands*
>
> *wishes redeemed*
>
> *no poet, but*
>
> *days in the sun*

He pinched the little scrap of her letter between his fingers, repeating it in memory . . .

Days in the sun. A garden. Allison lying in a whole bed of primroses. But she was the one he would pluck. His face was warm from smiling as he reached for her. But she sank away. Ever out of reach. The primroses died and the hole deepened as a grave. He could still see her, but her eyes were closed. There was knocking, like a body trapped in a coffin. Knocking, to get out. Knocking like—

Harry's eyes popped open to the muted light of the pre-dawn hour . . . or was it merely overcast? His eyes shot 'round the room. Another nightmare?

KNOCK

KNOCK

KNOCK

No. Not a nightmare. He didn't remember standing, but suddenly there he was, stalking to the door.

KNOCK

KNOCK

He was halfway to it when it opened on its own.

"Ah. I see you feel safe enough not to lock the door. That is progress, I think!" Allison's words washed over him like the chipper answer to a game of Buoyant Belle.

She drew her smile between her teeth as though it threatened to take her over if left unchecked. Her blonde waves were stacked messily into a wending golden ribbon—no sign of a lady's maid's touch. She wore her white chemise gown as she had that day in the mews, an open robe over top of it. And there. In her hands. A modest case.

She caught his eyes lingering on it. "Before you think me completely reformed, I should inform you that Hayden has left two large trunks at the foot of your building's stairs."

Harry could not hope. Could not dare. "You are here because . . .?"

Allison stepped toward him, right up under his chin, and lit him from below.

"I am here, Harry, for our days in the sun."

Epilogue

June 1787

Staring down at the basket in her hands, Allison had regrets. What a silly thing, bringing Faulkner another basket. Could society not conceive of better gifts for grieving? Allison frowned. A lack of imagination was not the world's fault, but her own. The ripe apples on top of the basket stared at her so quaintly that she wished to hurl one against the nearest tree, but she stayed her hand.

The chance that Faulkner would even see her was slight.

He'd locked himself into his townhouse since the night of his father's death, many weeks before, in April. The dukedom bypassed him as a revealed bastard, going straight to his cousin, instead. Rumor was rife that creditors had been sniffing about.

Allison rounded the street corner and spotted his townhouse looming silent and white. She hurried her pace, ready to be done with an errand that was sure to be painful.

The knocker felt like ice in her hand as she slammed it into the plate.

"Nobody is home."

She nearly tumbled from the stoop, startled as she was. And more startled yet as she saw it was Lord Faulkner himself who sat below street level on the steps to his tradesman's entrance.

She hurried down to meet him and he made space for her on the narrow steps.

He sat only in his shirtsleeves and waistcoat, almost unrecognizable without his immaculate, silken husk. His riding gloves in one hand, he slapped them against his palm. "Lady Allison."

"Lor—" Her lips cleaved the word. "Faulkner."

He smiled at her in a way that did not make it to his eyes and slapped the gloves to his palm again. "What have you there?"

She looked at her little basket and blushed. "Something rather inadequate for your losses, I fear."

He took one of the apples from the top. "Nonsense. I may never see ripe fruit again. Small things suddenly feel very adequate indeed." He bit into it as she found a spot to kneel on the step below him. She looked up just in time to see a pair promenading past and sneering down at them.

"Does it not bother you to be seen with a fallen duke?"

"Should it?" she asked. "I was certain I already consummated my ruin when I married a common man."

Faulkner's thick, dark eyebrows lifted in the center. "You truly did it then? You wed your Runner?"

She allowed a bashful smile to answer for her.

"Admirable. You have my felicitations."

It was easy to bask in his kind words, however formal, because *felicitations* on the lowering of her status were hard to come by. But she was not there to bask in congratulations.

"Does your own fall from grace not come with any . . . how shall I say . . . freedoms?"

"Freedoms? What could you possibly mean?"

"You owe no one an heir and no one has any influence over who you—I just thought you might be able to be with Miss Lyons."

Faulkner looked between his boots and began to shudder with a rueful, ironic sound. He flashed the terrible laughter at Allison before shaking his head.

"Oh, Allison. She does not want me. Not without a title. My godmother always warned me, *'Stephanie Lyons is flirting with the dukedom, not with you,'* and dash it, the monster was right."

He'd not said *mother* but *godmother,* a stark reminder of the newness of the truth. Lady Merton had been shipped off in exile to Denmark, the very same day that Faulkner's illegitimacy had been verified by the Crown.

Lady Merton had warned Allison at the theater that Miss Lyons did not love Faulkner. Her presence was eerily felt at the revelation she was correct.

"I am so sorry."

"Me too." Faulkner slapped his gloves into his hands again. "How does your mother find your marriage?"

"We have not spoken."

"You are disowned, then?"

Allison had grown used to the fact as best she could, but *"disowned"* seemed so permanent a word. She shook her head. "I do not know." For now, she could stomach that hole in her life, but was finding it difficult to stomach another. She steeled herself to ask what she most wished to know. "Faulkner. May I still call you a friend?"

Faulkner set aside his gloves and apple and put a hand on Allison's shoulder. His crystal blue eyes locked with hers.

"I know you well enough to understand you feel guilt, Allison. But yours was not the hand that killed my father's wife. You did not conceal my bastardhood from me, nor deny me a mother. Your husband did not murder my father nor my unknown brother. I was unaware my origins were rotten, but the rottenness did not spring from thin air."

"It is just, when you did not see me before, I—"

"I needed *time*, Allison." Faulkner picked up his things and stood, offering an uncharacteristically sticky hand to Allison. "If I deny your request for friendship, I fear I will die without any friends at all."

Allison's eyes wandered up the facade of a house that was no longer his. "Where will you go?"

"I'm not certain. But I will write you a letter one day."

"Letters have not always been reliable in my life. Promise to write at least two before giving up."

"I will write you ten. Ten letters to—"

"To Eight Dryden Street."

His face was a desert of expression. It was hard to believe she *would* see him again, but she could not press him for more.

"I truly wish you the best, Lady Allison."

"It is just Allison now."

He smiled, recognizing perhaps a thing they had in common. "So it is."

He took the basket from her hands and moved to the trades-man's door rather than accompanying her back up to the street level. He opened the door and Allison could not bear the sight of his back.

"Faulkner—!"

He turned.

"Happier times will find you. I promise it."

"Thank you, Allison. I will hold those words close."

The door shut behind him.

"You will be all right," she whispered. To the door. To him. To herself.

Frequent, grueling ascents to the apartment had made Allison's legs strong. Now, she could fairly take them in bounds. Yet she was still nearly out of breath as she reached the door.

The home had been restored to order and the dormer windows were open all day, leaving the breeze to swirl around the fresh flowers and herbs, which were kept in vases on the sill.

She'd sold a necklace to buy their marriage bed and Beth had sent them a quilt. *"Do not mistake it for my own skilled craftsmanship,"* she'd reminded Allison. *"As you know, I have none."* It fast became Allison's most favored thing to wear in the mornings, during that hour when Harry could not decide if he wished her dressed or undressed.

They had made love in every corner of the room, through every stage of its recovery. It had grown difficult to lay eyes on him without imagining his body against hers. One such thought gave her a pleasant shiver as she walked in, noticing his back to her by the fire.

He was reading in one of the upholstered chairs he'd bought on credit from the same carpenter whose son he'd once rescued. He leaned forward as she entered, his eyes quickly skimming a passage. It was what he always did when he had something to tell her but could not be torn from his book.

"Something came for you." It rushed excitedly from his lips the moment his book clapped shut. He hurried across the room to point to a letter on their little table.

She rushed over, wondering what letter could have excited her husband so, but she went cold upon recognizing the curls and swooshes of her mother's hand. She looked from the letter to Harry. "Do you think it is good news or bad?"

He lifted the letter and pressed it into her palm. "My Primrose, it was *hand* delivered."

Allison pictured her mother, the great Lady Weldon throwing herself up the flights of steps, past every dark door and loud noise. Had she truly?

The parchment crinkled in Allison's shaking hands as she studied her mother's cautious words.

Lady Weldon was not yet ready but, in the letter, swore she would be. *With time.*

Allison's heart leapt as she continued reading.

There followed some mundane passages on days at the townhouse and gossip at balls. There were reminiscences of their time on the Continent. There were musings on—on future grandchildren!

And it all ended with the plea to write. Everyone, it seemed, wished to write her.

She looked over the top of the parchment as she finished reading. Harry's face was plastered with an expectant smile as he awaited the news, hanks of hair falling into his eyes as ever. Those bright and hopeful eyes.

Months ago, she had lamented over his last letter. Back before the world had twisted itself in knots to turn their words into flesh. Into *love.*

She folded the parchment, enjoying the crispness of it as her heart filled with a hope so innate to her. She would write any number of letters if it kept her family near. She met her husband's eager eyes and knew her own were filled with hope.

Beautiful things came from letters.

Acknowledgments

Thank you again to my brilliant critique group: Brianne Gillen, Amanda Pereira, Jillian Graves, and Genevieve Kersten.

Julie Ganis, I don't know how I'd ever find copy editors without you. Thank you.

A special thanks to Jacob, who knows how much my writing means to me and shows up to support me with bells on. It's meant so much.

Lastly, I'm grateful, as ever, for my family's support. Thanks, Mom and Dad, for all your faith in me.

Bio

Daria Vernon grew up in the Southwest in houses brimming with antiques. Playing dress-up in old clothes, reading old books . . . is it any wonder she developed a passion for the historical?

Graduating into a recession and a writer's strike with a screenwriting degree didn't get her too far, but it led to the slew of odd jobs that would fuel her imagination for a lifetime, and for that she is grateful.

She writes from her well-nested (but woefully cat-less) introvert's cocoon, emerging mostly to twirl around at the local ice rink.

www.dariavernon.com
daria.vernon.romance
AuthorDariaV

For updates and excerpts from new books

go to:

www.DariaVernon.com

Thanks for reading!

—Daria